OPERATION
DESTINY

"It is not in the stars to hold our destiny but in ourselves."

...William Shakespeare

OPERATION DESTINY

Donald J. Lloyd

Library of Congress Control Number: 2021905828

StarLight Press
ISBN   978-0-9673887-3-1

"It is a mistake to look too far ahead. Only one link in the chain of destiny can be handled at a time."

...Winston Churchill

Table of Contents

Chapter 1
May 31, 1954

Matt Kane lay face down in the muddy field, barely clinging to life. Even close to death, his first reaction was one of irritation because he should have seen this coming. His eight years as an Army intelligence officer, including his service as a member of the Bletchley Park *Special Services Unit*, and certainly his last seven years as a freelance investigative journalist should have prepared him for this eventuality. He had upset many powerful people and organizations over the last decade and should have known that someone might look for retribution at some point.

While he had been in physical danger as a covert operative during World War II, he always felt that he had an advantage because he studied the enemy and understood their tactics. Obviously, he had lost some of that edge since he left the Army in 1947. For some reason though, he simply never considered the possibility that he might be the subject of a *professional hit*. *Who was she, and why me,* he thought? Matt struggled to remain conscious, but two bullet wounds to the chest made it difficult to think. *How can I stop the bleeding, will anybody find me before it's too late?* Then everything went dark.

Jacob Foster and Haley, his black-and-white border collie, were taking their nightly stroll through the Commons Park on Lake Minnetonka when two loud cracks sliced through the cool spring night, causing Haley to jerk her leash and bolt. The generally calm but inquisitive five-year-old, while initially startled, ran in the direction of the sounds.

"Haley, stop, sit! Come back," Jacob yelled several times to no avail. She was on the run through the mud-splashed grassy field. Jacob, uncommonly vigorous at age sixty, while no match for Haley's speed, chased after her at a brisk trot. After two or three minutes of pursuit, he saw his canine companion jumping and barking almost a hundred yards ahead. He also saw a fleeting figure running from the scene. Instantly, he knew something was wrong.

Jacob cautiously approached the frantic pet and froze. The twilight sky produced enough light so he could see a man lying face down in the mire. He quickly regained his faculties and turned the man over, revealing two bullet wounds, one in the lower right quadrant of the chest, obviously piercing the liver and lung, and the other, almost mid chest, just slightly below the Xiphoid process. The man was bleeding profusely and was unconscious but still alive. *I haven't done this in years,* Jacob thought, as he took off his jacket, then ripped off his shirt to pack the wounds and stop the bleeding. It was in the Ardennes in late 1918 that medic Jacob Foster had last performed this task. *Geez,* he thought, *it's been more than thirty-five years since I treated a gunshot wound.*

Okay, remember the ABCs...*airway, breathing and circulation.* Jacob's mind raced as he assessed the airway. *No obstruction there,* he thought. *Breathing is shallow, the bullet collapsed his right lung...I've got to stop the air from getting sucked into the chest cavity. Circulation seems tolerable, the bullet must have missed the artery and spine, but time is of the essence,* he ruminated. He then immediately packed the wounds with the shirt and wrapped his jacket around Matt to seal the wounds as best he could. Then the next problem. *How am I going to get him back to the street and to the hospital?*

"Sir, can you hear me? Stay with me! Sir..." the ambulance attendant screeched repeatedly as Matt lapsed in and out of consciousness, as Jacob looked on. His foggy mind wandered at warp speed as he attempted to make sense of what was happening to him. *Why was I at the park on Excelsior Bay?*

The investigation into cancer drugs and possible fraud in pharmaceutical industry research...would they kill me over that? He was experiencing an avalanche of disjointed reflections and emotions, which convinced him that the end was near.

Matthew Seiberling Kane...only child...born Minneapolis General Hospital...St. Louis Park...on a snowy February night in 1914, he contemplated. *My father...physician and German immigrant...fled to America on the eve of World War I... a job at Fort Snelling...provided medical services to officer training candidates...his Army stories that stimulated me to go to law school and the intelligence service.*

The flood of memories continued. *A comfortable life...a devoted mother and stern, but fair and supportive father...many leadership positions...a championship athlete...class Valedictorian at St. Louis Park High School in 1932...top ten in my law school class at the University of Minnesota...Major in the U.S. Army early in 1943...ironic...classic Aryan look at six-feet-two, blond hair, blue eyes, athletic body...served me well during my WWII escapades...Marie Spenser...my team in the SSU...toppling of the shadow government...the construction industry analysis...the civil rights series...could that be...?* Then total blackout.

Three days later, Matt weakly opened his eyes and there sat his mother and father, Mary and Friedrick, with looks of grave concern. He was on a ventilator and couldn't speak, but at least he was apparently still alive. *Who found me and how,* given that his meeting place was off the beaten path? He again lapsed into oblivion. It would be another twelve hours before he regained some trace of sustained consciousness.

That night, when he regained a semblance of coherence, Matt, realizing that the tube in his throat rendered him unable to speak, motioned for something to write with. "How did I get here?" he scribbled. "How long have you been here?" he wrote as he looked at his worried mother and composed father.

"A dog found you, and his owner saved you. Apparently, Mr. Foster heard the gunshots, ran to you and packed your wounds with his shirt," responded his father in his typical stoic manner. "Fortunately for you, he's a World War I vet with medical training, so he knew how to stem the bleeding." His father resumed, "Another stroke of luck was that two teenage boys rowing on the bay heard Mr. Foster calling for help and stopped to see what was happening. They carried you to a house on First Avenue, where the lady called the ambulance, and you were rushed here to Minneapolis General."

"As for us, we came immediately," related Dr. Kane. "Frankly, we were fearful that you wouldn't live. We thank God that you're still alive."

An intelligent and erudite man with great presence, Dr. Friedrick Kane was the sentinel influence in Matt's life. While a man of strong beliefs and expectations, he was a reasonable and compassionate father and physician. He was born in the mid-1880s in Schallstadt, Germany, roughly forty miles northeast of Basel, Switzerland, where he often went for recreation. He pursued his education at the University of Freiburg, where he attended medical school and developed his strong sense of community and service to humanity. Traits he passed on to his only son, Matthew. It was there that Friedrick Kane met the comely Mary Seiberling, a Swiss national who he married prior to fleeing to the United States in late 1913.

A somewhat prescient Friedrick Kane saw the seeds of war being sown in Europe long before the assassination of Austrian Archduke Franz Ferdinand and his wife, Sophie, in the summer of 1914. The youthful Kane concluded that the constant tensions between countries would ultimately lead to war. It seemed obvious to him that the formation of the Triple Entente Alliance that included Britain, France, and Russia, and the Central

Powers Alliance that included Germany, Austria and Hungary were essentially the fuse needed to light a European conflagration. He felt that once he finished his medical education, the only reasonable course was to escape to America.

The young Dr. Kane took a civilian job at Fort Snelling in the Minnesota suburb of St. Louis Park and treated officer-training candidates until he was mustered into the U.S. Army. He was promptly sent to France, where his knowledge of the German language and cultural heritage, and ability to develop a significant rapport with enemy soldiers proved to be valuable to the Allied powers. In late 1917, Dr. Kane helped treat and interrogate wounded German soldiers in France, and his stories sparked a curiosity in his son that set Matt on the path to Army Intelligence and ultimately into the field of journalism.

"How bad is it?" wrote Matt.

"Bad enough, son," responded a composed Dr. Kane as he lapsed into his typical dispassionate bedside manner.

"You were very fortunate, though. First, the bullets missed the thoracic and abdominal aorta, which would have killed you instantly. Second, the bullets hit you at an angle rather than straight on, so they missed the spinal cord and pancreas but caught the right kidney," he continued with the precision of an experienced surgeon, which he was.

"Also, your stomach and esophagus were spared. The bad news is that they weren't able to repair the kidney and had to remove it. The liver was significantly damaged, as well as some injury to the large intestine. The surgeons were able to repair those injuries. Fortunately, your liver will regenerate and essentially be normal in a month or so."

"Your ribs, however, are going to be a problem. The bullets splintered the seventh through the tenth ribs, so some parts of them were removed. It's going to be awhile before you're back on your feet. Maybe several weeks."

"Frankly, Matthew, you're blessed to be alive at all with those wounds. The major concern now is the prevention of infection. The penicillin in your IV should do the trick. But you're going to have to take it easy for a while and let your mother and I take care of you."

Matt just sighed and drifted back to sleep.

Chapter 2

The Interview

Still groggy from the pain medication, Matt guardedly tried to ease himself awake. *Marie Spenser*, he thought. *I must be in heaven.* He slowly regained some sense of mindfulness as nurse Ruth Chessman asked, "How do you feel this morning, Mr. Kane?"

"I guess I'm still alive," he responded in a raspy voice as he realized that the breathing tube had been removed. It seemed extraordinary that this nurse looked so much like Marie. Roughly the same size and look; five feet-four, sandy blonde shoulder-length curly hair, and the inquisitive blue eyes.

"What day is it?" he asked.

"It's Saturday, Mr. Kane," answered nurse Chessman. "You've been here since Monday night. You had a pretty rough go of it, but happily things look a lot better now. How is your pain?"

"Still pretty intense," responded Matt, "but I don't want to keep taking the morphine. I saw during the war how addictive it can be. How long do you think I'll have to be in the hospital?" he asked.

"I don't know, it will be up to the doctors to decide that, but you'll be here for several more days for sure."

"I've got to get back on my feet soon so I can find out who shot me, and why," Matt reacted forcefully.

"You may be a really tough guy, Mr. Kane, but you're going nowhere for a while," Miss Chessman responded gently.

Decidedly different than most of the other nurses on the ward, Ruth was thirtyish, attractive, and spoke with a kind and sympathetic tone, as compared to his preconception of most nurses who looked and sounded more like the drill sergeants he encountered in the Army. He was grateful that she was assigned to his case.

Ruth Chessman was among the new wave of nurses entering the profession. She wasn't trained in the hospital like most nurses, but earned her bachelor's degree in nursing from the University of Minnesota in 1948, where she developed expanded skills in critical care and the use of advanced technologies now being employed in many hospitals. Her expertise was important in managing Matt's several medical crises in the first three days after the shooting.

Just as Ruth finished taking vital signs, changing linens, checking his indwelling catheter, and cranking up the top of his bed to a near sitting position, a muscular looking man with stylish black hair and definite military bearing pulled back the screen that separated Matt from the other three beds in the ward.

"Mr. Kane, I'm Detective Captain Richard Johnson from the Minneapolis Police Department. Do your feel like talking about your attack? I'll come back later if you're not up to it, but I'd like to get started as soon as possible to avoid losing any memories you may have."

"We can talk now if the nurse doesn't mind."

"Just for a few minutes, Mr. Kane. You need your rest."

"We're gathering information from the crime scene," Johnson continued, "but there's still a lot of pieces to put together. We have the bullet they took out of your chest. It's at the ballistics lab now. There's probably another one out there but we haven't found it yet. We're also following up on the information given us by the man who found you."

Detective Johnson, a no-nonsense, fact-driven, veteran of the Minneapolis Police Force moved from Los Angeles to the Twin

Cities in 1948, after marrying Ann Brooke, a St. Paul native who he met at the Hollywood Canteen USO Center in 1944. She had moved to Los Angeles to be with her brother who was serving in the U.S. Coast Guard in Southern California.

Johnson, a Marine Major, met Ann when he was on his way to Saipan to command native scouts for the U.S. 6th Provisional Military Police Battalion. They had an immediate connection and corresponded while he was serving in the South Pacific.

After being wounded in the leg by sniper fire on Saipan in the spring of 1945, Johnson returned to California to convalesce, where Ann was a frequent hospital visitor. Once he was discharged from the Marines, he joined the Los Angeles Police Department and they were married.

Life then took a bizarre turn in 1947 when the L.A. police officer was assigned to the large task force investigating the brutal murder of Elizabeth Short, better known as 'The Black Dahlia'. Her body had been severed at the waist and largely mutilated. After nearly a year of following futile leads, the gruesome nature of the crime had an overpowering effect on Rich and Ann. There was simply too much crime, corruption and police misconduct in the city, so they decided to move back to her home state of Minnesota.

Rich Johnson found the wholesomeness of the Midwest a welcome relief from the unrelenting death of gang war and depravity in Southern California. He quickly rose through the ranks of the Minnesota Police Department and developed a reputation for being detailed and persistent. The crime rate in the area was modest, and the acuity of the crimes in the community was low. Their quality of life was clearly better. His success in solving the few major crimes that did occur made him the perfect choice to work on the attempted murder of a noted war veteran and journalist like Matthew Kane.

"I'm still not really sure what happened," replied Matt gingerly, still a little light-headed. "I'll do the best I can, but I'm not sure if I'm clear enough yet to be of much help."

"We'll take it slow and see where it goes," replied the detective.

"Early on Monday morning I received a call from a young-sounding woman who said she had confidential information that would help my drug industry investigation. She said it would be dangerous for her if they found out she was talking to me. She suggested that we meet near the large Elm tree in the back of the park on Excelsior Bay at 10:00 p.m. I should have known something was up when she wanted to meet that late in a secluded place."

"Did she give a name?" asked Detective Johnson.

"No. It was a short and somewhat anxious call, like she was troubled about something. I agreed to meet, and she hung up."

"You said she sounded young. Why do you say that? How young, teen-aged, twenties?"

"I don't know, maybe in her early twenties," Matt responded.

"Any distinguishing voice characteristics?" Johnson continued.

"Now that you mention it, her intonation was somewhat different."

Rich Johnson quickly countered, "You mean she had an accent."

"Yes," Matt replied excitedly as though they had their first meaningful lead. Suddenly Matt felt energized and was becoming more lucid. The stimulation was clearly good for his brain.

"Can you identify the type of accent?"

Matt thought for a moment. "It sounded foreign, possibly German."

"What makes you think it was German?" quizzed the detective.

10

"The way she pronounced the word *where*. There was a hint of a *V* instead of a clean *W*. That was the kind of idiosyncrasy we looked for in Army intelligence during the war."

"Perhaps I'm just looking for something," Matt cautioned, somewhat deflated. "It could just be a local with a European background. In fact, my parents emigrated nearly forty years ago and still have some German inflection in their speech. Maybe that's not what I heard at all."

"It's a start, Mr. Kane; it's a good start. We'll check it out. No detail is too small. Little things often lead to big discoveries," consoled Detective Johnson.

"Did you get a good look at the assailant? What did she look like...assuming that it was this woman you talked with on the telephone?" he continued.

"Yes, it was a young woman, but things happened so fast, I can't give you much detail about her. She was maybe a little above average height, and I think she was wearing a dark leather jacket and slacks. It looked like she had dark hair, but things happened so quickly I can't be sure."

"Was she heavy or slim?" quizzed Johnson.

"On the slim side. She looked athletic."

"Why do you say that?"

"I can't really say why. She just looked agile."

"What did she say, if anything?"

Matt paused and took several deep breaths and tried to make himself more comfortable as he strained to evoke more details of the encounter with the mystery woman.

"Not at first. She was just standing next to the large Elm tree on a hill near the shoreline where we agreed to meet. When I got about ten or fifteen feet away from her, I could see an odd smile on her face, and then she just said, 'Remember me'? and raised the gun and began firing."

"When did you see the gun?" Johnson asked.

"Just as she raised her arm. When I realized what was happening, I tried to dive for cover toward another tree. I was only able to move slightly before I felt a searing pain in the chest and that was it."

"As I understand it, that slight move saved your life."

Captain Johnson continued to solicit details. "What kind of gun? And do you remember which hand the gun was in?"

"I don't know what kind of gun it was, but it was definitely in her *left* hand," Matt retorted with renewed vitality.

"Can you remember anything else about her demeanor, looks or voice?"

"I'm afraid not now. Maybe later I'll think of something useful."

Detective Johnson was now ready to move on to possible motives.

"Can you think of anyone who has a personal grudge against you? You're a journalist...any exposé from the past couple of years that might be threatening enough for some organization to want you silenced?"

"I can't think of any personal enemy. I get along with most people just fine. I'm currently working on a story about the slow progress of cancer research and possible mismanagement in the pharmaceutical industry, but I can't really characterize it as an exposé. Although it may have some critical elements in it, I can't imagine that industry criticism would be a strong enough reason to risk committing murder. Being mixed up in a scandal like that would only bring about more scrutiny."

"Maybe not, but tell me about your drug industry story anyway," prodded the investigator.

"It's complex, but I'll try to be brief, Captain Johnson."

"Please, call me Rich. We're likely to see a lot of each other in the coming days so we should dispense with the formalities. Can I call you Matthew?"

"Matt is just fine."

"As you know, cancer treatment is a relatively new frontier for the pharmaceutical industry. While scientists have been working on treatment modalities for years, we still haven't seen much in the way of success in finding cures for tumors or blood disorders. The foundations of cancer treatment came a few years before World War I, but it was probably twenty years before any significant breakthroughs occurred."

Matt was now in full instructor mode.

"A pharmacologist named Murray Shear directed the effort to improve cancer research in the 1930s. He began his work at the U.S. Public Health Service, and later moved to the newly created National Institutes of Health. He developed a model to screen chemical compounds for effectiveness against certain types of cancers that looked very promising. Unfortunately, only two of three-thousand compounds tested actually made it to clinical trials, and his program was terminated a year or two ago. Notwithstanding his failures, Dr. Shear is recognized by many as the father of chemotherapy."

"The crux of the matter is this; these drugs are highly toxic, and many critics don't believe the future of cancer care is in chemical treatments. The criticism is that we don't know how to effectively test or use these chemicals in humans. That's why I'm investigating potential malfeasance in the industry. Are they stonewalling because of some economic pressures or has something gone wrong in their research? I don't know that yet, and that's why the call I got from the mystery woman was so appealing."

"Do you have some notes I can take a look at?" asked Johnson. "I'll follow up with some of the people and organizations you're investigating."

"You're welcome to the notes, but I still don't think you'll find much there," responded Matt.

"How about past stories?" pressed the detective.

"I wrote a series of articles last year about racial segregation, Jim Crow laws, and discriminatory public policies that clearly agitated a large segment of society. I asked why the dark color of one's skin was a disqualification for reasonable education, transportation, employment, medical services, housing or voting. There was a lot of blowback by organizations like the Ku Klux Klan at the time...and some threats, but I don't know why I would be singled out as a target now, given the current wave of support for the civil rights movement. There are plenty more high-profile targets for them to pursue. The KKK or some other hate group could actually be behind this, though."

"We'll definitely pursue that lead," replied Johnson. "Anything else?"

"I wrote an analysis of anti-communist persecution of some prominent elected leaders, but I can't imagine...*ugh!*"

Suddenly, an excruciating pain shot through Matt's right side that took his breath away. He yelped in agony and grabbed his chest in an attempt to diminish the pain. His shriek startled Rich Johnson, and quickly brought Ruth Chessman to his bedside, where she immediately repositioned her patient to relieve the discomfort.

"Sorry," whispered Matt. "The pain got the best of me for a moment. Give me a minute and I'll be okay."

"We can stop and talk again later if you're uncomfortable Matt," offered the detective.

"No, Rich, I'd like to continue so we can get to the bottom of this. I need to get out of here and get to work."

"Oh, no you don't," commanded Ruth. "It's time for some rest. Can you come back later, Captain Johnson?"

"That will be fine. I'll go back to the office and see what our officers have found at the Park and check on the forensics. Is 3:00 p.m. okay?" he reacted respectfully. "On second thought...I think I have enough information to keep me busy for a day or two. What about Monday morning? That will give Matt a chance to gain some strength and perhaps recall more details that can help in the investigation."

"Matt, don't press it, just let things come back naturally. Write down any details you can think of and we can discuss them on Monday. Take it easy until then," added Detective Johnson as he turned to exit the ward.

The nurse quickly suggested that Monday would be fine and moved in to take care of her patient.

"Why don't you close your eyes and ease your mind for a little bit, Mr. Kane. You have plenty of time to address the attack. It's going to take a while for your physical wounds to heal, and it may take even longer for your mind to process the event. You shouldn't try to do too much right now. Give it some time."

"I understand completely, Mrs. Chessman. I just need to understand this whole ordeal. By the way, all my friends call me Matt...you should too."

"I'm not married...and you can call me Ruth."

"It's a deal," he responded, as he closed his eyes and drifted back to La La Land.

Matt's session with Rich Johnson had generated a great deal of adrenalin, which in turn had revitalized and exhausted him. He slept soundly for almost three hours until a nurse's aide brought his lunch.

"Do you feel like eating something, Mr. Kane?" asked the short, stubby middle-aged woman. "This is the first real food you've had since your accident, so you might want to take it slow," she instructed in a somewhat brusque manner. She then put the platter on the tray table, wheeled it in front of him, and abruptly walked away.

Matt was still fuzzy as he eyed the plate in front of him. He warily lifted the cover to reveal a concoction of what looked like marginally cooked chicken smothered in some kind of white sauce, two brownish stalks of broccoli, an ice-cream scoop of mashed potatoes, a cup of orange Jell-O, a hardened roll, some butter, and a cup of hot tea. *I should have died*, he mused, as he put the lid back on the plate and decided to go back to sleep.

Several minutes later, Matt awakened to the sound of Ruth Chessman's voice. "You didn't touch your lunch, Mr. Kane...*ah*, Matt."

"Not very appetizing," he mockingly responded.

"I don't blame you, but we need to get you back on solid food. How about a couple of bites of broccoli, some mashed potatoes, and the Jell-O?" she quizzed gently.

"I agree with you about the chicken, though. I wouldn't eat it either," she chuckled.

Ruth's response raised Matt's spirits and he dutifully ate a few bites of everything except the chicken.

"Can you sneak me in a hamburger...with lettuce, tomato, onions, pickles and ketchup?" he chided.

"Well, it looks like somebody's beginning to regain his sense of humor," she responded cheerfully. "I'll see what I can do tomorrow. Now it's time to get you into a wheelchair and take you to physical therapy. You can't just lay here forever," she scolded Matt jokingly.

Realizing that he'd been set up by her kindness, Matt responded with a mock, "*ugh...*you nurses are all the same. It's about inflicting pain on us poor innocent patients!"

Ruth laughed.

"It won't be so bad for a strong man like you...just a little exercise, massage and maybe some traction. Better get used to it, though. We can't let you out of here until you're quite functional."

With the help of the stern aide, Matt was redeployed to a wheelchair and headed off to the first of many daily physical therapy sessions.

Chapter 3

The Investigation

Captain Rich Johnson and his squad were busy during the first week of the investigation into the attempted murder of Matthew Kane. The team conducting the inquiry included Johnson, two uniformed officers, and one other detective who arrived at the Commons Park within an hour of the shooting. As expected, the scene was chaotic.

As fortune would have it, weather played an important role in the initial investigation. Monday had been a comfortable day with a high temperature of sixty-eight degrees, ten degrees above normal for the date, but a significant rain in the early morning provided a treasure trove of information for the forensics team. The three quarters of an inch of rain had created a slushy surface that crusted over as the wind increased to nearly fifteen miles an hour throughout the day. Even the heavily grassed areas of the park provided a favorable foundation for scientific investigation.

While the immediate area around Matt Kane's body was contaminated by blood, multiple human footprints, and paw prints, the area a few feet west of that spot yielded several unique footprints that confirmed the assailant was indeed a female. The boot prints enabled the forensics lab to estimate the likely height and weight of the attacker.

It was determined that the boots were manufactured in Britain, which affected the size-height ratio. The assailant's British size five boot and the depth of the imprint indicated that she weighed approximately one hundred and twenty-five to one hundred thirty-five pounds. It also suggested that her height was between five feet-six and five feet-eight inches tall, demonstrating that the female was indeed taller than average.

Further examination indicated that the boots were a unique ankle-high chukka style with a full wedge heel that indented toward the middle of the foot and gradually widened out to the toes. The indention was the key element that enabled the lab to narrow down the manufacturer and size. Further, the right heel had a notch where the assailant probably stepped on the shell casing as she was fleeing the scene.

The array of her footsteps indicated that she was looking for the shell casings, but couldn't find at least one of them because it was buried in the wet grass. This stroke of luck enabled one of the policemen to recover the casing that delivered another useful piece of evidence. The headstamp on the casing confirmed that it was a nine-millimeter shell manufactured in Belgium in 1944. That discovery led Rich Johnson to suspect the would-be killer might be a foreign national.

Officer Kenneth Simmons found a nearly pristine bullet in the ground about thirty feet from the incident site. Blood on the projectile allowed forensics to verify that it was the missing bullet that passed through Matt Kane's chest. The ultimate advantage of the wet ground was the ability of the investigators to trace the direction of the attacker as she left the scene. The trail took her from Solberg Point southwest to First Street where the muddy footprints turned left toward downtown. The mud-spattered trail gradually dissipated but indicated that the assailant proceeded on foot toward downtown Excelsior.

On Tuesday morning, Officer Simmons and his associate, Officer Michael Coyle, systematically canvassed the neighborhood, talking with residents and business owners to see if anyone remembered seeing a tall, slim woman with black hair, wearing dark slacks, a black leather jacket, and ankle-length boots on the previous day. Their exhaustive inquiries over the next few days yielded nothing. The trail had gone cold.

While Officers Simmons and Coyle were attempting to trace the movements of the mystery woman, Captain Johnson and his partner, Detective Colin Young, were pursuing other avenues of inquiry. Detective Young focused on the Hennepin County construction industry critique that led to legal action against some prominent companies in the industry.

In late 1952, Matt Kane had written a series of seven articles for a national magazine about the lack of proper construction oversight by some county inspectors, the use of substandard building materials, overall shoddy workmanship by several contractors, and payola. The U.S. economy had surged after World War II, but the housing industry was in crisis. There was a lack of materials and experienced residential builders, and construction companies were not able to meet the overwhelming pent-up demand, causing builders to cut corners in an attempt to supply enough inventory.

The cost of housing in cities throughout the U.S. rose so rapidly that many families could no longer afford to live in larger municipalities. A rapid transition to the suburbs resulted in strong pressure on building inspectors to overlook 'minor flaws' in construction in order to produce enough housing. There was also a greed motive for builders. Minnesota was no exception.

Matt Kane meticulously researched construction companies and the relationship between builders and inspectors in Hennepin County, which revealed that some inspectors were being paid to overlook code violations and what were deemed 'inconsequential' defects in construction. These supposedly minor imperfections included unstable foundations, poor framing, damaged wall studs, faulty wiring, missing or insufficient insulation, unreliable plumbing and defective roofing. These flaws were prevalent in many new homes built in the late 1940s and early 1950s. His series highlighted seven particular companies and a handful of inspectors, resulting in charges being brought against individuals in the industry and termination of the guilty inspectors.

Detective Coyle spent most of the week conducting personal interviews with many individuals involved in the housing scandal, probing for hints of malice that might warrant an attempt on Matt's life. He found none. No individual could reasonably have made contact with a 'foreign' assassin, and he saw no possible collusion between either builders or the fired inspectors. While many were still quite irritated that Matt had meddled in their business, resulting in job loss, fines, and even bankruptcy, there was simply not enough hutzpah among the group to undertake such drastic action as murder. Another dead end.

On Monday morning, Detective Johnson returned to the hospital where he found Matt sitting in a chair chatting with Ruth Chessman. His catheter had been removed and he only had an intravenous line in his left arm containing a nine-percent saline solution to provide proper hydration. He looked markedly better than the previous Saturday.

"How's he doing this morning, Miss Chessman?" asked the detective.

"Much better, but still a long way to go," Ruth replied.

"We've made progress in the first week of our investigation..." Johnson began.

"Did you catch her yet?" Matt interrupted in a semi-serious tone.

"Not quite. But we do know a little more about her and her movements than we did last week. She left the park and it looks like she headed downtown. We've lost her trail for the moment, but our officers will continue their search and see if we can turn up something. We did find the second bullet in the dirt about thirty feet from where you were shot. It's in really good shape, and a quick comparison with the one that was taken out of your chest confirms that it was a nine-millimeter shell, which is somewhat common, but does help narrow down the type of weapon. We also found a shell casing that indicates the bullet was manufactured in Belgium a decade ago."

"Belgium? Maybe that's it," exclaimed Matt. "Some of the pharmaceutical companies I'm investigating are located there. I must be on to something for them to try to silence me. *Thérapeutiques Recherche, Inc.*, *JSS Pharmaceutica*, and *PIO Pharma* are three leading companies with a heavy emphasis on biochemical treatments. I suspected that they were up to something, and I feel like I was just about to close the loop when I got the call."

Rich Johnson had reviewed Matt's research notes on the pharmaceutical investigation, and Matt's reaction further piqued his interest. His response was typically measured, however.

"Good information, Matt, but let's not get ahead of ourselves yet. While the evidence we have thus far does suggest a foreign connection, I still want to follow-up on the KKK and other possible avenues. My gut tells me there's something we're missing. And I'm still searching for a clear motive."

"Detective Young has completed his investigation of the construction industry and we've effectively ruled them out. I'm going to work on the Ku Klux Klan angle this week while he does some preliminary work on the Belgian companies. If that avenue looks plausible, we'll have to call in the FBI and perhaps even the International Criminal Police Commission. On second thought, I already have a friend in the Washington Office of the FBI who may be able to give me some information on KKK activity. I'll keep you posted on any further developments."

"What about the assailant? Matt queried.

"We'll stay on that also. Just take care of yourself and I'll see you in a few days. In the meantime, give me a call if you have any other thoughts."

"This is Detective Captain Richard Johnson from the Minneapolis Police Department," he related in a professional voice to the FBI operator in Washington, D.C. "I'd like to speak with Agent James Rosino."

"Just a moment, sir. I'll ring Mr. Rosino's extension."

"Agent Rosino...how can I help you?"

"Hi, James. It's Rich Johnson. How are you? I'm calling because I need some assistance with an attempted murder case."

"Well, hello, Rich. It's been a while. I'm well. How about yourself?" responded the agent. "Straight to the point, as always," he continued.

"I'm fine, James. It's been too long. You need to get back to Minnesota so I can buy you that dinner I owe you for helping me on the check kiting case."

"We'll see, Rich. Now tell me about your problem."

"I'm working on what looks more like an assassination attempt than a simple murder. The victim was lured to a quiet spot on Lake Minnetonka and gunned down. He survived, and has been able to give me some possible perpetrators with legitimate reasons for taking him out. We've already ruled out a local group and are following up on two leads that may have national or international origins."

"What does your victim do that would suggest a murder-for-hire?"

"He's an accomplished investigative journalist with a background in military intelligence. He's smart, persistent and relentless, and has clearly stirred up somebody."

"So, what can I help you with?"

"At this point, we're looking at the Ku Klux Klan and some drug companies in Europe. He wrote a couple of inflammatory articles warning of the dangers of Jim Crow laws and the KKK in 1952 and is presently working on possible misconduct in drug research. Right now, I'm looking for intelligence on the Klan."

"You just happened to call me at the right time, Rich. I was assigned to Klan activities after the murder of the Florida

NAACP Executive Director, Harry Moore, on Christmas Day in 1951. I also have some reliable informants in the Klan who may be able to help us. I have some pressing business I need to take care of for a couple of days, but I'll be on a plane Thursday and we can get to work."

"Thanks, James. I'll see you then. Dinner is on me."

"Glad to assist, Rich. Stay out of trouble until I get there, my friend."

North Central Airlines Flight #104 landed at Wold-Chamberlain Field at 3:44 pm on Thursday, June 10th, and FBI Agent James Rosino bounded down the stairs and hurried toward the terminal to meet Rich Johnson. A balding, tan, and athletic man of medium height, he was seemingly always in a hurry. He had a new task and was ready to get started. His Bureau colleagues described James Rosino as tenacious, strong-willed, detail-oriented, and perfectionistic. His major flaw was impatience. When he saw a problem, he wanted to fix it immediately, and while this proved fruitful much of the time, haste was not always effective. Rich Johnson, on the other hand, was the picture of patience and precision. Consequently, they had the makings of a very effective team.

"Hi, James, it's good to see you again. How was your flight?" greeted Johnson.

"Some delay in Chicago, but otherwise fine. It's actually good to get away from Washington with the McCarthy *Red Scare* fiasco and unrest over the Supreme Court decision in *Brown v. Board of Education* a few weeks ago. I fear that we're going to see some violent repercussions from that verdict."

"That's exactly what our victim predicted in his Klan articles a year ago. It seems reasonable to think that his assassination attempt could be linked to the *Brown* decision."

The two friends left the airport and headed directly to Rich Johnson's favorite restaurant, located in one of the oldest buildings in the city on Sixth Street in central Minneapolis. Opened in 1946, Murray's was reputed to have the best steak in the state and service unmatched anywhere. The proprietors, Art and Marie Murray, were said to be excellent hosts who treated their guests like family. The ambiance was warm and cozy, which allowed for pleasant dinner conversation. After their lengthy dinner discussion, ranging from family and friends to wartime experiences, Rich took James to the Nicollet Hotel just a few blocks away in the Gateway District. The hotel choice would later prove to be providential in advancing the investigation into Matt Kane's attempted murder.

"Have a good night, James. I'll pick you up at 8:00 a.m. We can catch some breakfast and then go to the hospital to see our victim. I think you'll find him to be very helpful."

"Thanks for dinner and your hospitality, Rich. I'm ready to get to work. See you in the morning. Take care."

After breakfast at Vernon's Kitchen in St. Louis Park, the Minneapolis detective and FBI agent headed to Minneapolis General Hospital to see Matt Kane. The four-bed ward was again full, with three new patients having been admitted on Tuesday. Matt was sitting comfortably in a chair, IV in his arm, reviewing some case notes from his Ku Klux Klan series and pharmaceutical inquiry. He was also writing down recollections from his investigations and the shooting incident as he tried to establish a motive for the shooting. Having been off the morphine for a couple of days, Matt was again thinking clearly.

"Hi, Matt," greeted Rich Johnson. "You're looking pretty good. "Either the hospital food is better than I remember, or the nurse is doing wonders with your psyche," he joked. "This is James Rosino, my friend from the FBI that I told you about. He's been in charge of monitoring the KKK and white supremacist groups for the past two and a half years, and I think he can help us figure out if they are responsible for your attack."

"Hello, Agent Rosino. I appreciate any assistance you can give us," responded Matt.

"Please, not so official, Matt. All my colleagues call me James...my enemies call me other names," he laughed. "Rich tells me you've had a pretty rough go of it. I'm glad to see that you're doing so well given the trauma you experienced."

"James it is." Matt instantly liked the FBI Agent. He was convinced that this newly created team of three motivated professionals could get to the bottom of his shooting.

"After looking at my notes and thinking through the events of Monday night, I'm almost convinced that the mystery woman was sent here by the Belgian drug companies," Matt theorized. "Her brief greeting of *'remember me'?* has to mean that I met her at some time during my research on the industry. I can't see her being connected to the Klan."

"Again, let's not get ahead of ourselves, Matt..." countered Rich.

"He does have a point, Rich," injected Rosino. "She didn't think he would live to tell anyone so she may have simply let it slip."

"Possibly," retorted Johnson. "But we don't want to rush to judgment before we examine all the angles. It's too easy to get off track and waste valuable time. Patience, boys...we'll get there soon enough if we systematically eliminate other possibilities."

"Good morning, gentlemen," greeted Ruth Chessman. She introduced herself to James Rosino in a pleasant, but robust manner, that let him know she was in still in control of her patient.

Because the ward was full, Ruth suggested that they continue the conversation in a small conference room a few doors down from the patient care area. She then helped Matt up, steadied him for a moment, and firmly held his free arm and IV pole as she put him in the wheelchair and guided the three men slowly down the hallway to room 251. *She's a jewel*, Matt thought as Ruth helped him get comfortably seated.

Before launching into a discussion about possible suspects and motives, Matt felt obligated to tell the two law enforcement professionals why he chose to devote his life to exploratory and analytical commentary. It stemmed from his father's life experiences and his own personal observations in law school and during World War II.

Matt began by summarizing the influence of his father on his values, ethics, and sense of fair play. Friedrick Kane had seen exploitation of the working class by business and industry in his native Germany, throughout Europe, and even in the United States. He also observed the social mistreatment, abuse and persecution of certain groups due to heritage, religion or politics around the world. Finally, he watched government conspiracies and oppressive regimes in Germany, Russia, Spain, Italy and many other countries that had the effect of stifling social, political and economic freedoms. He encouraged his son to work toward creating a more just world. This led Matt to law school with the ultimate intent of representing beleaguered and disadvantaged people in the courtroom.

Matt went on to explain his alarm about the demonic dictators who appeared to be dominating worldwide politics in the 1930s, which significantly offended his sense of propriety. His intellectual curiosity and need to confront injustice grew as he studied case law and witnessed the growth of National Socialism and genocide of populations due to racial, ethnic, social or economic class. In short, he wanted a career that was broader than individual cases. Accordingly, after he was discharged from the Army in 1947, he chose to return to his Minnesota home to look for opportunities to identify social problems and propose solutions that would benefit all segments of society. Investigative journalism seemed to be the right vehicle for doing so.

The two-and-a-half-hour session flew by as Matt, Rich and James systematically reviewed Matt's Jim Crow and Ku Klux

Klan articles from the previous year. They each rendered their opinion on the motives of specific Klan leaders and the likelihood that this was only one of many such attacks to come in the wake of the *Brown* decision and the general unrest over racial segregation in the United States.

Matt Kane's articles in *Lifetime Magazine* were entitled *A Warning to America – A Divided Society* and *A Second Warning to America – The Ku Klux Klan: Violence and Intimidation*. In the first article published in mid 1952, Kane recounted the enactment of Jim Crow laws in the South in the wake of the passing of the Reconstruction Amendments to the U.S. Constitution, which were ratified in the five years after the end of the Civil War.

The Thirteenth Amendment outlawed slavery, the Fourteenth Amendment accorded citizenship rights to all individuals born in the U. S. and accorded 'equal protection of the laws', and the Fifteenth Amendment guaranteed all men, regardless of race or ethnic background, the right to vote. These protectionist revisions to the Constitution incited a strong backlash in the South, leading to various state laws intended to keep the races segregated and unequal.

The intent of *A Divided Society* was to raise awareness of how persecution of specific groups and segregation of the races not only violated our own Constitutional mantra that 'all men are created equal', but also fueled hatred and triggered a cycle of violence that affected every citizen socially, politically and economically. Indeed, Jim Crow laws largely prevented any direct relationship between Negros and Caucasians in every facet of life. For the remainder of the Nineteenth Century, violence against minority groups was widespread and largely sanctioned by law.

A Divided Society went on to document that the Twentieth Century saw little change until World War II, where the races were thrown together to fight the Nazis. After the War, the oppressed began to gain legal and social standing through the courts and legal marches, protests, and violent confrontations with police and white hate groups. He warned that the Harlem

Riots, and uprisings in Detroit, Beaumont, Mobile and Chicago were a sign of things to come if racial segregation was not ended.

As he hoped, *A Warning to America – A Divided Society* sparked widespread debate and praise from many enlightened white leaders for Matt's call for equality in jobs, housing, education, medical services and other facets of society in order to reduce poverty, and ultimately avoid the brewing violence that he anticipated. His article created enough impact that Matt decided to write a follow-up essay with a specific focus on the white supremacy concept and the Ku Klux Klan. He was also inspired by the newspaper columns railing against the Klan by W. Horace Carter of the *Tabor City, North Carolina Tribune.*

A Second Warning to America – The Ku Klux Klan: Violence and Intimidation was more scathing than his first essay, and generated both enthusiasm and pointed questions from Agent Rosino. A stickler for details, Rosino probed for clues to Klan involvement in the assassination attempt. The agent had devoted almost full time for over two years to monitoring KKK activities in several states, examining their methods of operation, and scrutinizing virtually every move they made. He had several paid informants in various Klan bodies and felt comfortable that he could help determine if the Klan was involved in the attack.

James Rosino was impressed with Matt's detailed history of the KKK over almost a century of activity. His article indicated that there appeared to have been two separate eras of the Klan, the first being in the immediate aftermath of the Civil War. Former Confederate soldiers led by General Nathan Bedford Forrest founded the alliance in 1866 in Pulaski, Tennessee. It was purported to be a social club, but its thinly veiled mission was to defy Reconstruction policies and cause white discontent in the South.

As the Klan migrated from Tennessee to most other states in the Deep South during the 1870s, their quest to restore white dominance included electoral politics, violence, murder, and bullying of black and white citizens, as well as retribution against unfriendly elected officials and law enforcement. Kane noted in *Violence and Intimidation* that the Klan had no central organization, but essentially acted as separate tribes of terror mongers. Gradually, as the Civil War moved into the background and Congress passed laws that addressed Klan activities, the group's influence subsided, only to be revived in the second decade of the Twentieth Century.

The essay went on to recount that the second era of the Ku Klux Klan was ignited by D.W. Griffith's 1915 movie, *Birth of a Nation*. The film detailed the Civil War and the Reconstruction, hailing the Klan as a savior of the nation. With the implicit endorsement of President Woodrow Wilson, Klan revival commenced in Atlanta, Georgia.

In late November, a few days before the film premiered, a group headed by a defrocked Methodist minister, William J. Simmons, burned a cross near Stone Mountain, thereby creating the distinguishing terror signature of the Klan. Matt explained that the next thirty years saw more viciousness and a broader application of the Klan's philosophy. The renewed mobs now spread throughout the United States and targeted Catholics, Jews, immigrants, adulterers and other non-Christian, non-white populations. Membership swelled to as many as four million people during this period.

The most illuminating element of Matt Kane's second article was his discussion of specific politicians and police officials who were actual KKK members or endorsers of their philosophy and tactics. Prominent names included West Virginia Senator Robert Byrd, Supreme Court Justice Hugo Black, President Harry Truman and several noted elected leaders, state governors and police commissioners. He even referenced current Imperial Wizards of the Klan in specific states including Eldon Edwards, a paint sprayer from Atlanta, Georgia; Sam Clark, a county sheriff from Meridian, Mississippi; Edward Maddox, a factory worker in Aiken, South Carolina; and Wallace Dryer, a lawyer from Hamilton County, Indiana.

The primary message of *A Second Warning to America – The Ku Klux Klan: Violence and Intimidation* was an admonition that the impending decision in *Brown v. Board of Education* could revive segregationist activity and revitalize Klan passion, sparking a third era of the Ku Klux Klan. That was Matt's major foreboding.

"I'll reach out to my informants in several states and see if they've heard any discussion of increased Klan activity, including assassination targets or attempts," offered Rosino.

"My initial instinct is that the Klan is not involved. One reason is that the decentralized nature of the state alliances is such that they probably couldn't effectively coordinate such a professional attack. The overriding reason, however, is that individual egos would not permit someone outside the Klan to handle their retribution...and certainly not a woman. Nonetheless, it demands careful investigation to eliminate them as conspirators in Matt's attack."

James Rosino's assessment was convincing to both Matt and Rich Johnson and they agreed to continue to look at all possible alternatives.

"Again, patience is the key guys. We need to remember to take it step-by-step, and we should continue to look for realistic motives, patterns of behavior, and what the antagonists' end game is," responded Rich. "I'm confident that we'll figure it out in time."

"It will take me a week or so to canvas all of my informants, so let's plan to get back together in two weeks. In the meantime, Rich, you can pursue the pharmaceutical angle and Matt you can concentrate on recovery and rehabilitation," concluded Rosino.

On cue, Ruth entered the room to usher her patient back to his quarters for dinner. Her presence immediately buoyed his spirits.

Chapter 4

The Mystery Woman

TWA Flight #919 arrived from Orly Airport in Paris early in the afternoon of May 23rd, where a statuesque and agile blonde woman in her mid-twenties stepped down the ramp and entered the terminal at Idlewild Airport in New York. She passed through customs with alacrity, hailed a cab, and went to her appointed hotel in the City. The cab took twenty-five minutes to get the young woman to the Plaza Hotel at the corner of 5th Avenue and 58th Street in Midtown Manhattan.

Stylishly dressed in a light-olive woolen skirt and ivory knit sweater with five buttons down the front and a flared collar, the mystery woman checked in almost unnoticed. Her room on the seventeenth floor afforded her a panoramic view of Central Park. She briefly surveyed the scene and marveled at the size and orderliness of the property. Since her flight to Chicago didn't leave until 8:45 a.m. the next day, she had a full afternoon of free time to explore the Park and observe some of the people in the 'Empire City'.

Before having lunch and trekking through Central Park, the secretive woman placed a long-distance telephone call to her benefactor in Aachen, Germany, approximately ten kilometers from the Belgian border, and less than an hour's drive from Liège, where *Thérapeutiques Recherche, Inc.* was located.

"Hallo," answered her handler.

"I arrived in New York," replied the woman in her native German language. "I'll leave for Chicago tomorrow and take the train to Minneapolis late in the day. I should have completed my first American assignment within a week. I'll call you when I reach Minnesota. "

"It is good that you are in New York. Be careful not to attract attention when you get to Minnesota. Finishing your first assignment this week is essential. You do not want to stay in the United States any longer than necessary. Also remember, from now on you must always speak English while you are there. No one should hear you speaking Deutsch. Call me tomorrow when you get to your next hotel."

"Yes, sir. Goodbye."

The professional assassin was educated at *Die Akademie der Auserwählten;* an exclusive boarding school located on the Avenue Georges Truffaut on the south bank of the Meuse River in the northwest section of Liège, Belgium. She was fluent in German and French, and spoke English *almost* perfectly, although her work had never taken her out of Europe. She was anxious to study these Americans and analyze their culture and behavior.

The mysterious young woman's temperament, background and education made her the perfect candidate for revenge indoctrination at an early age. She was attractive, athletic, intelligent and determined. She was also quiet and unassuming, but very crafty and resourceful...traits that suited her profession well. In short, she was an angry predator looking for retribution. But for what, and why was Matt Kane one of her targets? Only her handlers knew, and they used this enmity to further their goals.

It was a partly cloudy Sunday afternoon with temperatures in the high 60s as the woman stepped out of the Plaza Hotel, walked to the corner of Sixth Avenue, crossed West 59th Street and entered Central Park. After a few minutes, she paused briefly to watch the seemingly carefree passersby and admired the vastness of this tree-laden property before continuing on her way toward the lake. It only took a few moments for melancholy, then resentment, to overtake her. There were dozens of children on seesaws, swings and monkey bars, and other children throwing and catching balls or simply playing tag. These children were living an idyllic life compared to her wartime childhood...no bombed-out buildings, no famine, and no political upheaval or rampant crime as in her post-war world.

After regaining her sense of purpose, the woman resumed her hike, particularly examining the behavior of the young adults. She also noticed how the young women dressed, their hairstyles, and most importantly, their behavior. She was somewhat surprised at the frivolity of the women in her age group, and their keen deference to the young men. Her preparation had evidently been flawless, as she was able to move easily without attracting undue attention, but noted that she would have to curb her natural command tendencies if she was to aptly play her prearranged role during her stay in the U.S.

During the woman's journey through the park, it occurred to her that this type of setting would be ideal for trapping her prey and completing her first U.S. mission. She resolved to look for a similar site in Minneapolis in which to eliminate target number four. This would be her first task when she arrived in Minnesota.

The pensive woman spent more than two hours ambling through every area of the park, admiring many of its historic landmarks such as the Bow Bridge, the Ramble, the Angel of Waters Statue, Belvedere Castle, the Alice-in-Wonderland and Hans Christian Anderson statues, and the 106-acre Reservoir. Her tour of Central Park finally ended up at the world-famous Tavern on the Green restaurant.

After an of appetizer of shrimp cocktail, a main course of braised stuffed breast of veal with gravy, and a chocolate éclair, the satiated woman decided to head back to the Plaza Hotel, then abruptly changed her mind and hailed a green and yellow Checker Cab. She asked the driver to take her to the New York Public Library. While she could just as well have waited until she arrived in Minneapolis to look for an appropriate park in which to complete her task, she was anxious to get her research started.

The taxi proceeded west on the 65th Street Transverse through Central Park, turned south on Fifth Avenue and moved at a brisk pace to the main library branch located in the historic Stephen A. Schwarzman Building at the corner of Fifth Avenue and 42nd Street.

The massive exterior marble, with crouching lions and tall columns, reminded the mystery woman of the stately buildings in her home country that were destroyed by the unrelenting bombing during the war. Upon entering the building, she was struck by the vast expanse of the Rose Main Reading Room, with exquisite, gilded ceiling architecture and vast paintings, and endless rows of heavy oak tables. She then quickly returned to the task at hand. She politely asked the librarian where to find city maps, and was guided to the Travel Section, where she perused the stacks and found a Rand McNally Atlas of Minnesota, with bountiful details of metropolitan Minneapolis.

Intent on finding a suitable site for her attack on the assigned target, the clandestine woman carefully examined the map. She noted the extensive lake system and found what she believed would be the ideal location for her ambush. In less than fifteen minutes, she identified the Commons Park in the small community of Excelsior, Minnesota as her staging ground. Her quarry apparently frequented the area regularly and would likely be comfortable when she beckoned him to the park. She would stake out the area and plan her tactics when she arrived in Minneapolis.

Once the professional assassin was satisfied with her initial research, she exited the library and casually strolled north on Fifth Avenue toward the Plaza Hotel. The one-mile walk took less than twenty minutes. While it was still early in the evening, she was exhausted from her travels and the five-hour time change, and easily fell sound asleep.

The young woman arrived at Idlewild Airport thirty minutes before her 8:45 a.m. flight to Chicago, checked her luggage, and quietly boarded the plane fifteen minutes later. Shortly after takeoff, the chatty TWA hostess served a full breakfast of scrambled eggs, pancakes, sausage, fruit, orange juice and coffee. The clandestine woman ate most of the meal, but ignored the coffee. She contemplated the decadence of America since it was distinctly more prosperous than her native Germany. It was clear to her that the U.S. had suffered very little as a result of the war. Once again, she was annoyed and jealous at the same time.

Within an hour of eating the meal, the woman began feeling queasy and excused herself to the airplane toilet, where she heaved violently. Gathering herself, she returned to her seat and mustered enough grit to steady her mind, close her eyes, and endure the rest of the flight. It was obvious upon landing, however, that she would not be able to continue her trip to Minneapolis. She would have to find a place to stay in Chicago until she felt better.

Midway Airport, situated approximately eight miles southwest of the central business district, was bordered by 55th and 63rd streets and Central Avenue and the famed Cicero Avenue. The ill woman disembarked, recovered her luggage, and asked a porter for a hotel recommendation. Sensing that this was a woman of refinement, he suggested that she try either The Palmer House, The Drake or The Knickerbocker, all located within ten miles or so of the airport. She thanked him, tipped him two dollars, and moved toward the taxi stand. Upon entering the cab, she asked the driver which of the three hotels was closest, and was told it was The Palmer House.

They arrived at the hotel twelve minutes later. Now running a substantial fever and on the verge of retching again, she hurriedly checked-in, left her bags with the bellhop, and trudged to her room where she immediately vomited. She alternatively heaved and had diarrhea for the next several hours, and tried to decide whether or not to find a doctor. Sometime after midnight, dehydrated and drained, she determined that she had to see a doctor the next morning. The remainder of the night was fitful and difficult, although she was trained to endure worse.

Early on Tuesday morning, the erstwhile tough woman laboriously showered and dressed, called for a taxi, and headed off to St. Luke's Hospital emergency room a mile and a half away. Her wait was short, and she was quickly admitted and given IV fluids to ameliorate her dehydration. Given the recount of her day in New York and subsequent travel to Chicago, the doctor was pretty sure she had a bad case of food poisoning, probably caused by salmonella. He urged her to stay another twenty-four to forty-eight hours until her symptoms abated and she could get back on solid food.

In addition to being sick, the trained assassin was agitated and anxious because her timetable had been compromised, preventing her from getting on with her missions. Nonetheless, she realized that she wouldn't be fully functional for a few days and agreed to stay until the next day.

By Wednesday morning, the mystery woman felt somewhat better and informed the nurse that she wished to leave. The nurse contacted the doctor, and while he preferred that she stay another day, consented to discharge her after she ate lunch. Her appetite had not returned, but she agreed and resolved to force down some food so she could get back to her hotel and rest in private.

The young woman's next problem was paying the hospital bill. Her handler had carefully planned her international agenda, and had prepaid the hotel bills and left money on each room account for meals and toiletries. She also had a moderate amount of American currency, but didn't know if it would be enough to cover the hospital charges. She was relieved when she received a bill for two days totaling $21.50. That would leave her $23.50 in cash, which would be enough until she could request more from her financier.

Once back in her room at The Palmer House, the covert operative immediately placed a long distance call to her handler in Aachen.

"Hallo," answered the man.

"I'm sorry I couldn't call you sooner," spoke the woman solemnly in English.

"Where have you been? Have you completed your first assignment?"

"Nein. I became sick on the airplane and had to stay in Chicago. I had to go to the hospital for two days, but I am back at the Hotel Palmer House now."

"How did this happen? You are off your schedule," reacted the controller impatiently. "We will have to revise your schedule, and that will take time."

"I got sick from the airplane food and will need to rest for one more day," she retorted firmly, but respectfully. "I will take the train to Minneapolis on Friday. I will work on my plan and complete the mission on Monday, and take the train back here on Tuesday. I will need some more money. Please wire one hundred dollars to Western Union in Chicago. I will pick it up tomorrow."

"Okay, but you must complete the mission rapidly and silently. Call me when you get to the Nicollet Hotel on Friday. Auf Wiedersehen."

"Auf Wiedersehen."

By mid-morning on Thursday, the young woman was almost back to full health and walked two blocks to the Western

Union office to retrieve the money sent to her by her Aachen guardian. She then returned to The Palmer House, checked out, called a taxi, and proceeded to Union Station to catch the 1:00 p.m. train to Minneapolis-St. Paul.

The Twin Cities Hiawatha #101 train averaged roughly sixty-two miles per hour and made the four-hundred-mile trip from Chicago to Minneapolis in slightly less than seven hours. The luxurious train, with space to move about and gourmet dining, provided a quiet and peaceful break for the would-be assassin as she regained her composure and contemplated her assignment. She arrived at the Great Northern Depot in Minneapolis at 7:52 p.m., only a few minutes after the scheduled arrival time, hailed a cab, checked into the majestic Nicollet Hotel, and arrived in her room in less than an hour. Since it was close to 2:00 a.m. in Germany, she decided to wait until Friday morning to call her controller.

Friday, May 28th was an active day for the surreptitious woman. After apprising her overseer that she was in Minnesota, she dressed in a short-sleeved navy-blue dress with a light gray one-inch plaid pattern and modest V-neck, stylish flats, and a light blue sweater in order to look like the young women she saw in New York. After eating breakfast in her room, she set about crafting her strike, exploring transportation alternatives, casing Commons Park for the best staging area, and carefully observing her prey.

Her first task was to find the most efficient way to get to and from the park without being noticed. She looked at the map she was given by the hotel and planned her transportation alternatives. She decided to take a taxi on her scouting run, but concluded that it would be too risky on the night of her ambush. She was careful to mark the distance and time to the Commons Park so she could plan her exit after the confrontation with Matt Kane.

The cab driver proceeded southwest on Hennepin Avenue for fourteen minutes, passing the bus depot four blocks from the hotel, turned south on Excelsior Boulevard, and traveled for ten minutes to the community of Hopkins, then another eight minutes through Glen Lake, finally arriving at the municipality of Excelsior in another seven minutes. The passenger noted that the total trip of approximately twenty miles took less than forty minutes.

The cautious woman exited the taxi and walked up Lake Street toward the Commons Park, turned right on Water Street, and proceeded past the Tonka movie theater toward Excelsior Bay looking for a possible escape route by boat. While appealing, it was not practical because she would have to engage the conscious assistance of other people. She did not want to be noticed. While there, however, she saw a public toilet that would be useful on the night of her mission.

The mystery woman entered the park and walked along the water's edge to Solberg Point and turned toward the neighborhood streets that bordered the park. She was pleased that the trees would provide cover from onlookers. That, plus the dark of the moon, would allow her to ambush her quarry and exit with no witnesses.

As the scheming woman headed back toward town along Second Street, she saw a Twin City Bus Stop at the intersection of Second, Lake, and Mill Streets, and Morse Avenue. That fit her plan perfectly. She waited for the bus, inconspicuously got on, and went back to downtown Minneapolis. She now believed she had solved the transportation logistic.

The afternoon was spent reviewing her report on the personality and habits of Matthew Kane, as well as the information provided to her about his research into the pharmaceutical industry. By the end of the day, the would-be assassin had covered all the details necessary for a successful mission except one. She wanted to shadow her target for at least one day to get a better sense of his alertness, approachability, energy and overall serenity. All characteristics that might affect how she handled her ambush. Her briefing notes indicated that he was inquisitive, strong-willed, clever and tenacious. He was also reputed to be to instinctive, affable and confident. This target was special. She wanted to be absolutely sure.

Saturday and Sunday were spent following her mark, noting his habits and interaction with people and reviewing the dossier provided by her advance researcher. She already knew that he typically had breakfast at Nena's Diner on Excelsior Boulevard in St. Louis Park and decided to begin her surveillance there. While she was an accomplished motorcyclist, she felt that she would be too conspicuous, so she took a taxi to within a block of the diner and awaited his arrival. She observed his behavior and found him to be just as easy going as the report had indicated. The rest of his weekend activities were relatively simple to follow.

From Nena's he went back home to make some telephone calls and work on his current project until noon. He left home at 12:14 p.m. and proceeded to Old Lord's Restaurant on Lake Minnetonka to have lunch with friends. Since it was a warm enough day, the party moved to the marina where they boarded his boat and enjoyed the afternoon on the lake. She rented a canoe and trailed the party at a distance, again viewing his demeanor and weighing his temperament. The evening was spent at home reading, so the observer went back to her hotel.

Sundays were generally spent with his parents at their home in St. Louis Park. However, with May 30th being Memorial Day to honor Americans killed in war, the family gathered with other veteran families to watch the parade along Victory Memorial Parkway and the fireworks display at Victory Park late in the evening. The mystery woman took a taxi to the location and tolerantly watched her mark until almost 11:00 p.m.

The experience was riveting, but upsetting, because her country had been subdivided by the Allies and had no such remembrance. Nonetheless, having developed a good feel for her mark, she left the scene with a clear idea of how to approach Matthew Kane. She knew how to use his natural persona and easy manner against him in her telephone call to lure him to Commons Park on Monday.

"Hello, this is Matt Kane."

"Mr. Kane, I have information about the drug companies that is very important," replied the caller anxiously.

"Who are you?" he quizzed.

"I cannot tell you, but I know things about those companies that will help you stop them from hurting any more people," she conveyed in an urgent manner. "You must meet me tonight. I will be killed if they find out that I have talked to you, so we must meet in secret."

"Okay," Matt readily agreed. He was hooked. "Where and when do you want to meet?"

"The Commons Park, where the large Elm tree is on the hill in the northwest end near the water."

"What time?" Matt replied.

"After the sun sets, maybe 10:00 o'clock."

"How will I know you?" Matt asked.

"You will recognize me since we have met before," she countered, immediately regretting the reference.

"Okay, I'll see you..." She had already hung up the telephone.

Matt spent Monday feverishly analyzing his pharmaceutical company summaries, looking for any hint of the improprieties to which the caller had alluded. What did she know that would be that important? He wanted to be properly prepared so he could gather as many facts as possible in his secret meeting. Being a stickler for details, he didn't want to miss anything. He would also need to get corroboration before he finalized his story.

The assassin paced in her room throughout the day, pondering her impending mission, and carefully packed her attack bag, which included a **Walther P.38** automatic pistol and box of 9mm shells, her black wig, gray slacks, dark blouse, black leather jacket, and boots. She ate an early dinner at 4:00 p.m. in the hotel dining room and walked four and a half blocks down Hennepin Avenue to the bus stop. She boarded the bus at 5:15 p.m. and headed to the small town of Excelsior.

While the Twin City Lines bus followed the same route as the taxi from Hennepin Avenue to Excelsior Boulevard to Commons Park, the trip took almost fifteen minutes longer. The young blonde woman in a yellow print sun dress with her navy-blue sweater blended in well with the fifteen other passengers on the coach, but had some concern about the return trip because of the late hour. There would likely be only one or two other passengers and she didn't want to be remembered. Once in town, she marched down Water Street to the public toilet, stashed her attack bag, walked back to the Tonka Theater where she bought a ticket and entered the cinema at 6:25 p.m.

The movie, *Dial M for Murder*, an Alfred Hitchcock thriller, unveiled a husband's plot to kill his wealthy wife to get her inheritance. The carefully orchestrated plan unraveled and the would-be killer was nabbed...somewhat unnerving for the young woman. Fortunately, there were more than a hundred other patrons in the movie, many teenagers freshly out of school for the year, along with some young adults, which provided anonymity as she exited the theater in the middle of the next showing at 8:58 p.m.

The assassin unobtrusively strolled to the public restroom, retrieved her bag, changed clothes, donned her wig, re-stashed her bag, and stealthily slipped into the park. It took ten minutes to get to the appointed large Elm, where she perched behind the tree to await her victim.

Matt wanted to be early so he left home just after 9:00 p.m. and drove the twelve miles to Excelsior in just over twenty minutes. He parked on Lake Street and moved slowly along the pathway toward Solberg Point. It was not yet completely dark, but he saw no one, and he surmised that the remaining park goers were probably near the Water Street district. When he arrived at the appointed spot, he paused to look at his watch. He was fifteen minutes early.

The executioner stepped from behind the tree and Matt turned to approach her, looking for a familiar face. *I don't recognize her*, he thought.

"Remember me?" she mocked, as she raised her weapon and pumped two bullets into his chest.

Almost immediately, the killer heard a barking dog and knew she needed to leave the scene promptly. She hurriedly searched for the bullet shells, and found one, but not the other. Realizing that someone was coming, she abandoned the quest and ran through the trees toward First Street. As she fled the area, she saw a man chasing after the howling dog and realized that Matt Kane's body had been found. She had anticipated more time for her getaway, and while exasperated, she was confident that her plan was still viable.

The executioner ran three blocks down First Street to Center Street and turned toward the park. She saw no one until she reached the pathway behind the Tonka Theater, and quietly slipped into the public restroom. She had no time to clean the mud off her boots so she coolly grabbed her bag, changed clothes, took a deep breath, and exited to Water Street. Luck was with her. The late movie was just letting out and she was able to blend into the crowd as patrons were walking toward their vehicles. To her mild surprise, at least a dozen young girls, along with a few boys, headed for the bus stop. She heard the roar of sirens as she stepped onto the bus at 10:25 p.m., and knew that her getaway was complete.

While she was the last passenger on the bus, the driver did not appear to take conscious notice of her. She slipped off the bus by the rear door and marched, with a purpose, back to the Nicollet Hotel and into her room on the fourth floor. She was sure that she had avoided detection. She was exhilarated and exhausted, threw her bag on the corner chair, and fell onto the bed. Mission number four was complete, and she would head toward her next target in the morning.

The refreshed and reassured mystery woman woke up at 5:42 a.m. and showered, dressed, packed and checked out of the hotel in less than an hour. She walked northwest three blocks to the train terminal, bought a ticket on Twin Cities Hiawatha #6 train back to Chicago, and patiently waited for departure at 7:50 a.m. Before boarding, however, she dutifully called her controller in Aachen.

"Guten Tag," answered the handler.

"It is finished," responded the female caller, again in German. "I am leaving Minnesota and will be in Arizona tomorrow night."

"English...*English*...always *English!*" retorted her handler.

"Sorry, sir, I will call you when I get to Arizona."

Target number four, her principal antagonist, had been eliminated, and it was time to focus on number five. She had a train trip, an airline flight, and two days to plot her next attack.

Chapter 5

The Belgian Connection

Almost two weeks elapsed as Agent Rosino traveled throughout the deep South and lower Midwest to confer with his Klan informants. At the same time, Detective Johnson tended to a series of violent incidents attributed to a street gang turf war, while his partner, Detective Colin Young, began to probe the inner workings of Belgian pharmaceutical companies. Matt Kane continued his arduous physical therapy regimen and was healing more rapidly than his doctors anticipated. He fully expected to be discharged from the hospital before the end of June.

During the intervening fortnight, Rich Johnson stopped by periodically to see Matt, give him brief updates on both the KKK and pharmaceutical company investigations, and check on his recovery. During one visit, he chanced upon Matt and his father discussing a possible link to Belgian drug researchers. Dr. Kane suggested that the detective contact a former medical school classmate, Dr. Rudolph Steinhardt, an expatriated German pharmacologist from Cornell University. He was certain his old friend could provide background information on the pharmaceutical industry and current ongoing studies.

Dr. Steinhardt initially arrived in New York in 1938 and had been a prominent academic researcher in his home country. He had extensive experience in cancer research in both Germany and the United States, and was familiar with most American pharmaceutical companies and their current studies in blood disorders and solid tumors. Dr. Steinhardt was an early champion of the concept of chemical treatment for various types of malignancies, and devoted much of his time before the war working with pharmacologists, neuropathologists, biochemists, biologists and hematopathologists in cancer research. His team worked under the direction of the esteemed Dr. Otto Warburg during the 1930s until the political climate forced him to flee to the United States.

"Hi, Rich, it's James. I've finished my Klan investigation and I can get back to Minneapolis on Wednesday if that works for you and Matt."

"Okay, James, Wednesday, June 23rd is fine. I'll pick you up and we can get back together with Matt. He's recovering nicely and should be out of the hospital in a few days. He's disappointed that we haven't been able to get any meaningful information on the assassin, and is anxious to be discharged so he can be more helpful with the investigation."

"Anything of value on the drug company angle?"

"Maybe. Matt's father gave me the name of a cancer expert who might be able to provide some leads. My partner has been looking into the Belgian companies and thinks he's found some irregularities."

"Fine. I'll see you next week...and stay out of mischief until I get there. We can do it together," joked Rosino.

During the two-week hiatus, Ruth Chessman and Matt Kane began to develop an attachment that seemed to go beyond the normal bounds of the nurse-patient relationship. While he was almost seven years her senior, he found her to be mature, intelligent, and insightful. She found him to be resilient, confident and fascinating. Ruth understood that patients move in and out of a nurse's life with regularity, and that developing an emotional bond with them can easily lead to personal distress and psychological exhaustion. Nonetheless, she was drawn to him and felt that their connection was destined to go beyond a professional relationship.

Matt had not experienced a meaningful attraction to a woman since he left England in 1947. Marie Spenser was the secret love he was forced to leave behind after the war when she chose to return to university to finish her undergraduate degree in mathematics, and ultimately her Doctorate in Linguistics at King's College London. He somehow assumed they would eventually find each other again, but now he was developing a kinship with Ruth that he felt compelled to pursue. He wondered, however, if his feelings were a post-traumatic response or a genuine affinity for another woman. He resolved to be patient and see how their relationship evolved.

When time permitted during the normally hectic rush in the ward, Ruth would stop by and chat with Matt, and occasionally stay after her shift and take Matt outside on the terrace, where they would talk for half an hour. Their conversations ranged from how they chose their respective careers, interests outside of work, family, and Matt's extensive travel and World War II experiences. Ruth was also keenly interested in the shooting and the next steps in the investigation.

On Wednesday morning at 9:30 a.m., Rich and James entered the ward to find Matt sitting contentedly in the chair beside his bed, jotting down some thoughts about the Belgian drug companies. By now he was convinced they were the instigators of the attack. The issue was how to prove it. He rose from the chair and extended his hand to each of his new friends.

"Well...don't you look spry," quipped Agent Rosino with a roguish grin.

"I should be...this lady is a taskmaster, and has pushed me to keep up with her," Matt quipped with an admiring glance at Ruth.

"Okay, gentlemen. You know the drill. Off to the conference room," she countered in mock authority.

Matt rose from his chair and walked with purpose to the conference room, explaining along the way that he was ready to leave the hospital, but the doctors insisted that he stay another week to be sure his kidney function was normal and his restructured ribs were strong and secure. While Matt was anxious to get back in circulation, he was also ambivalent about leaving his new companion. He knew a moment of truth was coming in their friendship.

"Guys, I spent the last two weeks with several imbedded informants all over the South," began James. "And yes, there's great resentment over the Supreme Court decision in *Brown*, but there is no evidence that suggests undue animosity toward you, Matt. It seems more likely that they will go after Negro leaders. For instance, Thurgood Marshall, the black lawyer who argued the case against segregation before the Court, might be a target. Or Medgar Evers, the new field secretary of the Mississippi Office of the National Association for Advancement of Colored People. There are many more inviting marks than you, Matt."

"Their immediate focus seems to be on black people who try to attend white schools. I fear we're going to see a significant rise in Klan violence, as you predicted in your last essay. We appear to be headed for a race war. In addition, the Klan has a plan to mobilize white extremists to vote for political leaders who are committed to stalling integration through legislation and simple non-compliance with the inevitable court decisions that seem destined to come in the next couple of years. Integration is going to be a slow and painful process, and our primary task is to figure out how to tamp down the violence."

"In summary, Rich, I'm convinced that the Ku Klux Klan played no role in Matt's ambush. You mentioned that you might have found something in the drug research inquiry?"

"Yes, I think we may be on to something," responded the detective. "There appears to be some irregularity in the way drug experiments are being conducted by at least one of the Belgian companies. That avenue needs to be carefully explored. Unfortunately, that's out of my purview. My charge is to find the individual who shot Matt, and the way it looks now, she has left the city and I don't have the authority to pursue her. Given the facts, it's likely that she's a foreign national so it looks like the FBI should have jurisdiction over the investigation."

"Have you given up on the search, Rich?" queried Matt.

"Not completely," Johnson retorted apologetically, "but since we haven't been able to identify or track down the attacker in three weeks, our Police Chief, Weyman Larson, wants me to shift my emphasis to the local gang violence and let national authorities take over the case. It will remain semi-active and I can have Colin Young devote some time to it, but the majority of activity will have to come from the FBI."

"What about me? Can I do some digging and report to you or Detective Young?" implored Matt.

"I don't mind at all, Matt, but our team has combed the area, and talked to dozens of people who were in the park or in town that night, so I don't know how much good it will do."

"Let me worry about that. I don't quit that easily, and I'll find something if it takes a year." Matt was exasperated and determined to demonstrate his skill as an investigator.

"Okay, boys, I think I have a solution to the problem," interrupted Rosino. "Rich, how would you like to be temporarily assigned to the FBI to work with me on the case? Matt can work with Young locally, and you and I can pursue the case wherever it leads us...even to Belgium, if necessary."

A surprised Rich Johnson hesitated for a few seconds to fully comprehend James' offer. "Can you really do that?"

"Absolutely. Somebody get Ruth. I'll call Director Hoover and get it all arranged if you think you're up to it, my friend." A knowing smile then crossed his face.

Rich looked at Matt inquisitively, Matt nodded, and they both promptly agreed. Ruth directed the FBI Agent to a private telephone line in the hospital administrator's office where Rosino made a call to FBI Director J. Edgar Hoover. It took less than five minutes to persuade the Director that the Matt Kane case had a national, and perhaps international, scope, and that the extraordinary skills of Detective Captain Richard Johnson would be invaluable to the case. Hoover agreed to call Police Chief Larson to clear the way for the detective to be part of the team.

In less than an hour, Rich received a call from the Minneapolis Chief of Police informing him that an FBI task force was being assembled to pursue a case vital to American interests, and that he was being assigned immediately to that unit. His credentials would be forthcoming in the next day or two.

Agent Rosino knew the FBI Director well, and clearly understood Hoover's penchant for intrigue, particularly any international treachery that might affect the security of the United States. Convincing him to form the task force was easy. Rosino and Johnson would be on a plane the next day to interview the Cornell pharmacologist, Dr. Rudolph Steinhardt.

The task force leader and his new partner arrived at the office of Dr. Rudolph Steinhardt on the Cornell University campus at 4:00 p.m. on Thursday, having flown to New York City, rented a car, and drove to Ithaca. He indeed turned out to be a treasure trove of information as promised by Dr. Friedrick Kane. The two-hour interview confirmed much of the material contained in Matt's notes on the Belgian pharmaceutical companies, and yielded some other possible links to the case.

Dr. Steinhardt was an affable and loquacious fountain of knowledge, and was eager to share it with the FBI agent and Minneapolis detective.

"Gentlemen," began Dr. Steinhardt, "while efforts to develop chemical treatments for cancer started in the Nineteenth Century, the first major breakthrough came serendipitously during World War II as a result of data that came from the use of mustard gas by the Germans in the Great War. Researchers found that an accidental spill of sulfur mustards on troops during the bombing of ships in Bari Harbor, Italy in December 1943 caused bone marrow and lymph nodes of exposed seamen to be dramatically affected by the gas. This raised the possibility that alkylating agents might be effective in the treatment of malignancies if compounded properly."

Now fully engaged, the effusive professor continued his history lesson.

"Dr. Milton Winternitz and two other pharmacologists from Yale were engaged by the U.S. Office of Scientific Research and Development to study the potential therapeutic effects of the mustard compounds. They observed significant positive effects in the treatment of non-Hodgkin's lymphoma patients, which boosted hopes that alkylating-based chemical combinations could be effective in curing all types of malignancies. After their results were published in 1946, a crush of research developed around these compounds. Unfortunately, these amalgams only provided short-term and incomplete reduction in the progression of the disease."

Rich and James just looked at each other in bewilderment, but before they could stop the informative, but seemingly inconsequential monologue, the professor went on.

"While insulin and penicillin dominated the pharmaceutical industry between the two world wars, antibiotics and cancer drugs now occupy the front lines of chemical analysis. Despite the popular opinion that cancer is simply not curable by drugs, the quest for chemical treatments has continued unabated."

"Unfortunately," he indicated sadly, "the rush to develop cancer cures has attracted new pharmaceutical companies, some with questionable ethics. New drugs mean acclaim and profits, and because there is inadequate oversight of the industry worldwide, testing has largely become haphazard and there is no meaningful mechanism to protect an unsuspecting public."

After pausing briefly to catch his breath, Dr. Steinhardt pressed on.

"The search for effective cancer treatments involves a wide range of fields; everything from nutrition and folic acid analogues, to antibiotics, and antimalarial compounds. One antifolate that seems to have promise is a drug called methotrexate, which shows substantial promise in childhood leukemia."

While the history tutorial was fascinating and would inevitably provide great material for Matt Kane's current project, Rosino and Johnson politely insisted that their interest was focused on the Belgian pharmaceutical industry, particularly *JSS Pharmaceutica*, headquartered in Liège.

"Ah, yes. An interesting new entry into the research arena," exclaimed the doctor. "What is not generally known is that *Thérapeutiques Recherche, Inc.*, *JSS Pharmaceutica*, and *PIO Pharma* are all subsidiaries of an American holding company."

This now piqued the interest of the interviewers.

"How do you know this?" inquired Johnson.

"Some of my former German colleagues are employed by these companies, and one of them told me they formed the holding company to avoid the stricter regulations on human testing in the United States."

"So, you're saying that these three drug companies are frauds?" asked Rosino.

"Maybe not frauds, but they certainly have questionable operating philosophies. And in my opinion, while their research may ultimately produce some major breakthroughs, their methods might not be much different than the Nazi experiments during the war."

"Doctor Steinhardt, we're investigating the attempted murder of a journalist who was researching these companies for an exposé. In your opinion, do you think they would risk killing someone to keep from divulging their U.S. sponsorship and questionable operating practices?" probed James Rosino.

"I wouldn't be surprised," answered the professor.

James and Rich now believed they had found the key to the case. It was time to return to Washington, D.C. to design a strategy for working the problem. They knew it would be a complex investigation, with moving parts in both the U.S. and Europe, and identifying the source of the attack would likely hinge on finding the shooter.

Chapter 6

The Partnerships

Monday, June 29, 1954 may have been a cloudy and sticky day in Minneapolis, but for Matthew Seiberling Kane, it was a beautiful day to celebrate life itself. After four weeks and one day, he was leaving Minneapolis General Hospital. Matt was finally regaining his freedom and constructing a new life. Energy abounded, and he was looking forward to spending time on his boat during the summer and reinvigorating the local investigation into his attempted murder.

Friedrick Kane had picked up Matt's 1952 maroon Hudson Hornet Brougham from the Commons Park the day after the shooting, and came to the hospital to pick up his son and take him home to stay with him and his mother until he was fully healed. Matt would have none of it. He contended that while he had some physical limitations, he was well enough to take care of himself, and wanted to be able to work on the case from his own home.

The doctors told Matt that he shouldn't drive a car for another couple of weeks to avoid tearing scar tissue around his restructured rib cage. True to his resourceful nature, he found a solution to two problems. His new friend would be his driver until he was cleared to resume piloting a vehicle. Dr. Kane knew it was futile to argue with his headstrong son, and handed the keys to Ruth.

Matt lived alone in a house at the end of Decatur Avenue South in St. Louis Park, adjacent to the Minneapolis Golf Club. He reasoned that since his parents resided less than ten minutes away on Edgewood Avenue South, they could respond quickly if he had a problem. As it turned out, Ruth lived in an apartment house with one of her sisters and a friend just off Minnetonka Boulevard, approximately halfway between the hospital and Matt's house. A fifteen-minute drive either way.

In their after-shift discussions on the hospital terrace, Matt learned that Ruth and her two roommates shared a two-bedroom apartment and a 1950 second-hand Chrysler automobile they purchased from Kay Motors in early 1953. Ruth would drive the car to work one or two days a week. On the days that Ruth didn't drive, she took the bus to the hospital. She found out that Matt lived less than seven miles from her in St. Louis Park.

While Ruth felt somewhat uneasy driving and keeping Matt's car, she reasoned that it was a mutually beneficial arrangement; she didn't have to ride the bus and he had someone to check on his medical recovery. In addition, it would give them a chance to see if they could get past the nurse-patient relationship. Matt was pleased that she agreed to the plan because he enjoyed her company and wanted to see if his attraction to her was more than just a post-traumatic rebound.

For the next two weeks, Ruth stopped by to check on Matt each morning before her shift and drive to work. After work, she returned, sometimes with groceries or a meal, and would stay for a couple of hours. The friendship was clearly developing into more. They talked about high school and college years and personal interests, wartime activities and, of course, the attempt on Matt's life. He found out that Ruth had been an accomplished tennis player and enjoyed swimming and almost any outdoor activity. She learned of his athletic feats in football and basketball. They also both enjoyed solving crossword puzzles. Unmistakably, they had much in common.

Matt and Ruth were also different in complementary ways. He was a free communicator. She was more circumspect. He was restless and needed a constant challenge. She was a bit more cautious and settled. She was kind and giving. He had an edge. To the casual observer, they were complete opposites. In reality, it seemed as though Matt's influence could draw Ruth out of her conservative shell, and Ruth could moderate his impatience.

Perhaps the most definitive link came from their World War II experiences. Matt was able to tell Ruth that he had been an intelligence officer during the war, but was prohibited from telling her about his code-breaking activities and covert work with the Bletchley Park *Special Services Unit*. He talked about serving in Britain, France, Germany and Belgium in general terms without revealing the true nature of those assignments. Notwithstanding the vagueness of his stories, Ruth was perceptive enough to realize that he had been involved in top secret operations that perhaps changed the course of the war.

Ruth told Matt that she had an older brother, Robbie, who was killed in a bombing raid over the Regensburg Messerschmitt factory in Germany in August 1943. He had been a pilot in the Eighth Air Force, 100th Bomb Group, stationed at Thorps Abbots Airfield in Norfolk County on the North Sea.

Robbie's B-17 aircraft was assigned to Mission #84 as part of **Operation Pointblank**, the coordinated strategic daylight campaign to destroy Germany's military and industrial production capability. His plane was hit by ground flack and nosedived into another aircraft, exploding both and killing all twenty of the crew on the two planes. Like many family members of Americans killed during the war, she meticulously researched Robbie's unit and missions to help her cope with the loss of her brother. Matt could tell that talking about the loss was cathartic for her.

During the day, Matt tried to reconstruct the movements of his attacker. In the evenings, he and Ruth would discuss, and sometimes debate different possible scenarios. During these sessions, it became clear that their general perspectives and approach to problem solving were significantly different, creating a dynamic tension that made them a good investigative team. At first, this was uncomfortable for Ruth, but Matt enjoyed the give-

and-take, and actually encouraged Ruth to challenge his thought processes because he was more interested in solving the problem than being dominant in the relationship.

On July 4th, Ruth took Matt on his first daily outing. They went to the North Shore Marina on Maxwell Bay, where Matt docked his twenty-five-foot 1947 Chris Craft cabin cruiser. As a condition for the trip, Matt had to agree that Ruth would do the heavy lifting under his direction. They enjoyed a quiet day on the water and returned to his house. As she left for her apartment, they shared their first kiss. Both were now hooked, and their bond became a true partnership.

Matt was due to see his surgeon on Friday, July 16th, where he anticipated that he would be restored to full independence. His ribs were somewhat tender, but he was still healing and the doctor was confident that he would eventually regain full mobility and strength. His kidney function was good, and his liver was regenerating nicely. Forty-six days after his misadventure, Matt was cleared to resume normal, but not excessive, activity. Now he was ready to put his probative skills back to work.

Matt and Ruth went to Nena's Diner for an early dinner and then he drove to her apartment, where he finally met Ruth's older sister, Laura, and her friend Anna. Laura had earned an accounting degree from Gustavus Adolphus College in 1948, and worked as an auditor for a small accounting firm in downtown Minneapolis. While she was somewhat shy, she displayed an excellent analytical mind with great attention to detail. Anna was a secretary at Laura's CPA firm, Wilton, Taft & Oberlin. Outgoing, confident and attractive, she was a good communicator who kept clients happy and the firm running smoothly. Both were anxious to help Matt and Ruth with the investigation.

The willingness to help Matt solve the mystery was not limited to Ruth's roommates. During his two weeks at home, several of Matt's friends indicated a desire to help. After he returned home, he contacted a couple of close friends and arranged to have them meet at his house the next morning to hand out assignments for conducting his fact-finding operation.

"Thanks for checking in on me and providing moral support for the last six weeks...and your offers to help find the person who shot me," began Matt. "Not to mention the blood I got from John and Tony. We're truly related now," he cajoled. "Also, I want you to meet Ruth Chessman, my nurse and confidant during this ordeal. I don't think I would have survived without her. Plus, she had a great deal of input into our strategy for finding the attacker."

There were eight people in the room, including Matt, Ruth, Laura and Anna. Matt laid out the plan and handed out assignments to each. He wanted them to work in pairs to take advantage of the geometric awareness that comes from more than one perspective. The police had used one individual to question potential witnesses. Matt and Ruth believed their approach would be more effective and help ensure that small details were not overlooked.

"The police have already conducted a thorough investigation of that night, beginning at the park and leading toward town. They talked with cab and bus drivers, shop owners, and any other potential eyewitnesses they could find. No one apparently noticed the shooter before or after the attack. After a couple of weeks, they concluded that they were at a dead end and gave up the search. We want to retrace their steps and see if we can find anything they missed."

During one of their strategy discussions, Ruth suggested to Matt that the attacker might have been disguised, or perhaps even changed clothes before or after the assassination attempt. Did she wear a hat or maybe a wig? Did she slip into the park from the water and exit by land? Did she have a local accomplice who provided transportation? The assumption was that she was a professional killer, so she was likely skilled at blending in and covering her tracks. They reasoned that a professional assassin would likely not have a local accomplice. Where might she have made a mistake?

"As we canvas the area, we should ask if anyone saw a young, dark haired woman wearing pants and a black leather jacket, but we should also ask if they saw anyone who might be wearing a dress or coat...or have light colored hair...or someone who just looked out of place?" offered Ruth.

"Remember, guys...this is an investigation, not a personal crusade. Just gather information, don't try to do too much," Matt added. "We can start today, but I think we'll be better served if we work from Monday morning through Tuesday afternoon. If we're lucky, we may find someone who was in Excelsior or the park on those days who can shed light on the investigation. Let's get back together on Tuesday evening and see what we've learned. Again, thanks for your help. You've genuinely demonstrated the meaning of true friendship."

Laura and Anna took two days off from work to probe the transportation angle. They first considered the possibility that the mystery woman might have had a driver but decided to proceed with the public transportation angle first. Consequently, on day one they talked with any cab drivers who went to Excelsior on Monday or Tuesday. After several hours of research, they were confident the mystery woman had not traveled by taxi.

On Tuesday, one bus driver did remember an appealing blonde who rode the bus twice that day, getting on at the Hennepin Avenue bus terminal and getting off in Excelsior. He remembered her because she also took the last bus leaving Excelsior around 10:30 p.m. She got on with several younger girls and boys and sat quietly on the way back to Minneapolis. He assumed she was their chaperone.

"Did you tell the police about this?" inquired Anna.

"I never talked with the police," answered the bus driver.

"Why did you notice her, in particular?" asked Laura.

"She was young and pretty," he replied sheepishly.

"Tell us everything you can remember about her?" probed Anna.

"She had a blonde ponytail for sure...and I think she was wearing a yellow dress. That was a couple of months ago, so I'm not sure,"

"*Oh,*" he exclaimed, "She *was* carrying an oversized satchel that seemed a little out of place for a young lady in a dress."

Anna thanked the bus driver and they eagerly returned to their apartment to share their findings with Ruth. She wasn't there. They tried to restrain their excitement, but were convinced they had found a lead that the police missed. They would pass the information along to the group at the 6:00 p.m. meeting.

John and Sandy Oleson were among Matt's closest friends. John was a law school classmate who joined a prominent legal firm in Rochester, Minnesota to practice criminal law after graduation. He met Sandy at a dance on the University of Minnesota campus in 1937 and they married when he graduated the next year. She was a traditional housewife with two young boys to raise, and the couple were frequent companions on Matt's boating excursions. Their assignment was to explore the would-be assassin's transportation into the country from Europe, as well as her mode of travel from the point of entry to Minneapolis.

John began with the assumption that she would fly to the U.S. rather than take a ship because of the time element. New York or Washington would be logical access points. He also surmised that a good covert operator would then change her method of transportation to cover her tracks. A bus trip from New York or Washington would be laborious so he concluded that she would have taken the train, and perhaps even travel through an intervening city to conceal her ultimate destination. He and Sandy would start at the train station and airport and work backward.

Reasoning that the professional assailant would come a few days before staging her attack to familiarize herself with the city and decide on a venue for the attack, John and Sandy expanded their investigative period to one week. They began their canvas at Wold-Chamberlain Field and questioned ticket and gate agents and stewardesses and, as expected, found nothing useful. They moved to the train terminals in St. Paul and Minneapolis and centered their inquiry on ticket clerks and baggage handlers. John believed that if the executioner was indeed from Europe, she would be familiar and most comfortable, with train travel. He was on the right path, but this avenue was futile because too much time had elapsed and too many people moved in and out of Minneapolis daily for anyone to notice one lone female. Their trail ended there.

Another couple, Tony and Pat Erickson, were assigned the task of uncovering the attacker's lodging arrangements. Tony was a lifelong friend, having lived down the street from Matt on Edgewood Avenue South. They went through school together and were teammates on the St. Louis Park football team. Tony and Pat were high school sweethearts and married after they graduated in 1933. He immediately enlisted in the Navy, where he served for twenty years, beginning as a radioman aboard a destroyer, ultimately achieving the rank of Chief Petty Officer before retiring a year ago. He had been assigned to the USS Henley, a Bagley-Class Destroyer, on December 7, 1941, when the Japanese attacked Pearl Harbor, but his ship only sustained minor strafing damage during the battle. His entire career was spent in communications.

Tony and Pat began their quest on Saturday afternoon talking with hotel and motel personnel along Minnetonka Boulevard. It was obvious after two days of inquiries, however, that they were on a fool's mission. Too much time had elapsed and memories had dulled. Matt's attempted murder was now old news.

Business owners, workers and residents of Excelsior were eager to help Matt and Ruth in their investigation. While not a major celebrity, Matt did have some notoriety in the area as a result of his series of articles on the construction industry and, of course, most people were well aware of the attempt on his life. The incident had somewhat reduced the number of visitors to the town and park and everyone was anxious to have a resolution so business could return to normal.

Matt and Ruth spent most of Monday talking with residents on Lake and West Lake Streets, 1st and 2nd Streets, Grove, Courtland and Center Streets, West and East Drives, and School Avenue. The police had questioned these citizens during the first week, and found nothing useful. Again, they all regretfully reiterated that they had not seen or heard anything that day or night. An exhausting and disappointing day.

The pair began on Tuesday at the drug store on the corner of Water and Second Streets, and systematically worked their way up and down Water Street and toward the bay...Clausen's Garden Store, Tony's Barber Shop, Weisser's Lunch, National Food Stores, Minnesota Drug Company and many other shops and eateries. Finally, the Tonka Theater.

Mr. Sam Richards, the theater manager, was amiable and quite willing to help. It was late afternoon and there were few patrons in the theater, so there was time for the couple to talk with employees. Their timing was perfect. It was almost shift change time. Employees were beginning to arrive for the evening showings of *The Caine Mutiny*, a World War II thriller starring Humphrey Bogart and Van Johnson, so the manager collected day and evening shift workers one at a time to talk with Matt and Ruth. The afternoon ticket taker, concessions girl, projectionist and usher/custodian. Nothing. As they expected, nobody could remember anything unusual on that day. They then moved on to the evening crew. Once again, no luck...except for the ticket taker. The young man, in his mid-twenties, had a vivid memory of that night.

"What did you see that night that was so unforgettable, Gary?" asked Matt.

"I sold a ticket to tall, very pretty blonde that had not been to the theater before...or I would have remembered her." he responded.

"She came to the 6:30 p.m. movie by herself, and I saw her leave during the show. Then I saw her again on the bus after the last show and tried to speak to her. She seemed a little annoyed so I left her alone."

"So, don't you see lots of pretty girls, Gary? Why was this one different?" asked Ruth.

"She was just curious."

"What do you mean, curious?" pressed Ruth.

"She just didn't look like she was from around here," he responded. "She looked sophisticated and a little mysterious."

"That seems like a stretch, Gary," challenged Matt.

"Well, she looked like she was miles away...maybe she had something on her mind. Anyway, she brushed me off pretty good when I tried to talk to her on the bus."

"Tell us anything else you can remember about her?" continued Matt.

"*Well*...she had a blonde ponytail, blue eyes, and looked like she was about my age. She was tall, maybe 5'8" or so. Something else, too. Most of the other girls wore petal pushers or shorts and she had on a dress."

"What kind of dress? What color?" queried Ruth.

"Just a dress, a light dress. *Oh*, when she bought her ticket to the movie, she didn't have a pocketbook, but when she got on the bus she was carrying and big black bag."

"What kind of bag?" chimed Matt and Ruth in unison.

"I don't know...just a bag."

"How big was it," pressed Matt.

"Much bigger than a pocketbook," Gary related with some frustration.

"Tell us about the bus trip, Gary?" asked Matt. "What time did the bus leave? When did she get off?"

"The last bus of the night is usually around 10:40 p.m. I got off at the Glen Lake stop and she was still on the bus. That's the last time I ever saw her, Mr. Kane."

"One more thing. Did you tell this to the policeman who came to talk with you?" Matt prodded guardedly.

"The police never questioned us," interceded the manager. "You two are the first ones to ask about that night. I guess they thought it was a waste of their time."

"Thank you again, Mr. Richards. You and your employees have been very helpful."

"You bet. Anytime."

Matt quickly determined that they had found a real lead. Ruth was a little less optimistic. It was getting late and they rushed home, arriving right at 6:00 p.m. Everyone was already waiting and anxious to hear the reports of the other groups. Matt apologized for his tardiness, but indicated that he may have found a lead.

Anna was first to speak. She energetically recounted her and Laura's two-day investigation, finally revealing the bus driver's memory of a surreptitious blonde as though it was the final scene of a mystery movie. Ruth and Matt immediately looked at each other with a knowing glance. They were now convinced they had found the would-be assassin. When they revealed their discovery, the room erupted with excitement and a sense of accomplishment.

They were now confident they knew what she actually looked like and that she took the bus to and from downtown Minneapolis. Their next task was to find out when she arrived, where she stayed, and when she left. If they found her hotel, they should be able to get a name to go with her description. John and Sandy Oleson had to get back to Rochester, and Anna and Laura had to return to work. That left the assignment to Matt, Ruth, Tony and Pat.

Matt and Ruth began at the Hennepin Avenue bus terminal and worked a grid of streets northeast toward the Mississippi River while Tony and Pat concentrated their search in a crisscross pattern southeast along Hennepin Avenue. The assisting friends were destined for another exasperating and disheartening failure.

It took Matt and Ruth half a day to reach the Nicollet Hotel, four blocks north of the bus depot. Fortunately, Matt had a friend in management at the hotel who was willing to cooperate in his 'unofficial' investigation.

"Hi, Matt, I was sorry to hear about your ordeal," offered Daniel Price.

"Thanks, Dan...I'm lucky to be alive. This is my friend, Ruth Chessman. She's helping me in my search for the attacker."

Price extended his hand to Ruth and asked, "What can I do to help?"

"We're pretty sure that the attacker stayed in a hotel in Central Minneapolis, and we've been trying to track her movements. Can you look at your register from Saturday, May 29th through Tuesday, June 1st for us? We know the assailant was an attractive, tall blonde woman in her mid-twenties and was likely from Belgium. Maybe we can find something in the record that might give us a name and timeline."

"Let's go take a look, Matt."

Old registers were kept in a storage closet in the basement of the hotel. They contained guest name(s), room number and daily charges, including restaurant and room service orders, telephone, laundry and other incidental charges. In addition, they indicated the method of payment.

The hotel had more than five hundred rooms so the chore would be a lengthy one. Matt knew his friend was chancing a reprimand or even jeopardizing his job by violating hotel privacy standards, but Dan felt that the circumstances justified the risk. In order to hasten the process, Dan took the Saturday roll, with Matt and Ruth taking the Sunday and Monday records. Matt was the first to find something of interest.

"Dan...take a look at this. I see a Giselle Houlé in room 407 on Sunday night. She had breakfast in her room and ate dinner in the restaurant. Can you find her on Saturday? Ruth, take a look on Monday and see if she is still there?" Matt requested.

"She was here on Saturday, Matt," responded his friend.

"Ditto on Monday," Ruth added.

"Okay, Dan. See about Friday...and Ruth, take a look on Tuesday. I'll check on Thursday just in case," Matt suggested vigorously.

It took less than an hour for the trio to finalize the search and determine that they had identified the professional assassin. She had checked in at 8:42 p.m. on Thursday, made a telephone call to Aachen, Germany early on Friday, and checked out before 7:00 a.m. on Tuesday morning. While she had breakfast in her room most of the time, she did have dinner in the restaurant at 4:00 p.m. on Monday.

The puzzle pieces seemed to fit perfectly. The clincher for Matt was the call to Germany, and the fact that the hotel charges had been prepaid by a travel agency in Paris.

Matt was sure that Giselle Houlé was an assumed name and that she was actually German or Belgian. They had both telephone numbers. Matt and Ruth were anxious to transmit their findings to Detective Johnson and Agent Rosino. They wouldn't have to wait long. The pair was finishing their international investigation and would be back in Minneapolis on Friday.

Chapter 7

The Epiphany

After returning to Washington, D.C., James Rosino and Rich Johnson met with J. Edgar Hoover to introduce the detective to the indomitable FBI Director and brief him on the situation, since it appeared likely that international cooperation would be needed. After the session, they retired to James' office and began devising a plan for pursuing the Belgian pharmaceutical angle. Their plan was simple and direct:

First...bring Dr. Steinhardt to Washington to fully debrief him on the U.S. holding company connection and persuade him to provide the names of former colleagues working for *Thérapeutiques Recherche, Inc.*, *JSS Pharmaceutica*, and *PIO Pharma*.

Second...examine the holding company to see if any U.S. laws were being violated. Once they understood the relationships, they would interview company management to see how much they knew about actual drug company operations.

Third...notify the International Criminal Police Commission of the need for assistance from the appropriate Belgian, German and French law enforcement agencies. Since the ICPC was only an investigative agency, direct approval would be needed from the home countries for the legal authority to pursue a criminal in their countries.

Fourth...arrange meetings with Belgian, German and French police to clarify investigative roles and boundaries. Apprehension was the purview of home-country police, so close cooperation would be required.

Fifth...pursue local and U.S. leads in the event that Matt Kane's attacker was still in the country.

❖ ❖ ❖

Dr. Steinhardt was more than willing to share his knowledge of the pharmaceutical industry and give them names of German scientists in Belgium. The next morning, he caught a Greyhound bus in downtown Ithaca, made the one-hour trip to Hancock Airport in Syracuse, boarded the American Airlines Convair 240 aircraft and arrived at FBI headquarters at 2:55 p.m.

The fact-finding duo probed the professor for almost three hours, then took him to dinner at Old Ebbitt Grill on 15th Street, just a few blocks from the Justice Department and The White House. The self-satisfied Dr. Steinhardt spent the night at the Hay-Adams Hotel on 16th Street and dutifully reversed his course back to Cornell the next morning. The information session provided an excellent background for Rosino and Johnson's next phase of the investigation.

Knowing that Dr. Steinhardt was a sentinel historian of medical research, James and Rich gave their esteemed expert wide latitude to navigate the information session. The professor framed his comments by explaining the fundamental lessons learned early in the Twentieth Century concerning chemical cures for disease. Dr. Steinhardt began his narrative with the pioneering work of Nobel Prize winning German physician, Dr. Paul Ehrlich.

"Dr. Ehrlich's first research discovered the concept of histological dye staining of tissues and demonstrated how different types and dye colors bind to different cells. This allowed researchers to identify various categories of bacteria and led to significant advances in immunology, and ultimately chemical therapy."

"Paul Ehrlich's further staining work provided the basis for isolating the Tuberculosis bacteria and led him to a staff position with the world-renowned Institute for Infectious Diseases in Berlin. While there, he collaborated with Dr. Emil Behring to develop an antitoxin to treat Diphtheria and create a better understanding of immunization therapy. The 'magic bullet', however, came through this legendary physician's tireless research for a cure for the dreaded venereal disease, Syphilis. In 1909, Ehrlich's lab perfected an effective blend of arsenic and other elements to create the drug Salvarsan, the first chemotherapeutic treatment for combating the disease."

Again, Rich and James were a bit bemused by the depth of Dr. Steinhardt's account. Nonetheless, they now understood the value of his background information since they were going to have to be at least somewhat knowledgeable in order to effectively interrogate Belgian pharmaceutical scientists.

Professor Steinhardt continued.

"Dr. Ehrlich's lab fashioned a process and protocol that set forth fundamental standards for chemical testing. Their research demonstrated that biological therapies for treating disease were a real possibility, but realizing the potential of chemical treatments takes time, often to the consternation of medical practitioners and the public."

"Dr. Ehrlich's research group established that laboratory analysis on mice, rabbits or other small animals must be extensive before proceeding to clinical testing on human subjects. While Salvarsan yielded a cure for Syphilis, it also showed that drugs have side-effects that sometimes cause harm and death to patients. Consequently, adherence to a standard protocol, regardless of monetary cost or extended development time, is fundamental to the formulation of successful biological treatments."

"Dr. Ehrlich's primary lesson was that medicines must be safe and effective before routine use on people, and that the testing process cannot be rushed. Consequently," the professor forcefully emphasized, "any conclusions about the quality, safety or effectiveness of drug treatments must be based on solid science, and human testing must only be attempted when laboratory evidence demonstrates that a compound is highly effective with a minimum of side-effects."

The venerable Professor Steinhardt then meticulously weaved his way through the biochemical research history that followed Dr. Ehrlich over the next forty years, tracing the timeline of research model development, theories and analysis of thiopurines, antifolates, antibiotics, foods and nutrients, vitamins, and even environmental carcinogens. He praised the current U.S. work of Dr. Sidney Farber who, in collaboration with Dr. Harriet Kilte of Lederle Laboratories, produced the promising leukemia drug, methotrexate.

Dr. Steinhardt ended his recitation with a somber warning.

"Biochemical companies appear to be trapped in a continuing wave of paranoia, and I strongly believe that too many companies are cutting corners in their research protocols in order to beat their competitors to the market. Millions of dollars are at stake, and I fear that profits are more important than medical cures for cancer or other deadly and debilitating diseases."

"In short, I think these companies are shortcutting the laboratory stages and proceeding to human testing prematurely simply because of the greed motive. Further, *Thérapeutiques Recherche, Inc.*, *JSS Pharmaceutica*, and *PIO Pharma* are probably at the top of that list."

James and Rich concluded that Matt Kane's exposé of these companies would certainly be enough motivation to commit murder, and queried Professor Steinhardt further to ascertain the name of the American parent company operating *Thérapeutiques Recherche, Inc.* in Liège, as well as former colleagues working for any of the Belgian pharmaceutical companies. Dr. Steinhardt did not know the name of the holding company, but shared four contact names he believed could provide useful information on the innerworkings of these 'rogue' companies. Armed with a robust background of the world-wide pharmaceutical industry, they were now ready for phase two of their investigation.

It took less than a day for a member of Agent Rosino's task force to locate Dr. Paul Ludwig, lead cancer investigator for *Thérapeutiques Recherche, Inc.* Ludwig was wary of speaking to American authorities and would only entertain casual conversation about his work in cancer research. During the few minutes of dialog with the FBI agent, however, the cautious German scientist inadvertently revealed the name of *Thérapeutiques Recherche's* parent company...*MGJ Universal Applications.* The shell company, formed in 1947, was headquartered in Cambridge, Massachusetts, nestled within a seemingly insulated academic environment.

Armed with an FBI administrative subpoena, James Rosino, Rich Johnson, and five task force members presented themselves at the office of *MGJ Universal's* CEO Earl Hobson within twelve hours. They informed the executive that they were investigating an attempted murder, possibly involving an individual linked to his pharmaceutical company operations. The subpoena gave them the ability to converse with any employee of the company, and to examine all relevant documents on the company's business structure, research, manufacturing operations, and financial statements.

The two-day analysis yielded enough evidence to bring into question the legalities of the parent company's ownership and operations of all three Belgian pharmaceutical enterprises, but yielded no direct link implicating *MGJ Universal Applications* to Matt Kane's assassination attempt.

Close examination revealed that *Thérapeutiques Recherche, Inc.* was primarily involved with cancer drug development, *JSS Pharmaceutica* was focused on new antibiotic amalgams, and *PIO Pharma* centered its research on benzodiazepine, a promising compound for producing effective treatments to combat neurosis, anxiety and depression. Rosino and Johnson established that while the U.S. Justice Department should file charges against the parent company for fraudulent operating practices, there were no detectible grounds to pursue an attempted murder indictment. It was now evident that their next stage of the investigation was a trip to Belgium, beginning in Liège and *Thérapeutiques Recherche, Inc.*

The Federal Police of Belgium, called the *Gendarmerie* in the French speaking regions of the country, and the *Rijkswacht* in Dutch speaking provinces, were eager to provide support to the FBI task force in its probe of the Belgian based biochemical companies. Less than a decade after liberation by the Americans at the end of the Second World War, the thriving country was grateful for America's aid in rebuilding the country through the Marshall Plan. Also, being founding partners in the North Atlantic Treaty Organization and allies in the Korean War, the relationship and cooperation between the countries was strong. Accordingly, Agent Rosino and Detective Johnson were afforded the utmost courtesy and assistance by the *Gendarmerie* in Liège.

The first interviews with *Thérapeutiques Recherche, Inc.* executives and administrative personnel were full of obfuscations. While the Belgian directors and staff of the company were polite, outwardly compliant, and generally self-effacing, they were noticeably guarded and evasive in their answers. They avoided direct responses, either attempting to shield proprietary information or just waiting for the American interrogators to reveal the depth of their knowledge. It was apparent to James and Rich, however, that they had been instructed by their U.S. owner to reveal as little about company operations as possible.

Interviews with scientists proved to be more enlightening. The researchers openly had a stronger sense of submission to authority than the administrators, undoubtedly due to the Nazi culture and influence during the war. They were direct in their answers and less concerned with the political ramifications than explaining and vindicating their actions. They were on the verge of a major advance in cancer treatment, and were anxious to share what they believed would be as impactful as Dr. Paul Ehrlich's success with Salvarsan forty years prior.

The major breakthrough came during Detective Johnson's interview with Dr. Emil Peters, the junior member of the cancer research team. In the researcher's vanity to get credit for recent successful human testing of CA-CV-156, he carelessly disclosed criminal breaches in research principles and protocols that caused pain, suffering and death to several test participants.

Dr. Peters zealously explained that the research panel obtained the HeLa cancer cell line from Johns-Hopkins Professor George Gey in 1952 and injected the cells into a selected group of prisoners in Liège jails for experimentation. Many of these individuals developed various malignancies that were currently being treated using the experimental CA-CV-156 compound. The scientist described numerous failures with earlier versions of the chemical blend, but rationalized that the experiments were worthwhile and deaths of inconsequential hominids were justifiable when formulating trailblazing treatments for virulent diseases.

It was further learned through other researchers that while initial versions of CA-CV-156 were extensively tested on mice and larger primates, as the drug began to show promise, lab testing on animals was circumvented and experimentation moved directly to humans. It was also revealed that most patients were not informed that the drug administered to them was in an experimental stage. Toxic and sometimes fatal side-effects were simply considered a reasonable consequence of innovation. The matter-of-fact explanations of team scientists were alarming and appalling to the American and Belgian investigators.

One senior scientist, when pushed, indicated that his colleagues at *JSS Pharmaceutica* and *PIO Pharma* were being pressed by *MGJ Universal Applications* to follow the same abbreviated protocol in an effort to get new drugs into circulation more quickly. In the next few days, the investigative team traveled to Antwerp to evaluate *JSS Pharmaceutica* and Ghent to assess *PIO Pharma*, and repeated the same line of inquiry. The administrative and research personnel interactions notably repeated the communication pattern employed at *Thérapeutiques Recherche, Inc.* Agent Rosino and Detective Johnson were startled at the flagrant ethical and legal contraventions of these pharmaceutical companies, which had been concealed from authorities for several years.

Their trip complete, the exhausted investigators headed back to the United States to compile and assess the information they had gathered and see what, if anything, Matt Kane and his amateur sleuths had learned about the would-be assassin. They were positive the attempt on Matt's life had been engineered directly by *MGJ Universal Applications* or one of their pharmaceutical subsidiaries in Belgium. Their last step was to identify the executioner, track her down, then pinpoint and bring her sponsoring authorities to justice. Case closed.

Matt now had a major story that would not only bring public attention to fraudulent behavior in the biochemical industry, but could potentially revolutionize the clinical research process itself.

Matt arrived at the Minneapolis Police Department on Plymouth Avenue North at 8:34 a.m. on Saturday, July 24th to exchange information with his law enforcement partners and plan the final stages of the investigation. He was anxious to share his group's information on Giselle Houlé and find out what James Rosino and Rich Johnson had discovered about the Belgian pharmaceutical companies.

"You're looking well, Matt," began Rich as he extended his hand in a welcoming gesture.

"I've still got a ways to go, Rich, but at least I'm operational now," Matt responded.

"I understand that Ruth has been taking good care of you for the past couple of weeks," added James as he grasped Matt's hand. He also had a knowing smile on his face. Ruth had spent several nights at Matt's house.

"You probably didn't see them, but I had you shadowed by two agents just to make sure the predator didn't stick around and try to take you out again."

"I thought I was paranoid, James, because I felt like there was someone there several times. I just couldn't quite pinpoint it. Ruth told me it was just a post-traumatic stress reaction. I'm glad I'm not completely crazy," Matt emphasized with a sigh of relief.

"I believe we've identified the attacker," Matt continued. "We know what she looks like and we know she has a contact in Aachen, Germany. She also flew into New York from Paris on May 23rd, arrived in Minneapolis on May 27th, and presumably left town on Tuesday morning after the attack. Now we just need to see if we..."

"We know all that, Matt," interrupted the FBI agent. "Colin Young told us all about your adventures in the last few weeks."

"Your information fits perfectly with what we learned in Belgium," explained Rich. "You were certainly on to something with the misconduct on the part of those drug companies. They've committed serious breaches in testing drugs and clearly wanted you out of the way. What we don't know is how they found out you were examining them and that you knew so much about their operations when the authorities in Belgium had no knowledge of their crimes."

"You're going to have a helluva good story to tell once the case is closed," exclaimed Rosino.

"So...how do we catch her?" asked Matt.

"I'll work on the Aachen and Paris travel agency angle," responded James, "and Rich can work on the U.S. travel perspective. Hopefully, we can find her before she leaves the country, although that's probably a pipe dream. A seasoned professional would likely have exited the U.S. within a day or two after the attack, and is probably now sunbathing on a beach in the south of France. Nonetheless...we'll get her. I guarantee it!"

"I'll work with Rich," responded Matt.

"You still need to take it easy," responded the detective. "I'll have some taskforce members do the leg work, and you can work on your exposé."

"Not on your life, Rich! I'm not going to be left out of the investigation. I've got a vested interest here. This woman nearly killed me, and I'm going to find her with or without your sanction."

Matt was clearly exercised and Rich relented. He reluctantly agreed that he would find an appropriate role for him in the quest to locate the erstwhile Giselle Houlé.

Matt and Ruth spent Saturday afternoon aboard his boat, *The Rose*, enjoying the peacefulness of the lake, simply reading his weekend array of big city newspapers and listening to music. The radio was softly playing *Stranger in Paradise* by Tony Bennett when Matt's bellow pierced the serenity of the lake.

"*It can't be*...it can't be a coincidence!" he shrieked. "That's it...we need to call Rich and James."

"What in the world are you talking about?" retorted the startled Ruth. "Are you okay?"

"I'm fine, but Lew Tarquin isn't!"

"Who's he?"

"A very important part of my past. He was an integral part of my team during the war...and he was killed yesterday in Arizona. Look at this," Matt roared as he tried to catch his breath, pointing to a short article in the Los Angeles Times.

> Lewis Tarquin, a distinguished UCLA professor and WWII veteran, died from gunshot wounds suffered outside the *El Trovatore Motel* in Kingman, Arizona. A witness described the assailant as a person on a motorcycle dressed in a black leather jacket, who was possibly a woman. The fifty-five-year-old professor was on his way to Chicago with his wife, Josette, when...

Ruth gasped. They had it all wrong.

Matt quickly fired up the engine and sped back to the marina and pay phone by the front door. He deposited a nickel in the slot and dialed *zero*.

"Hello...how can I help you?" responded the telephone operator.

"Connect me to the Minneapolis Police Station on Plymouth Avenue," Matt answered hastily.

"Just a moment, please."

The phone rang three times before the desk sergeant answered.

"This is Matthew Kane. I need to speak to Detective Rich Johnson."

"I'm sorry, sir, but Captain Johnson and his FBI associate left a several hours ago."

"I have critical information and I need to speak to him as soon as possible. Can you get in touch with him and have him call me at home? I'm at Lake Minnetonka now, but I'll be home in forty-five minutes. Time is of the essence."

"I'll see if I can locate him, Mr. Kane."

"Thanks," replied Matt as he hung up the phone.

It took Matt and Ruth thirty-four minutes to traverse the route from the North Shore Marina on Maxwell Bay to Matt's house in St. Louis Park. He and Ruth sat anxiously on the couch in the living room waiting for his new colleagues to call. The next twenty-two minutes seemed like a lifetime. It only took half a ring before Matt picked up the phone.

"Rich...is that you?"

"What's so important that it couldn't wait, Matt?"

"We had it all wrong, Rich," Matt thundered. "It's not the drug companies. It has to do with my military service in Germany."

"How do you know that?" asked the detective guardedly.

"A teammate of mine during the war was gunned down yesterday in Arizona by a woman on a motorcycle. She was wearing a black leather jacket. It has to do with some covert operations we engaged in late in the war. We need to go to Kingman, Arizona right now to sort this out, and catch her before she gets out of the country."

"Hold on, Matt. Why are you so sure this is the connection?"

"I can't talk about my wartime assignment, Rich. We signed an oath of secrecy concerning my team's activities during the war, but I'm sure that's the connection."

"It may or may not be related to your military actions, but it sounds like it may be the same perpetrator so I agree that we need to get to Arizona and see if we can pick up her trail," agreed his friend.

"It's been eight weeks since your attack. It doesn't make sense that an international assassin would stay in the country for that long between hits. I wonder what she's been up to?"

"Do we need to call James and get his perspective?"

"He left for the airport an hour ago. I'll see if I can catch him before his plane takes off. I'm sure he can help us. Pack some things and I'll get back to you as soon as I talk with James."

"In the meantime, Rich, I'm going to get in touch with as many of our team members as possible and let them know they're in danger," Matt responded hastily.

Chapter 8

The Confirmation

Ruth kissed Matt goodbye and drove away from Wold-Chamberlain Field in his Hudson Hornet. Matt's mind was racing as he met James and Rich on the tarmac. He was exploding with information and was anxious to get started in the hunt to stop the alleged Giselle Houlé.

His calls to former *Strategic Services Unit* team members confirmed his suspicions that the professional assassin was the instrument of some lingering Nazi conspirators. He wasn't sure who was behind the treachery or why, but he intended to find out and bring them to justice no matter how long it took. James Rosino and Rich Johnson were seasoned veterans and competent law enforcement officials, but *he* was an expert on the Nazi war machine and its obvious remnants. He was now back in command.

The three partners boarded the Northwest Airlines flight to Chicago, where they would pick up an American Airlines flight to Phoenix Sky Harbor Airport the next morning. The short trip would give Matt enough time to give them a general briefing on the situation. Once settled in the back row of the aircraft, Matt began to reveal his findings.

"Men," Matt began in an authoritative tone, "There is no doubt that the assassin has been engaged by a contingent of remaining Nazi officers. I'm unable to tell you what I did during the war, but I can tell you that we had a team of nine members who conducted some sensitive, top-secret operations in Europe. I tried to contact them all this morning. Including Lew Tarquin, four of them have been killed in the past nine months. I presume I was number five. Of the remaining four, two are female...one who lives in Boston and the second in a small town in England. The other two teammates are male, but I lost track of one of them a few years ago. I was able to warn Duncan Giles."

"I spoke with Abby Findlay in Boston, but wasn't able to get in touch with Marie Spenser or Hugh Kensie. I told Abby that she was in danger, and she indicated that she, her husband, and two kids would vacate immediately and go to a safe location. She told me she would leave a telephone number with my father so I can reach her next Saturday to talk further about the case."

James and Rich were astounded by the revelations, but were perhaps more impressed by the proficiency, organization and authority shown by intended victim number five.

"Okay, Matt...I'm satisfied that you're probably right about the war connection, but we need to know more about the activities you were engaged in if we're going to catch these conspirators," pressed the FBI agent.

"I signed a secrecy oath, James. Violating the oath could mean prison."

"I can easily fix that. I'll call Director Hoover as soon as we get to Chicago and have him arrange for Rich and me to be given clearance."

"Okay. Once I get written authority, I'll give you a complete picture of my team and details of our war related assignments and activities."

"Fair enough," replied James.

"What can you tell us now about the four other victims. You said they were killed. How...and where?" asked the Minneapolis detective. "Any witnesses? Evidence? The more details we have the quicker we can find the killer or killers?"

"Killers? More than one?" asked Matt.

"My gut says this is more than a one person show," observed Rich.

"I agree," added James. "This sounds like a well-organized and financed force that's bigger than a few murders. If you're right about this being a Nazi descendant group, your team isn't the only target. This is big, and I'm sure Mr. Hoover will give us all the resources we need."

The one hour and fifteen-minute flight landed at 10:10 p.m. Central time. They checked in to the Skylark Motel, a three minute walk from the Airport, and Agent Rosino immediately went to the pay phone and called J. Edgar Hoover at home. Initially annoyed by the late hour call, the Director's interest in the case grew dramatically as James explained the possible Nazi resurgence. Matt made another call to Marie to no avail.

Hoover assured his agent that he would contact the appropriate authorities and get Matt his release letter. In the meantime, he ordered the team to pursue the stalker wherever her trail took them, and he would go directly to the top. While the *Brown* decision had caused some strain between the Director and President Eisenhower, their relationship was still amiable enough. This is where he would start. He told Rosino that it would take a few days to get the completed correspondence, but the priority was tracking down the assailant before she could kill another war hero. He also instructed his agent to keep him apprised of the pursuit daily.

It was ninety-five degrees with a dry, biting wind when American Airlines flight #955 from Chicago arrived in Phoenix at 1:30 p.m. on Sunday, July 25, 1954. Matt, Rich and James promptly made their way to the Hertz Car Rental desk and secured a pale blue Chevrolet Bel Air for the trip to Kingman, Arizona. The nearly two-hundred-mile trip took just under three and a half hours in the blistering heat. Matt had insisted on driving, but was overruled by Rosino. It was just as well, since Matt was significantly fatigued and experiencing some discomfort in his reconstructed ribs, which he naturally hid from his compadres. He slept most of the way.

The trio's first stop was the Kingman Police Department just off U.S. Highway 93 on Route 66, where they met with Lt.

Paul Ashton, the primary investigator on the case. He respectfully shared all the photographs of the murder scene, as well as accounts of three witnesses who either directly saw the event or the perpetrator as the motorcycle sped away. The two bullets that had been removed from the body of Lewis Tarquin, along with three shell casings found on the pavement in the parking lot of the El Trovatore Motel, were sent to the Phoenix FBI Office for forensic analysis two days prior. He expected to get the results at any moment.

In early June, Lewis Tarquin, Ph.D., a noted Papyrology scholar from the University of California at Los Angeles had been contacted by a wealthy collector of ancient Greek artifacts and documents in Paris to interpret several ancient Curse Tablets from Athens court cases. It was summer and Dr. Tarquin and his wife of nine years decided that a two-week business/vacation trip to Europe would be a pleasant break in his academic regimen. It would give him and Josette time to reconnect with relatives they hadn't seen in many years before returning for his graduation speech at the University of Chicago in August.

It was to be a leisurely summer of travel and relaxation for the former wartime companions. He and Josette had almost three months to themselves, and wanted to make the most of it before embarking on another academic year in September. So, after arriving back in Los Angeles, the couple decided to take a ten-day drive to Chicago via historic U.S. Highway 66, also known as Route 66 or *The Mainstreet of America*. It was on day two of the trip that the attack occurred.

There were three witness statements, which were simple, clear and consistent. According to Josette Tarquin, she and her husband arrived at the El Trovatore Motel late Friday afternoon. They left Los Angeles on Thursday and stayed overnight in Amboy, California before continuing their journey toward Chicago the next day. They checked into the motel, freshenedup, and were going to have dinner at Casa Linda Café, just a few blocks down Route 66. They were walking toward their car when a motorcycle pulled up fifteen or twenty feet away and the gunman pulled out a pistol and started firing.

According to the police report, the widow was unusually composed and coherent, given the trauma she had just experienced. What they didn't know was that Josette Beaulieu had been an active Resistance fighter in the war, and it was through those activities that she met her soon-to-be husband in 1944. Grief stricken...yes, but courageous and stoic because of her wartime activities. She had been well trained to observe her surroundings, and had been awarded the *Médaille de la Résistance* by The French Committee of National Liberation for her valor during the French occupation. Her life had depended upon her awareness. She would mourn in her own way at the appropriate time. The priority now was to catch the killer.

Mrs. Tarquin described the attacker as medium height, wearing black pants, a grey-shielded helmet, and a black leather jacket that looked like it was fashioned for a female. The assailant also wore gloves, but while the hands weren't visible, the body movements were clearly feminine. She was confident that the murderer was a woman.

When the firing began, Josette Tarquin dived behind the car as one bullet tore through the sleeve of her blouse, narrowly missing her shoulder. The motorcycle then sped west down Route 66, and she immediately raced to the aid of her husband. He was already dead. He had taken one shot in the throat and the other directly to the heart. He died instantly.

It did not appear to be a random shooting, according to the observer. She was sure she and her husband were intended victims. Why? She didn't know. This would become clear in a couple of days when her old colleague from the *Special Services Unit*, Matt Kane, appeared on the scene.

Witness number two was a young male who had just arrived at the motel after stopping at the Mobil filling station down the road. He turned into the parking lot when the motorcycle passed him and came to a screeching halt. As he was getting out of the car about fifty feet away, he saw the motorcyclist open fire at a middle-aged couple walking through the parking lot. He was startled, disbelieving what he saw. He also indicated that the rider was wearing a helmet and black leather jacket, and had quickly fled the scene after firing three shots. For some reason, it looked to him like the couple was being targeted. He had no opinion about the attacker's gender.

The third witness was a local resident driving by the El Trovatore Motel on his way to the Railroad Station for his evening shift as a freight handler. The fifty-one-year-old man told Lt. Ashton that the motorcycle passed him two or three miles back on the highway, and caught his attention because of its high rate of speed. He watched it disappear in the distance and then reappear as though it had either slowed down rapidly or stopped. He initially thought the police had spotted the vehicle.

As the driver passed the motel, he saw a woman tending to a man lying on the ground bleeding profusely. His first thought was to stop and render aid, but he instinctively wanted to follow the motorcycle. He glimpsed the bike turning off the highway heading down a dirt road a block from the train depot, but quickly lost sight of it in the dust. He then stopped at the train station to call the police and report what he saw. They asked him to return to the motel and give them a statement.

Just as they completed a review of the witness documents, the lieutenant received a call from the Phoenix FBI forensics lab. They confirmed that the 9mm bullets taken from Lew Tarquin matched the bullets taken from Matt. The shell casings were also identical to the one found in The Commons Park when Matt was attacked. Any doubt about the connection with Matt's *Special Services Unit* was now erased. The question was who, and why nine years after the end of World War II?

The Kingman Police found the motorcycle and helmet fifty yards off the road behind a bushy, eight-foot yellow paloverde tree, less than a mile down the dirt road where the freight handler had last seen it. It was stolen, helmet and all, from a garage not far from the train station. It seemed obvious to law enforcement that the female executioner arrived and departed the city either by train or bus since both modes of public transportation were housed in the same building. What the trio of pursuers didn't know was whether she went east or west. They, of course, were wrong.

From this point forward, FBI offices from Los Angeles to Chicago would be involved in the manhunt, following both train and bus routes between those cities. Matt, James and Rich would head east by automobile, reasoning that the killer was likely headed to Chicago, and ultimately on to New York for a return to Europe. The chase was on.

Chapter 9

The Chase

The alias Giselle Houlé entered the United States on May 23rd, and exited the country as an angry and frustrated hunter five days after her attack on former Army Major Matthew Kane. She traveled from Minneapolis to Chicago by train, bussed to Midway Airport, and took an American Airlines DC-7 flight to Los Angeles. She spent two days searching for Captain Lewis Tarquin, only to find out that he left the U.S. the day before on his way to Paris for a conference. Had she not lost the better part of a week recovering from food poisoning in Chicago, she would have been able to dispatch her prey according to schedule. Her illness had completely upset her timetable. The exasperated tracker had no choice but to return to Germany to have her plan recalibrated by her handler.

The aforementioned Giselle Houlé returned to the United States under another assumed name, Clare Lyon, forty-three days later, intent on completing her previously aborted mission, then moving on to target number six in Boston, Massachusetts. The youthful twenty-four-year-old woman easily passed for a college student. Her blonde hair, white blouse, plaid cotton skirt, white sox and penny loafers rendered her indistinguishable from any other coed at UCLA. She prowled the campus in search of Professor Tarquin, seeking to learn as much about his behavior as possible.

The pretend college student located Professor Tarquin's office, only to find that he would be away for much of the summer. She quickly made friends with two female graduate students who had taken his class in Greek Classic Literature; and one undergraduate who had taken his Introduction to Papyrology course. This was a stroke of luck because the undergrad was actually a student assistant in the Classics Department. Together, they unknowingly provided the fictitious college student with vital information about his demeanor and habits...and even the kind of car he drove and where he lived in Westwood.

Clare Lyon also learned that the professor and his wife were leaving Thursday on a driving trip to Chicago where he was to share his Curse Tablet findings from the Paris excursion with University of Chicago faculty members. The student assistant even knew the professor's itinerary, which she willingly shared with her new college friend. This was the break that Clare needed. Rather than eliminating him in Chicago, she would ambush him in an unpopulated area and inconspicuously move on to Boston for her next assignment.

The predator had a day to adjust her plan and initiate her pursuit. They would be driving, so she reasoned that following them by automobile would allow her to easily choose the time and place of her attack. She left the campus, walked a few blocks down Gayley Avenue and found a used car dealer. It took less than an hour for her to find a high mileage 1949 Ford four-door sedan at a bargain price of four-hundred-ninety-five dollars. The navy-blue vehicle would serve her limited needs, and blend in nicely with other cars on the road. She produced a phony driver's license, completed the minimal paperwork, paid cash, and was on her way to shadow her quarry.

She had dinner at Carl Andersen's Chatam Restaurant in Westwood Village near UCLA, famous for its Scandinavian cuisine, and spent the night nearby in a comfortable motel in the Village. She rose early, drove to Captain Tarquin's house, parked and waited for him to emerge. She toyed with the idea of simply killing him then, but didn't want to involve the renowned Los

Angeles Police Department in the investigation. She would follow him to a remote spot and complete her mission.

The couple appeared just after 9:30 a.m. with suitcases in hand, packed their pale-yellow Mercury Monterey, and set off for Chicago. Clare Lyon followed at a safe distance. She learned from the undergraduate that they were going to stop for the night in the Mojave Desert town of Barstow, California, roughly a hundred-forty miles from their home. She would ambush them somewhere in the desert before they reached their destination.

All went well until the female hunter stopped to get gas just outside San Bernardino, California. After filling up, the worn-out Ford wouldn't crank. Furious, Clare had no choice but to ask the attendant for help. He quickly diagnosed a faulty starter, and said he could fix it in a couple of hours. In the meantime, her objective was getting away. She arrived in Barstow in the late afternoon, but couldn't find the couple. She would have to wait until the next morning.

Clare Lyon was now both annoyed and anxious. She drove up and down the highway looking for Tarquin's automobile in motel and café parking lots. No luck. She then calmed herself, reasoning that she could find her prey on the road to Kingman, Arizona the next day. She stayed in the Route 66 Motel, rose at 6:00 a.m., ate breakfast at the motel restaurant, and was on her way to Kingman by 7:25 a.m. The predator would get ahead of her mark, find a suitable spot in the desert, and wait for him to come to her. What she didn't know is that Lewis and Josette Tarquin decided not to stop in Barstow, but continued on to the small community of Amboy, California, some eighty miles east. They stayed at Roy's Motel & Café and would be ahead of her all the way to Kingman.

The long desolate road and summer desert heat were a new experience for the assassin. Having checked her map, Clare decided to make her way to Sitgreaves Pass about five miles from Oatman, Arizona. The three-hour drive was scorching and arduous, but she was confident this was the best place to waylay her prey. She would shoot out his tires at the top of the mountain and send the vehicle off the cliff into the abyss where it may never be found.

The chaser waited for another three hours and grew ever more agitated. It finally occurred to her...*they must be ahead of me!* She was hot and hungry, and fatigue was now impairing her judgment. She raced through the winding mountain road and long straight-away twenty-five miles to Kingman and began a frenzied search for the yellow Mercury.

On her third trip from the train station past Hualapai Mountain Road and back, the self-appointed Clare Lyon spotted the target getting out of his car and heading into the El Trovatore Motel. As she passed the motel heading west back toward the train station, she was considering her options when she saw the stylish Harley-Davidson FL Hydra-Glide motorcycle parked next to a garage just off South 4th Street. It came complete with a shielded helmet. This both emboldened and motivated her, since she was an expert rider and the helmet would obscure her identity.

She proceeded down the dirt road less than a mile, parked the Ford, changed into her attack clothing and walked back to the garage. She skillfully connected the starter wires, cranked the bike, put on the helmet, and sped off in the direction of the motel. She cruised by slowly, watching people trickle in and out of the motel and restaurant, and decided to test out the machine to gauge its speed and handling before staging her attack. Clare Lyon was restless and resolute. She would go back to the motel, sit across the street and wait for her prey to emerge, strike quickly, take the Harley back to where she parked her car, change clothes, and be on her way to Flagstaff, Arizona to spend the night.

Luck was with the assassin. She sped past several cars heading west on Route 66 and was preparing to stop when Captain Tarquin and his wife were leisurely striding toward their car. She instinctively screeched to a stop, retrieved her weapon, and fired two quick shots into the center of her male prey. She also fired one shot at the female who was trying to flee. The female went down and Clare believed she hit her in the neck or shoulder. She then executed her escape plan and was on her way to Flagstaff, Arizona within twenty minutes.

The exhausted Clare Lyon checked into the new Western Hills Motel and Restaurant just after 8:00 p.m., went to her room, fell on the bed and didn't awaken until after 6:00 a.m. on Saturday, July 24th. Still tired, but more in control of her wits than the previous day, she got up, bathed, dressed and waited for the restaurant to open at 7:00 a.m. She realized that she hadn't eaten for twenty-four hours and would need to get to Albuquerque and rest for a day before moving on to Boston to complete her last U.S. assignment. She ate heartily and began the mesmerizing three-hundred-plus mile desert drive to New Mexico. While less stressful than the previous day, Clare was wind-blown from the drive and drained when she arrived in the city just after 4:00 p.m. She was grateful that the temperature had cooled to the low eighties.

The executioner searched for a suitable hotel for a two-day stay while she recuperated and prepared to confront her next victim in Boston. She found the four-story Hilton Hotel on Second Street. It was perfect. She could come and go without being noticed while she decompressed and planned the strategy for her Boston attack.

The former Giselle Houlé, now Clare Lyon, grew up hating America, and she resented the prosperity of the country compared to the poverty and postwar struggles of her countrymen. However, in her two trips to the United States she had observed robust and undamaged cities and towns, a seemingly contented citizenry, and plentiful food, shelter and recreation. As she moved around the country, she was also developing a grudging admiration for the tranquil nature and apparent serenity of its people. In short, she was becoming somewhat conflicted. Her youthful education and indoctrination railed against the Allies, particularly America. What she was seeing didn't comport with those teachings. Notwithstanding, the overall goal of her organization was more important than her personal feelings. She just wanted to complete her last mission and go home.

James Rosino was coordinating the communication between FBI agents along the suspected route the evasive predator was likely taking to Boston. James, Rich and Matt decided to get to Albuquerque as quickly as possible, and would catch a plane to Logan Airport and wait for the woman to arrive. They planned to have her in custody within a week. Because the trio was already two days behind the perpetrator, they decided not to stop in Flagstaff, but continue through the night to Albuquerque. The grueling nine-hour drive ended just before 7:00 a.m. on Monday morning. They would sleep for a few hours and take an afternoon flight to Boston. Unsuspectingly, they also chose to stay in the Conrad Hilton Hotel.

Sunday was a day of physical and mental rest for so-called Clare Lyon. She spent the day exploring old town Albuquerque and taking a vigorous hike to the top of the ten-thousand-foot Sandia Crest. She enjoyed the freedom and was now ready to resume her trek to Boston on Monday morning by airplane. As she began her descent from the second-floor, the stalker froze. She saw the ghost of Major Matthew Kane standing with two other men in the lobby of the hotel. She immediately retreated to her room to think.

Is this possible, thought a disbelieving Clare? *I shot him twice in the chest. He could not have survived.* She caught her breath and decided that it was a mirage. She would calmly proceed to the front desk, check out, and drive to the airport as planned. Within a few minutes, she again grabbed her bags and headed down the stairs, surreptitiously passing by the three men. The object was looking in the other direction, but she was now sure it was Matthew Kane. Her mind raced.

How did he survive? What does he know? Are they after me? Do they know who I am or what I look like? Should I go to Boston? Should I abort the mission and go back to the continent, or should I wait here and eliminate them all? Her adrenalin surged, causing her heart rate to spike, pupils to dilate, breathing to accelerate, and sweat to pour down her face. Her knees buckled...the clandestine Clare Lyon's flight or fight stress reaction was in full dominion. *Just get to a safe place quickly,* she thought.

Okay, the young assassin deliberated. *I've experienced this before. Be calm. Breathe. Remember your training. Just check out and go to the car. I will figure it out.* She mopped her brow and continued to the front desk. Clare was instantly annoyed with herself for the panic attack. She was often told by her instructors that plans go awry, and that she would have to improvise sometimes. She had to recover her full senses, and realized that it might even take an hour before she could think clearly again. She waited for the threesome to get in the elevator, then checked out and hurriedly took her bags to the Ford, entered and looked for an out of the way café for breakfast. *I'll be fine once I have something to eat and time to calculate my options,* she told herself.

The three pursuers were so tired they failed to notice the attractive, tall blonde who quickly passed by them in the lobby. Sleep deprived, they were barely functioning. They checked in, went to their rooms, and agreed to meet at noon in the hotel restaurant. They would then go to the airport and proceed to Boston by the quickest route possible. Little did they know what the redoubtable hunter had in mind for them.

Chapter 10

The Failures

Clare Lyon drove down Central Avenue, found a local café and had a burrito with hash-brown potatoes and a cup of tea for breakfast. A treat she had never experienced before. Again, she was aggravated and envious of the bounty available in America. Her first three...or four operations, if you count Major Kane, had gone off without a hitch. Now it was turning into a cat-and-mouse game. With her sensibilities returning, she decided to call her tutor, a former high-ranking Nazi *SS-Obergruppenführer*, for instructions.

"Hallo," answered her controller.

"Major Kane ist nicht tot," retorted the irritated caller.

"English...always *English*, my dear. What do you mean he is not dead?"

"He is here with two other men. I saw them in the hotel lobby."

"Are you sure it is him?"

"Ja...I mean *yes*. I walked right by him and I am sure."

"This means they know why he was targeted. We will have to change our plans. Did you eliminate Captain Tarquin?"

"Yes...I hit him twice in the chest. I am sure he is finished."

"Okay...how about the woman in Massachusetts?"

"Lieutenant Findlay is...*was*...last on my list. Should I go to Boston and finish her? What about Major Kane?"

The taskmaster thought for a moment before he responded. He wanted Kane and Findlay dead as quickly as possible. Their plan was already behind schedule. Clare Lyon, while his prized pupil, was like all of his acolytes, expendable. If she failed, he would just send another agent to complete the assignment.

"Can you take care of Major Kane and the other men today?" he commanded rather than asked. "Find a way to eliminate them today and go to Boston and terminate Findlay. This has taken too long. It is time to finish the American operation and get back to the homeland."

"Yes sir," Clare responded obediently. "I had to buy a car in Los Angeles so I will need more money. I will collect it in Boston. I will finish the assignment in two or three days and return home for my next mission."

Clare had to work fast. She needed to quickly find a place on the road to the airport to ambush the three men since she was sure they were going to fly to Boston to get there before her. She also had another problem. She only had her **Walther P.38** pistol, and needed an automatic rifle for this type of attack.

After the war, American military materials were in great supply, and a previously small industry grew into a staple in most cities...the Army/Navy Surplus store. Clare had been instructed that she could get weapons and ammunition at one of these stores, if necessary. She walked to the phone booth at the corner of Central Avenue and Locust Street, opened the telephone book and found Romero's Military Surplus a few blocks away on San Pedro Drive.

She got in the car, exchanged her dress for pants, boots, and a grey blouse, put on her black wig, and marched to the dusky stucco building in a run-down looking section of town. The proprietor, a Hispanic man in his sixties, looked warily at this young female, wondering if she was lost. Military surplus was a man's domain, and he was suspicious of this interloper. Clare eyed him distrustfully too, but had no choice. She needed a weapon, and needed it now.

The cagey female slowly wandered around the store and saw some American rifles hanging on the wall, mostly **M1** and **M2** .30-caliber carbines. Both were lightweight and easy to use. The **M1** was a true semi-automatic weapon and employed either a 15-round magazine or a 30-round banana clip, and while it was touted to be effective at three-hundred yards, its reliable accuracy was closer to two-hundred yards. It also had a wind adjustment mechanism to improve accuracy. Its primary flaw was the larger ammo clip. If it was not seated properly, it was prone to jam. The **M2** was an updated version that operated as either a selective-fire or fully automatic weapon. Either would suffice...until she saw the German-made **G43/K43 Karabiner**.

The **Walther** long rifle was designed for both infantry use and, with a 4x magnification scope, was an excellent sniper weapon. It was gas-operated and used .31-caliber ammunition similar to the American rifle. The gun utilized a 10-round magazine and was accurate up to four-hundred yards. The weapon was not in pristine condition, having obviously been used in combat. Nonetheless, Clare was familiar with the weapon and made her decision.

"Let me see the **Karabiner**," she ordered.

"Do you know anything about weapons?" responded Romero.

"Yes. Can I see the weapon?"

"Okay, but are you sure you know about this one?" he pressed.

"Do you want to sell a gun today?" she shot back. She was in a hurry and had no time for an inquisition.

The old man reluctantly took the rifle off the wall and handed it to Clare. She inspected it closely and demanded, "I need to test it before I buy it."

Romero was taken by surprise, and found himself agreeing before realizing it. It was rare that he allowed someone to fire a weapon before a sale. Nonetheless, he handed her a clip and pointed to the door leading to the open field behind him. She scanned the landscape for some kind of target, and found a grouping of prickly pear cacti about two-hundred yards away. It had a burst of small red blooms that provided the exact element she needed to test the weapon. She injected the clip into the rifle, took aim and squeezed the trigger three times. Two red blooms erupted in a cascade of color. She was convinced.

The proprietor was astonished. She was clearly not a weapons collector. The strange young woman handled the rifle like an experienced professional, and he suspected that she intended to use the gun for a malevolent purpose. Romero didn't want to sell her the gun, but was genuinely afraid she would kill him if he refused. Bargaining didn't take long. She paid a hundred and twenty dollars for the rifle and thirty rounds of ammunition, and was out the door in a rush. Señor Romero promptly called the police.

Clare now believed she was the hunted and reasoned that the trio of men would be headed to the east coast as quickly as possible to apprehend her. She calculated that they would likely be headed to New York or Washington, D.C. and would take TWA flight #92 to New York at 1:40 p.m. since the next flights to either city were more than five hours later. It was now almost 11:00 a.m. and time was of the essence.

She intended to eliminate them on the way to the airport and take the flight herself. She would simply leave the car at a strategic site near the airport and, after the mission was complete, would return to the vehicle, change clothes, and casually drive past what was sure to be a police checkpoint. She would purchase her ticket and be on her way while there was confusion at the ambush site. Clare was also sure the Ford would not be noticed for several days. By then she would be back in her homeland.

The road to the airfield was off the main highway, but there were three smaller roads that ultimately led to Miles Avenue, where the driver would have to take an awkward left turn approximately half a mile from the airport. It provided an excellent location for the ambush. The female predator parked the car just off South Walter Street, not far from the intersection of Ross and Miles Avenues. She found a good spot behind a broken-down adobe dwelling a few hundred yards from her desired attack position.

The assassin stealthily made her way back to find the best vantage point. While not an ideal position, Clare found a clump of old Juniper trees slightly less than a quarter of a mile north of the turn in the road. The sun was on her left and would be almost in the driver's eyes as he negotiated the quirky intersection. She cradled the rifle, drank some water and waited.

The telephone rang in James Rosino's hotel room at exactly 11:50 a.m. It was FBI Agent Donovan Early from Washington, D.C. He had important information to share regarding the identity and itinerary of the female fugitive. Another FBI agent had contacted the Paris travel agency and inquired about airline and hotel reservations made for Giselle Houlé in the past three months. The information provided by the agent enabled the FBI to track her movements during late May and early June, but the bureau had no further communication regarding her beyond that. Further investigation did reveal that someone from the same telephone number in Aachen, Germany had called to make airline and hotel reservations in Los Angeles for a Clare Lyon.

James Rosino gathered his belongings and hurried to the dining room to share the information with Matt and Rich. The task force now knew their executioner's name, where she was from, and had been able to track many of her movements over the past week. The most vital information was that she currently had reservations at the Parker House Hotel in Boston from Tuesday, July 27th to Thursday, July 29th, and had a late afternoon flight on American Airlines to London. The three men quickly ate lunch and proceeded to the airport to catch the TWA flight to New York, where they would connect to American Airlines for the jaunt to Boston.

Two shots rang out as the Chevrolet was traversing the sharp turn toward the Albuquerque airport. After a couple of loud pops and hard thunk, broken glass sprayed throughout the vehicle. Rich Johnson lost control of the car and it careened off the road, eventually coming to a stop in a large clump of tumbleweeds. Blood was seemingly everywhere but miraculously, none of the occupants were mortally wounded. Shards of glass showered all three men, although Matt Kane only had a few slivers in the left side of his face and neck. James Rosino took the brunt of the blast in the face, chest and left arm. Rich Johnson was hit on the right side of his body, with a couple of significant fragments getting lodged in his war-wounded leg.

The first bullet hit the metal window framing on the driver's side of the vehicle, and the second projectile struck the sedan a few inches below the windshield about mid-way between the driver and passenger, spewing glass ubiquitously. Unbeknownst to the three travelers, the German-made rifle had jammed, preventing the sharpshooter from emptying the magazine into the car.

Clare Lyon was furious. While she did not know the extent of the damage she inflicted, she did know that her aim had been off. At the instant the automobile turned and she was about to squeeze the trigger, a giant flash of sunlight reflected off the windshield and temporarily blinded her. She jerked slightly, causing the first bullet to miss high and right. She quickly adjusted, but not enough to accurately pinpoint the driver. Then the unthinkable. The weapon jammed, thwarting her attack.

The exasperated hunter saw the three men gingerly exit the vehicle and knew her mission had failed. Now it was a matter of survival for her. She would not be able to fly but would have to make her way back to her car, change her appearance, and drive her way out of danger.

A city truck was patching cracks in the pavement on the airport road not far from the location when the shots rang out. The three workmen instinctively looked up on the rise toward the noise and then quickly ducked behind their vehicle. They could see a figure running northwest away from the trees, and realized that they were not the targets of the attack. In a few seconds, they noticed the Chevrolet as it came to a stop off the road. The foreman pointed to the airport and ordered one of his crew to call the police, while he and the other laborer ran to the aid of the injured men who crouched behind the automobile.

Matt knew exactly what had happened. Somehow, the German executioner had found them and wanted to finish the operation she began two months ago. With his mind racing, Matt returned to military mode. He immediately looked for the enemy and saw her racing away from the scene. He then turned to Rich and James to assess their wounds.

Rich was unconsciously wiping the blood from his face while tending to the more serious wounds of his FBI partner. The two workmen arrived on the scene where one of them noticed the blood streaming from Rich's leg. He took the sweat towel he was carrying and wrapped it around the wound, being careful not to plunge the glass further into the victim's leg. Matt and the foreman concentrated on James. He was conscious, but dazed...and mad as hell.

An ambulance arrived on the scene in less than fifteen minutes, with the police not far behind. While not life-threatening, James' wounds were not inconsequential, and he and Rich needed immediate attention. They were helped into the emergency vehicle and transferred to the Lovelace Clinic and Hospital a few miles away for treatment. Matt's wounds were slight, and he remained behind to explain their situation and brief police on the attack.

The senior officer informed Matt that they had received a warning about a hostile female who purchased a German automatic rifle earlier in the day, and appeared as though she was eager to put the weapon to use. The description of the woman confirmed that it was indeed the elusive Giselle Houlé, aka Clare Lyon. Matt told the officer that she had clearly been in disguise, and that they should be looking for a young blonde, not someone with black hair and dark clothing.

Two more police cruisers arrived and at the checkpoint, and the officers were dispatched to search the area where the ambush originated. An All-Points-Bulletin was also initiated, although the authorities had no information concerning her mode-of-transportation or direction of travel. The Albuquerque police rapidly set up roadblocks on major thoroughfares leading in all directions and police were dispatched to several public transportation hubs to prevent the attacker from fleeing the city.

Authorities reasoned that the fugitive would have to use U.S. Route 66 to travel east or west, or U.S. 85 or State Road 47 to go north or south. Roadblocks were established at the intersection of U.S. Highway 66 and State Road 194 heading west, and on Route 66 just east of the University of New Mexico. In addition, barricades were established at the Barelas Bridge on U.S. 85 and three miles south of the Municipal Airport on Highway 47. The northern route was covered by barriers at Highways 85 and 47 at Menaul School Road.

Once the interview was complete, one of the officers transported Matt to the hospital for treatment. He learned that Rich had sustained several cuts in his face that required a total of nine stitches, and two serious gashes in his right leg, each requiring substantial suturing.

James was simply a mess, having taken the brunt of the assault. His face required nearly twenty stitches, as did his neck, arm and chest, but he was adamant that they catch the next flight to the east coast. The doctors ordered the patient to remain in the hospital for a few days. In addition, they maintained that Rich's leg wounds prohibited him from any kind of travel. James protested, but Matt sided with the physicians and instructed the FBI agent and Minneapolis detective that they were going nowhere until their lacerations were clearly under control.

Matt was released to travel back to Minneapolis while his two partners were confined to the hospital for the rest of the week. He chose to stay with his compatriots. The chase for Clare Lyon would have to be delegated to other members of his FBI task force until they were physically able to continue. Another frustrating setback for the impatient Matt Kane.

James grudgingly grabbed a telephone and called Washington to brief members of the task force on the incident and give them instructions to monitor air, rail and bus transportation into and out of Boston. He also instructed them to screen all airline and ship manifests on the east coast for a single female passenger with a foreign sounding name traveling to Europe. He emphasized that Clare Lyon must not be allowed to leave the United States.

It took ten minutes for Clare to reach her vehicle. She swiftly took off her wig, changed clothes and headed north on South Walter Street on a trip to nowhere. While the Mexican border was only two hundred and seventy-five miles south, Clare reasoned that authorities would be looking for her in that direction. She also knew she couldn't go east to another big city. If she could avoid police through the city, she was satisfied that she could evade her pursuers by traveling north to Canada. She was correct.

Clare proceeded north on South Walter, turned on to South Broadway, crossed Route 66 and continued north until she found a dead end at Menaul School Road, where she spotted the police setting up a blockade two blocks west of her. She found an unnamed dirt road thirty yards west and followed it for a mile or so until it intersected with U.S. 85. Within an hour of the ambush, the hunter turned fugitive had evaded the dragnet and was on her way to Santa Fe.

Clare stopped briefly to refuel on the outskirts of Santa Fe. She turned the key to start the engine. Nothing. "Is it the starter again?" she mumbled. She waited a couple of minutes to avoid flooding the engine and anxiously turned the key again. Nothing.

The service station attendant approached the Ford and told the young woman it sounded like the battery was dead. He, of course, was willing to sell her a new battery. "American cars," she muttered to herself. It took fifteen minutes and six dollars to replace the power source. She took a few deep breaths and was hurriedly on her way. But where? Clare looked at her map and decided that she would head for Denver, sell the car, and take a train to Canada.

After a tedious five hour drive up the Sangre de Cristo Mountain highway, the escapee arrived in the small community of Raton, New Mexico, where she found a picturesque motel to spend the night. Reality also became apparent. Getting to Denver, and further north to Canada, was going to be a grueling trek that would likely take a week or more. It was now a matter of patience and guile. She convinced herself that she was cool and resourceful, and was determined to show her tutor that she could survive under hostile conditions.

Tuesday, July 27th was another wearying day as Clare Lyon traversed the two-hundred and twenty-five miles through Pueblo, Colorado to Denver. It was late afternoon and the clandestine female was anxious to rid herself of the flawed American vehicle. As she hurried in the direction of Union Station where she intended to catch the next train to Denver, the young woman kept her eyes open for a place to sell the Ford. When she turned on Colfax Avenue, she spotted a used car dealership not far from Lincoln Park, turned in and was immediately met by a heavy-set, rumpled man with a two-day beard. He, of course, wanted to sell her a car, but she quickly turned the tables on him.

"I want to sell my car," the woman decreed. "How much will you give me for it?"

The salesman looked quizzically at the woman and asked, "Do you want to trade for another automobile? We have some very nice deals. I can give you more for your automobile if you buy one of ours," he continued.

"No. I just want to sell my car. How much?" she answered curtly.

The disheveled double-dealer motioned her to follow him into the office, where he picked up and thumbed through his Kelly Blue Book to find the actual value of the 1949 Ford. Four-hundred-twenty-five dollars.

"I can offer you three hundred dollars for your car, lady," offered the shifty salesman, cocksure that he had a *live one*.

"You can do better than that," she responded. "I paid four-hundred-ninety-five dollars a few days ago."

"You paid too much," he snapped. "I can go as high as three hundred and forty-dollars. Take it or leave it."

"I will take it."

Half an hour and a few signatures later, the parties to the transaction went their separate ways convinced they had bested the other.

It was time for the calculating Clare Lyon to go off script. On Wednesday morning, she boarded the Denver Zephyr at Union Station on her way through Omaha to Chicago, where she switched to a Greyhound bus that took her to Detroit. Her trek took almost thirty-hours and she was mentally and physically fatigued. Nonetheless, she had one more task before she could find lodging for the night. Crossing the border into Canada.

Clare Lyon took the Tunnel Bus to Windsor, Canada. Another identity was required. Border authorities had no difficulty admitting Christa Osen, a Belgian student on holiday for the summer, to their country. Finally, the crafty fugitive had managed to evade the American law enforcement dragnet. The downside was that she used her last passport, and would be unable to change her identity again until she returned to Aachen.

Aka Christa Osen found a Howard Johnson's Motel just off the main road in Windsor and crashed for the night. On Friday morning at 10:55 a.m., the formidable young woman stepped on to the Canadian Greyhound bus bound for Montreal. The nearly twenty-hour journey on Highways 401/403 took her through several small towns and dropped and added passengers in Hamilton, Mississauga and Toronto. She found the stretch along Lake Ontario between Toronto and Kingston particularly peaceful, with the glimmer of light off the water in the darkness presenting an enjoyable hiatus from the flight from her pursuers.

Upon arrival at the bus terminal in Montreal, the determined Christa Osen took a taxicab to Montréal–Dorval International Airport, where she looked for any flight to Europe. She found BOAC flight #607 to London, departing at 7:15 p.m., and paid the extra fifty dollars to reserve a sleeping berth in first-class on the Stratocrusier. The overnight flight was quiet and Christa Osen was relieved to be back in familiar territory. The ferry to the continent and her homeland would be easy.

While Rich Johnson was not overjoyed to be under house arrest in a hospital, he was familiar with the drill, and comported himself in an obliging manner. His stay in military hospitals taught him that open antagonism was non-productive. Not so with James Rosino. His spirited Greek-Italian nature simply wouldn't let him rest. He fidgeted, grumbled and paced. He couldn't stand being sidelined while the task force closed the deal. He wanted to be the one to catch the redoubtable executioner, and wanted everyone to know how exasperated he was. Five days seemed like five years.

On Saturday morning, the three walking-wounded arrived at the Albuquerque airport to the stares of airline personnel and fellow travelers alike. Clare Lyon, or whoever she was, had not been captured and Matt, Rich and James were forced to limp back to Minneapolis and Washington, D.C. to lick their wounds and contemplate their next steps. It would be two weeks before they could resume their pursuit of the elusive professional executioner.

Giselle Houlé, aka Clare Lyon, aka Christa Osen, did not eliminate Major Matthew Kane or Lieutenant Abigail Findlay, and the FBI task force had missed its opportunity to apprehend her. All parties in the drama were dissatisfied. Failure had temporarily won the day.

Chapter 11

The Special Services Unit

Ruth Chessman stood at the gate and watched as passengers deplaned from Northwest Airlines flight #109 from Chicago. It was Saturday afternoon, a few minutes after 1:00 p.m., and she was planning to coax Matt into having lunch, going to the lake, and spending a quiet afternoon on the boat. After several minutes watching people surge down the stairway, Ruth was stunned into reality.

Matt looked like a ghost, and Rich Johnson had a pronounced limp as they gingerly made their way down the ramp. Matt called Ruth on Friday night and asked her to pick them up at the airport the next day, and while he told her they had been waylaid by their quarry, she was not prepared for what she saw. It was clear that both men would need time to recuperate before they could continue the chase. She could only imagine what James Rosino looked like.

Ruth's first stop was the Johnson household, where Ann Johnson was equally disquieted by the appearance of her husband. After a careful hug, she chastised him for not being careful. She had seen his war injuries a decade earlier, but certainly never expected him to experience that kind of trauma again, since policing in Minneapolis was a relatively safe place for his work. She regretted giving Rich her approval to be part of the FBI task force.

The trip to Matt's house was a quiet one, as Ruth contemplated her 'I told you so' speech. She had strongly advised him to let the FBI agent and detective handle the investigation and not to go to Arizona because he was not yet fully recovered from his brush with death two months ago.

"You're going straight to bed," Ruth chided.

"I'm okay, but I admit that the trip took more out of me than I anticipated," Matt replied.

"Matt, you need more time before you're able to physically take on this kind of strenuous activity. Right now, you need rest."

"*Okay*...I know you're right, but this thing is obviously bigger than we thought, and time is of the essence."

"You are *absolutely* correct, I was right...and you're going nowhere for at least two weeks!"

Matt was too worn out to argue. He would debate the issue tomorrow. Right now, he just wanted a breather. Ruth took his vital signs, made him a sandwich, and spirited him off to the bedroom.

The next week was a quiet one for Matt, Rich and James as they each recovered from their near fatal encounter with the female executioner.

James flew back to Washington, where one of the task force members picked him up and took him to his apartment not far from Rock Creek Park. He was an avid runner and the park offered a convenient setting for him to engage in his passion. At thirty-seven years old, he lived alone but spent many evenings and weekends with colleagues and friends, both male and female. This week there would be no socializing or athletic endeavors. He would remain alone and marginally ambulatory, and spend his time working on a strategy for apprehending the foreign agent.

While James was no stranger to female companionship, he had not yet met a woman who understood the necessary commitment to the job, long workdays, the constant on-call status of an FBI agent, and the hyper-vigilance necessary to succeed in a dangerous profession. He almost married in his mid-twenties, but his fiancé, while thrilled with the prestige of being an FBI spouse and the camaraderie of agents and families, dreaded the persistent danger and lack of a normal life. In short,

James Rosino didn't think his current role was conducive to a successful marriage. Maybe someday, but not now.

Detective Captain Richard Johnson patiently spent some much-needed time with Ann and his two boys, Robert and Michael. He also communicated daily with his MPD partner, Detective Colin Young, to discuss progress on the gang violence case and a series of burglaries and vandalism in the Riverside neighborhood that was heavily populated by immigrants from Sweden, Germany and Bohemia. While he was temporarily assigned to the FBI, he was still a Minneapolis police detective and didn't want to get out of touch with his community.

As a professional law enforcement officer, Rich was viewed by his peers as a stoic and purposeful man who focused on case facts rather than personalities or emotive behavior. Courts relied on facts, and he solved cases by unraveling small details that ultimately led to the arrest and conviction of his perpetrators.

His family saw Rich as a caring husband and attentive father. His job required odd hours, but when at home, he provided structure, generous support, and affection for his children. Ann was his best friend, and as a true partner, he routinely sought her counsel and included her in his decision-making. Not this time, however. He was on a personal mission and was determined to see this international case to its lawful conclusion.

Ruth spent virtually every waking hour between shifts tending to Matt. He could not legally share his *SSU* summary with her, so he worked feverishly on it when she was at the hospital. She was highly curious, but didn't press her companion to violate his secrecy oath. It took most of the week to complete, and all he needed was a release letter from the Secretary of Defense so he could share this vital information with his two colleagues. He was anxious to bring his new partners into his wartime drama so they could fully understand the situation.

After eight days of recovery and reflection, all three men were stir-crazy and ready to resume their search for the elusive female killer.

"Hello...this is Agent Rosino."

"Hi, James, it's Matt. How are you doing?"

"Hi, Matt. Still a little sore, but anxious to get back on her trail. I've devised a strategy for tracking her down, and I'm ready to get to work as soon as Rich is able to travel."

"What about me?"

"I don't know if you should be taking on an international assignment right now, given how taxing our last sojourn was. Why don't you..."

Matt's blood pressure rose sharply and his tone became combative.

"*Oh, no you don't!* I'm not sitting this one out. I have critical information and a personal stake in the outcome. You're not leaving me home. If necessary, I'll go by myself and take Ruth with me to monitor my health. Probably not a bad idea for her to take care of you and Rich, too."

"*Okay*...okay, don't get bent out of shape. As for Ruth, it's too dangerous for her to be put in the line of fire. By the way, I have your release letter from Secretary Wilson. As it turns out, Director Hoover called the White House and talked with President Eisenhower a couple of weeks ago and the President committed to waive the secrecy oath in this case if the Secretary of State and Army Chief of Staff George Marshall agreed that the circumstances warrant the exception. The letter states that you have the authority to share the information with others on a need-to-know basis."

"Great," responded Matt. "Why don't you come back to Minnesota when you feel up to it, and I'll brief you and Rich on the *Special Services Unit* and the covert operations that seem to be the catalyst for this conspiracy. Then we can get back in the hunt. Too much time is being wasted."

"I'm ready to go now," countered a resurgent Rosino. "I'll call Rich and check on his status, and let you know when I can get there."

Wednesday, August 11th was a banner day for the three trackers. Each still sported the scrapes and scars of their encounter with Clare Lyon...or whoever she was, but were impatient to resume their mission. James and Rich were intrigued and mesmerized by Matt's hour-long summary of the members of the *Special Services Unit* and sketch of his team's secret operations.

Matt reminisced that it was late September 1943 when he entered the office of British Major General Stewart Menzies, Chief of the Secret Intelligence Service, and found eight assorted individuals who also had no idea why they were there. He described the general as cordial, but typically British, having opened his monologue with an apology for keeping everyone in the dark...*literally*. Each specialist except Marie Spenser was transported individually to the site with a hood over his or her head so no one could see them and they could not see where they were going. Marie was already a regular at the complex.

Secrecy was paramount. While it seemed that thousands of workers entered, exited, and moved freely within the compound, their existence as a group was destined to be unusually secretive because their assignments were to be kept outside the established chain of command.

Menzies explained that everyone in the room had been selected for a small, top-secret covert operations unit, whose task was to undertake intelligence missions that could shorten the war by years. Each person came highly recommended by their superiors after being carefully watched and vetted for several months. He indicated that they had been selected for their specific skills and knowledge, resourcefulness in problem-solving, athletic background, overall physical fitness, and guile.

Matt smiled as he recalled a marked change in tone after the general's introductory ego boost. He became solemn and official, and decreed that he could not disclose any details about the exact structure or activities of the unit until all nominees had signed the confidentiality oath required by the Official Secrets Act...whether or not they agreed to be part of the group. He stressed that participation was strictly voluntary, and that the nature of the assignments would require travel behind enemy lines and be highly dangerous. Furthermore, no one in the room would ever be able to reveal their participation in the project or discuss any of the unit's operations, presently or after the war.

Menzies clarified that if anyone decided not to stay, he would arrange for them to be transported back to their previous situation with no recriminations or loss of status. After everyone signed their secrecy oath, the general asked if there were any questions or if anyone wanted to be excused. Matt said that the six men and three women paused, looked at each other probingly, and finally Abby Findlay took the lead. He recalled her comments almost exactly.

"General, pardon the impertinence, but I believe I know where we are and have some idea about the type of work you have in mind. I want you to know that I'm all in." Everyone concurred, and at that moment, the Bletchley Park *Special Services Unit* was officially born.

General Menzies then launched into a summary of the Government Code and Cypher School run by the British Secret Intelligence Service. He told the group that it was a clandestine code-breaking operation located near the city of Bletchley in Buckinghamshire, England on a fifty-eight-acre estate, just over seventy kilometers northwest of London. The Victorian mansion was the center of a mass of huts and blockhouses where thousands of gifted men and women worked to intercept and decrypt German, Japanese and other Axis country communications. He stressed that no one outside the compound knew of its activities except for the Prime Minister and a small group of highly placed military and government leaders. The citizens of the small railroad town of Bletchley and the many outside communities that housed and fed the workforce thought the outpost was a specialized university, training young people for war-related assignments.

Then Matt dropped his bombshell.

"Bletchley Park was the code-breaking epicenter for the Allied forces throughout the war. They worked closely, albeit suspiciously, with the American code-breaking operations centered in the Washington, D.C. area, and were able to decrypt virtually all German and Japanese communications worldwide."

"General Menzies revealed to us that Germany and Japan were using complex electromechanical cypher machines for industrial, ambassadorial and military communications, and that their coding schemes and machines were thought to be unbreakable. However, Germany and Japan were unaware that their *Enigma* and *Purple* machines had been captured, and their codes had been broken. Menzies said he was confident that the Allies were virtually reading enemy communications before commanders in the field had them."

"The General also divulged that Bletchley Park was staffed by thousands of diverse individuals from completely different social and educational backgrounds, and that young women comprised almost three-quarters of the codebreakers. I can tell you from my experience that they were indeed an eclectic group of data gatherers and codebreakers that included actors, attorneys, college professors, logicians, mathematicians, linguists, engineers, all types of military strategists, university and non-university-trained women, and thousands of other exceptional individuals from around the free world. Interestingly, the common link between them seemed to be that they all had natural inquisitive talents, and many were crossword puzzle aficionados."

"The General went on to explain that there was a tunnel of communications from cryptologists that were fed to a select few individuals who determined how the information was to be used and who would receive it. The complicating issue was how to employ the intelligence to counter Axis moves without alerting Germany or Japan that their communications were being read."

As an illustration, Matt detailed the heavy feeling in the room when Menzies described a specific incident that outlined the intense ethical dilemma faced by military decision makers.

"General Menzies told us that the *Enigma* machine allowed the Germans to use a modified typewriter to encode plain text messages utilizing an electromagnetic combination of lights, revolving rotors and accompanying plugboards that converted messages into an unintelligible string of letters. This provided something like a hundred-and-fifty million *times* a hundred-and-fifty million different combinations of letters...obviously too complex for any number of human beings to unscramble. Not to mention that the Germans changed the rotor settings daily. It was an impossible task and the enemy thought it was too intricate for anyone to break their codes."

Rich and James looked at each other with astonishment.

Matt paused and then continued.

"The first *Enigma* machine had three rotors that provided initial keys to unscrambling the cypher text by the receiving unit. We were told that a small group of Bletchley academics built a machine called a *bombe*, which was effectively the first computer. The contraption made it possible for us to identify the daily rotor settings and decipher the messages. However, in early 1942, the Germans began using a modified version of the machine with four rotors for their naval codes, which completely shut us off. The mathematicians told Menzies that the new machine had *one-hundred-thousand-billion-billion* combinations! Prior to that, we had been able to significantly reduce our convoy losses in the

Atlantic, enabling us to get crucial food, equipment and heavy weapons to Russia and the continent."

"At that point, we were in big trouble because we didn't know where the U-boats were and our convoy losses were escalating dramatically. The General told us that late in the year we captured some key code books from a sinking sub and regained our capability to decode U-boat communications when the wolfpack began communicating again."

"At the last minute, the codebreakers were able to locate the wolfpack and could have warned two large convoys of merchant ships moving from New York to British ports of an impending attack. Command decision makers were faced with a moral/strategic dilemma. Save known ships and lives or sacrifice them to prevent the Germans from learning we had broken their code. They chose not to use the information in order to retain a broader strategic advantage, which resulted in twenty-two ships being sunk, and the loss of more than three hundred seamen. This apparently happened with some frequency across military theaters."

"Ultimately, when plausible and convincing alternate explanations for countering U-boat or troop movements were developed...like air reconnaissance, the decision to safeguard the codebreaking coup proved to be the correct strategy. Although families who lost someone because of withheld warnings, as well as the general public, might have taken exception to the policy. Not making reactions to message intercepts too blatant allowed the secret to be kept, and thousands of lives were ultimately spared."

"Remarkable, Matt," proclaimed James, "But how does that codebreaking feat relate to your *Special Services Unit*?"

"Okay...I'll get to that," Matt responded.

"Apparently, in 1940 the Prime Minister concluded that Britain couldn't win a conventional war with Germany, and that some kind of subversive force was necessary to disrupt Axis operations and create havoc on the continent. Churchill reasoned that a specialized group could coordinate resistance activities in occupied countries and incite guerrilla warfare, thereby diverting troops away from the conventional battlefield. As a result, he established the *Special Operations Executive*, a secret militia to infiltrate France, Germany and every other country in Europe."

"The *SOE* eventually had about five-hundred trained agents who conducted operations throughout the continent based on information gained from Bletchley. These *SOE* agents were highly trained in everything from reconnaissance, communications, and camouflage, to hand-to-hand combat, weapons and explosives, sabotage, and subversion. They effectively carried out clandestine operations that provided vital information to Allied leaders that altered troop movements and undermined enemy operations, and generally confused the enemy. However, some people had doubts."

"Notwithstanding their successes, General Menzies and many other high-ranking officials didn't approve of Churchill's private army. If I remember correctly, Menzies actually called the *SOE 'amateur, dangerous, and bogus'*. Furthermore, too many of their agents were being captured and used against the Allied effort. Once they were no longer useful to the Germans, they were killed. The weak link appeared to be the lengthy wireless transmissions necessary to convey information to London. Agents were tracked, caught quickly, and used to send false reports, raising questions about moles in the network. That's why Menzies decided to form his own covert section...the *Special Services Unit*."

"Okay, that's the hook!" quipped Rich Johnson.

"This information is still protected by the British Official Secrets Act and the American Espionage Act," added Matt. "Thousands of Americans, British, Canadians, French and other countries' ordinary citizens played a momentous role in the war but are prevented from ever revealing their contributions to the war effort."

"Unfortunate," opined Rosino. "But necessary because some techniques are still being used against the Soviets and other communist countries. In addition, many of those secret operatives are probably still active."

Matt handed Rich and James a copy of his summary of *SSU* members. "This is a brief bio of each SSU member. Only these individuals and probably five or six others knew the unit existed and the operations they were engaged in. In addition to these nine, only General Menzies, Bill Donovan, head of the American OSS, Generals Eisenhower, Bradley and Montgomery were in the loop. There may also have been a couple of other key leaders, but the circle was intentionally small to prevent any leaks that would compromise our projects."

"What about Roosevelt and Churchill?" asked James incredulously.

"They were definitely not included because they both tended to talk too much and shared information with their confidants too freely."

Rich and James poured over the document to familiarize themselves with the assassin's targets and get a handle on their traits and skills.

Bletchley Park Special Service Unit Personnel

- **Duncan Giles** – Born 6/1894 – Colonel in the British Army...Intelligence Officer in charge of Special Services Unit (*SSU*)...WW1 veteran of Gallipoli, Somme and Passchendaele campaigns... British Army light-heavyweight champion four consecutive years in the mid 1920s ...*SSU* Team 1 leader...code name **Flanders**. Led *SSU* Covert operations (Sub-Ops) *Mouse Trap*, *Weasel* and *Temptation* in 1944/1945.

- **Andrew Brant** – Born 9/1912 in Stuttgart, Germany ...emigrated with his mother to Pennsylvania in 1922...schooled in US...tennis player and linguist at Harvard...returned to Germany after the war...SSU Team 1 ...code name **Ten**...participated in Sub-Ops *Mouse Trap*, *Weasel* and *Temptation* in 1944/1945.

- **Gale Fraser** – Born 1/1911...French citizen who fled to London with family in 1940...Bletchley Park codebreaker...numismatics hobby...fluent in French, German and English...snow skiing instructor in 1930s...code name **Harley** (loved to read mystery books by George Harley) ...*SSU* Team 1... participated in Sub-Ops *Mouse Trap*, and *Temptation* in 1944/1945.

- **Matthew Kane** – Born 12/1914...University of Minnesota Law School...Intelligence officer and codebreaking specialist in the US Army... worked with William Friedman in the *Signal Intelligence Service* (*SIS*) at Arlington Hall in Virginia...football and basketball at UM...Father/Mother immigrated from Germany just before WW1...*SSU* Team 2 leader... code name **Candy**...led Sub-Ops *Thrust*, *Replace* and *Screen*.

- **Marie Spenser** – Born 9/1921 – British code breaker at Bletchley Park... worked with Joan Joslin converting accounting machines into codebreaking machines... mathematics student at Durham University...eventually graduated with PhD in Linguistics from Kings College London...accomplished competitive swimmer...*SSU* Team 2...code name **Rose**... participated in Sub-Ops *Thrust*, *Replace* and *Screen*.

- **Patrick Kendall** – Born 1/1908...Father British, Mother French...raised in France...French Resistance operative... Chess champion and French soccer goalkeeper...*SSU* Team 2...code name **Earl**... participated in Sub-Ops *Thrust, Replace* and *Screen*.

- **Abigail Finlay** – Born 11/1912 – Engineering Degree from MIT... highly intelligent and superior leadership skills... *bombe* specialist in the U.S. Naval Communications Command...avid swimmer...lives in Boston...senior analyst for the National Security Agency...*SSU* Team 3 Leader...code name **Cato**...led Sub-Ops *Spoof* and *Retrieve*.

- **Hugh Kensie** – Born 4/1902...British Commando, Major...Mathematics Degree at Cambridge University... Olympic Fencer in 1936 in Berlin ...*SSU* Team 3...code name **Sunnyside**... participated in Sub-Ops *Spoof* and *Retrieve*.

- **Lewis Tarquin** – Born 1899 in France...moved to U.S. in 1914...Papyrology professor at UCLA...Doctorate from University of Chicago...minor league baseball player for the Chicago White Sox in the early 1920s while pursuing PhD...Married to French Resistance operative Josette Beaulieu ... *SSU* Team 3...code name **Grant**... participated in Sub-Ops *Spoof* and *Retrieve*.

"An interesting group," offered Rich.

"Yes, and dedicated and effective," replied Matt. "Good friends all. Unfortunately, I've gotten out of touch with them over the years."

"We spent a few weeks in late 1943 training at Bletchley and then ten weeks at Camp X, a secret training facility on Lake Ontario in the Canadian wilderness. No one there knew we were a unit. We were simply a group of individual trainees just like everybody else in the compound."

"Our instruction included everything from intelligence gathering to espionage...and virtually every other skill in between; from physical combat tactics to psychological warfare."

James, Rich and Matt spent the next two days in Rich Johnson's office on Nicollet Avenue formulating and debating the merits of several pursuit plans to apprehend the female assassin and get to the bottom of what appeared to be a wider conspiracy.

The trackers settled on a strategy to contact the remaining four members of the former *Special Services Unit* and get them together in London to analyze their covert operations and try to pinpoint the link to the stalker and the underlying motivation for eliminating *SSU* members. Once they had a better understanding of the situation, they would re-engage the International Criminal Police Commission, and coordinate with appropriate intelligence and law enforcement agencies in Britain, France, Germany and Belgium.

After a weekend of further recuperation, Matt Kane, Rich Johnson and James Rosino were on their way to London. Unexpectedly, Ruth Chessman would be there to meet them.

Chapter 12

The Gathering

"What are *you* doing here?" barked a startled Agent Rosino.

Rich and Matt just looked at each other and laughed. They knew her too well by now. On the surface, Ruth Chessman was unassuming and more comfortable in the background. In reality, in the last two months she had revealed a side of her that was inquisitive, adventurous and persistent, as Rich and Matt had discovered. James was also rapidly finding out.

"I'm on vacation," Ruth responded nonchalantly.

"It's too dangerous for you to be involved," James countered.

"Who said I was involved? I'm here as a tourist...*and* perhaps as a trauma nurse, based on your last escapade."

"Where are you staying?" asked James.

"The same place you are...the St. James Hotel near Buckingham Palace. What a coincidence, huh?"

The exasperated FBI agent grabbed her arm and spirited her off to catch a taxi to the hotel with his amused partners.

Prior to catching their flight to London, James had assigned two members of the Kane Task Force to track down the four other members of the *Special Services Unit* and arrange to have them transported to the MI6 offices at 54 Broadway in London, just ten minutes from the St. James Hotel. Early on Monday morning, August 16th, James received news that confirmed Matt's theory that his assault was indeed part of a wider conspiracy to eradicate all the members of the *SSU*. The puzzling question was why?

Four members of the *SSU* had been killed in the past seven months, but their deaths were not linked by law enforcement since the murders occurred in four different countries, and because there was no apparent reason to connect the victims. The group behind the attacks neatly scripted the sequence of events to mask their strategy and remain hidden. James concealed this information until the remaining five *SSU* members were present in a secure conference room at MI6 for an afternoon briefing.

Present were the retired Chief of MI6, aka, the Secret Intelligence Service, General Stuart Menzies; current Chief of MI6, General John Sinclair; former *SSU* agents Duncan Giles, Abby Findlay, Hugh Kensie, Marie Spenser and Matt Kane; as well as Rich Johnson and James Rosino.

"Matt was right, it seems evident that there's a concerted effort to liquidate everyone in this room, except maybe General Sinclair...but he may also be a target of the plot, we just don't know yet," began the FBI agent. "Four of your colleagues have been killed in the last several months, and Matt has barely escaped twice in the last three months. We need your help to identify the assassin and expose the conspiracy."

"Here's what we know now. Andrew Brant was gunned down last December as he was returning to his apartment in Düren, Germany. There were no witnesses and no apparent motive. He spent the first three years after the war back in the U.S. working as a professor at Harvard, but took a leave-of-absence to return to his hometown in 1949 to participate in the re-development of the city after its total devastation in late 1944. Many cities in Germany are still dangerous places because of the poverty and political upheaval, so the authorities in Düren simply didn't expend too much effort to find his killer."

"Gale Fraser was shot twice in the chest at close range at night outside Gare de Dijon-Porte-Neuve train station in late

January. She had just arrived from Paris to visit her sister and was standing outside the Dijon station on Junot Avenue waiting for her brother-in-law to pick her up. He had been delayed because his tires had been slashed. A witness told the Sûreté that a greyish, late model Peugeot drove slowly by and he saw two flashes of light and watched as the victim fell to the concrete. He was about twenty meters from her and rushed over to render aid, but she was already dead. He noticed that the vehicle had no license tag. He didn't see the driver."

"Miss Fraser was a banking supervisor for the main office of Crédit Lyonnais in Paris," James continued. "According to some of her co-workers, she lived alone and didn't socialize much outside of work. The Sûreté investigators told FBI agents that she had hundreds of books in her apartment, which seemed to validate the fact that she didn't get out much. Neighbors said she was pleasant and quiet, but seemed somewhat melancholy."

"We did catch a forensic break, however. The two bullets taken from her body matched the bullets from Matt's attack and our fourth victim, Lewis Tarquin. Clearly, the same female operative is in play in all of the attacks," Rosino emphasized.

"The third victim discovered was Patrick Kendall, who continued in British intelligence with MI6 after the war. His cover employment was as an assistant coach on the British soccer team. Kendall disappeared after leaving practice last November and his remains were found on March 20th near Hastings in a cave used as an air raid shelter during the war. Evidence confirms that he was severely tortured before being shot."

"What kind of torture?" quizzed Abby Findlay.

"His body had no clothing, which indicates that he was dehumanized before being tortured. Forensic analysis revealed that his fingernails and toenails were ripped out, both legs were broken and his genitals were mutilated. Need I go on?" snapped the FBI agent in a sickened tone.

Undoubtedly, this was a classic Nazi SS interrogation. Now the former SSU operatives clearly understood the situation.

"Patrick Kendall's assassination, however, may provide some foundation for establishing a motive for the systematic elimination of you all. General Sinclair, do you want to share the nature of his assignment with the group?"

"Yes, thank you Mr. Rosino. Remember, you are all still under the privacy restrictions of the Official Secrets Act, and anything you hear in this room must never be discussed or revealed in any way. Since the war's end, there have been rumblings about a resurgence of the Nazi Party. We know that some key SS leaders escaped justice in 1946 and went underground for a few years, probably to reorganize and recruit new extremists to the Nazi cause. Mr. Kendall was head of the division probing the new faction. MI6 did not make the connection to the *Special Services Unit* until the American FBI contacted us a week ago. These murders corroborate our intelligence regarding the new Nazi Party, and this conspiracy must be quashed before it gains any significant traction."

James resumed by summarizing the May attempt on Matt's life, the shooting of Lewis Tarquin in Arizona, and their subsequent encounter with the mystery woman in the desert. He also indicated that the brutalization of Pat Kendall was evidently intended to identify any World War II intelligence agents who might have knowledge that could derail the reincarnation of the Nazi organization.

"Given the information we have now, I suggest that we find out how many of the three hundred surviving *SOE* agents have died in the last year or two, and the circumstances of their deaths," decreed General Menzies. "If there's to be the birth of a Fourth Reich, it's inevitable that the cabal would want to purge them also...along with General Sinclair and anyone else who has intimate knowledge of Nazi personnel, strategic and tactics."

"Excuse me, General," interrupted Matt. "I think we all agree that there's a vast conspiracy at play here. But my experience in Minnesota felt personal. Looking for a woman who has a particular grudge may be very revealing as we try to uncover the motive for eliminating *SSU* members. We need to look at our 1944 and 1945 operations and see how the personal angle fits."

"That's our next step, Matt," interrupted James. "We'll spend the next day or two examining the covert operations each of you engaged in and see if there's an exploitable pattern. Your assignment for tonight is to jot down some notes on each of your missions so we can get a better picture of why you are targets of the conspirators."

Agent Rosino concluded the briefing by laying out the combined task force strategy for protecting the former *SSU* and *SOE* agents and other important actors, identifying the female assassin, and ferreting out the leaders and legions of the suspected new *Waffen SS*. Much to the chagrin of the former *SSU* agents, each was to be assigned two guardians to shadow them for the foreseeable future. Matt, of course, would have James Rosino and Rich Johnson as his protectors.

"We've traced the movements of the female assassin through a travel agency in Paris, and telephone calls between the agency and a telephone number in Aachen, Germany. We're aware that all of you have put your spy days behind and moved on in your lives, but any of you who are willing to assist in our investigation can be added to the task force. Again, it will be a dangerous undertaking, but your knowledge and covert operation experience will be invaluable in the search. Do we have any volunteers?"

Abby Findlay couldn't respond quickly enough. "I have a nice job and family, but none of us...or our families, are safe until we uncover and dismantle the conspiracy."

Unexpectedly, Marie Spenser also offered her services. "I agree with Abby. I think I can help, and I can take a leave of absence from my position in the Language Department at Durham University."

"My civic responsibilities prohibit any travel, but I'm willing to help you from the U.K.," added Hugh Kensie.

"I'll do anything necessary to catch those buggars," bellowed a robust sixty-year-old Duncan Giles. "I may be retired, but I can still out-wit and out-fight those jerry bastards. Just point me in the right direction and I'll take care of the Nazi hooligans."

With a mixture of jocularity and solemnity, the group left the conference room and boarded a lorry for the ride to the Criterion Restaurant in Piccadilly for dinner.

Chapter 13

The Reunion

When the group entered the popular World War II restaurant at 5:33 p.m., *Moonlight Serenade* was wafting through the sound system of the Criterion Restaurant. Matt and Marie immediately looked at each other. At that instant, Matt's heart raced, his faced flushed, and he struggled to catch his breath. He then faltered slightly, clutching a counter near the doorway. Rich steadied Matt briefly before the inimitable Ruth Chessman appeared and hurried to his aid.

"*See*...this trip is too much for you, Matt," scolded Ruth tenderly. "You definitely need a keeper."

"I'm fine, Ruth. I just felt a little dizzy for a moment. Where did you come from anyway...and how did you get here?"

"I'm a pretty good detective, too. I persuaded the bus driver to reveal his destination," she responded with a smile.

"Not you again!" roared James. "What am I going to do with you?" He thought for a minute and responded. "*Okay*...If we can't get rid of you, I guess I'll have to include you in the task force as a medical attaché so I can keep an eye on you...but you'll have to sign a confidentiality agreement, and anything you see or hear during this *vacation* can never be revealed or discussed with anyone. Is that clear?"

"Yes sir!" Ruth responded with an air of unconquerable satisfaction.

"Now, finish with your patient and join the group for dinner. I'll deal with you later," the FBI agent commanded in bewildered authority.

Matt, however, knew that his bout of syncope was caused by Marie and the music, not his medical injuries. He was now in a quandary. He had hyperventilated before, early in his relationship with Marie Spenser in 1943 and a few times in the ensuing weeks until he got used to her presence. He was simply captivated by her from the first moment he saw her, but with several years' separation, he was convinced he was over her. Obviously not.

During the past three months since the shooting, Matt had drawn close to Ruth, and frankly, he thought his time with Marie had passed anyway. She earned her Doctorate in Linguistics and had a promising teaching career...and as far as he knew, a husband or suitor.

As fortune would have it, the only two seats left at the table of eight were next to Marie, so there he was, Marie on his right and Ruth on his left. As poised as he typically was in communicating and managing prickly situations, he was bumfuzzled and noticeably failed to command the situation. James bailed him out.

"Everyone, this trouble-maker is Matt's personal medical aide. She nursed him back to health in Minnesota, and again took care of him after our mishap in New Mexico. Apparently, I can't keep her away, so I decided to add her to our task force. In addition to monitoring Matt's health, she may actually come in handy if any more of us run into trouble during our pursuit of the conspirators."

"Welcome, Ruth. I'm Marie Spenser. Glad to have you with us. As you have undoubtedly found out, Matt can't seem to stay out of mischief."

"Hi, Marie...*now* I understand why he thought I was you when he first regained consciousness. We do actually look a lot alike. I'm looking forward to getting to know you."

"Likewise, Ruth. I think we just might become friends."

Matt was flabbergasted. *What now*, he thought? He desperately wanted to spend some private time with Marie and figure out how to handle this now touchy situation. He quickly regained some sense of balance and told himself that the first order of business was catching the assassin and thwarting the new Nazi plot. The reunion would have to wait.

The dinner conversation between Marie and Ruth was cordial and informative for both, and while their backgrounds and career paths were disparate, their respective interests and personality characteristics were indeed similar. It appeared as though a genuine friendship could be forming.

Meanwhile, Matt was distracted and tried to avoid the genial interplay between the Ruth and Marie. He was deep in thought as he journeyed back in time to when he first saw Marie. He recalled that she was slightly built, with piercing blue eyes and sandy-blonde hair with abundant natural curls. She sat quietly in the briefing room and listened intently to General Menzies. He noticed that she looked to be the youngest person in the room, and he had openly wondered what special skill she might bring to the unit. He later learned that she was uncommonly smart, observant, and intuitive. She could take a jumble of data, assimilate it, turn it into information, and create usable knowledge very quickly.

At the conclusion of the meal, General Sinclair introduced each former agent to their MI6 protectors and explained how they would shadow them during the investigation. They then boarded the coach for a return trip to the St. James Hotel for the night. Matt took Ruth by the hand and headed for the back of the vehicle, studiously avoiding any further conversation between the two females.

Matt sat pensively during the twenty-minute bus ride to the hotel. It was obvious to Ruth that something was wrong. Having gotten to know him over the summer, she knew that pressing him would do no good, however. She would wait for him to ask her for assistance if he needed it. As they left the bus, she asked if he wanted her to monitor him over night. He declined, and said that he just needed to get over his jet-lag and would be fine in the morning. He walked Ruth to her room, gave her a gentle kiss good night, and strolled up to the third floor.

Upon reaching his room, Matt turned around, walked back to the first floor and exited the hotel. He meandered down St. James's Street to Marlborough Road, and ultimately found himself at St. James Park. He walked into the park and found a bench near the lake and sat down to ponder his predicament.

His mind wandered back to the fall of 1943 and Woburn Abbey, where the new *SSU* recruits were billeted. The community of Woburn was situated just over eight miles from the railroad town of Bletchley, and each day lorries took hundreds of staff to and from the Government Code and Cypher School (GC&CS) at Bletchley Park. While Matt had been formally introduced to the other new agents by General Menzies during his orientation sessions, it was on the nearly thirty-minute morning and afternoon bus rides between Woburn and Bletchley Park that he became increasingly enamored with Marie Spenser.

He learned that Marie came from a conservative middle-class family who lived in the historic city of Durham, situated in the northeast quadrant of England. Rich in cultural landmarks dating back to medieval times, the town of roughly twenty-five thousand offered ample opportunities for historical exploration and study, with its abundance of castles and cathedrals that bordered The River Wear. Marie and her older brother, Andrew, were curious children who took full advantage of the many reconnaissance adventures available in the community, often to the chagrin of their mother, Isabella.

Marie's father, William, worked as a Divisional Superintendent for the London & North Eastern Railway, and Isabella provided part-time secretarial services for a mathematics professor at Durham University. Andrew, having shattered his left leg when he fell from a fifteen-foot cliff on one of his and Marie's many excursions, was unable to serve in the military, but spent the war as a bridge and track inspector, as well as a signal maintainer for the LNER railway.

Because her mother recognized Marie's quick mind and penchant for learning, she insisted that Marie go to university, and with the recommendation and support of Dillwyn Knox, master scholar and cryptologist, Marie was admitted to King's College London to study mathematics in 1939. Isabella's father had befriended Knox in the 1920s and the eminent papyrologist had known the Spenser family and Marie for many years.

'Dilly' Knox, as he was known, was a sentinel codebreaker at the Government Code and Cypher School. He recruited Marie for service at Bletchley Park in early 1942, cutting short her academic pursuits. Her first assignment was in Hut 8, the cryptology center charged with breaking the German naval *Enigma* messages. She moved with the team into Block D a year later, and ultimately to Hut 11, where she supervised *bombe* operators decrypting enemy communications until her reassignment to the *Special Services Unit.*

Matt reflected that it was a cold and rainy Thursday morning in mid-December 1943 that he first hyperventilated in her presence. Marie was seated near the back of the bus and touched his hand briefly while he was getting settled. He mused that it took him by surprise and was clearly noticed by Marie. She had inquired if he was ill. He smiled as he recalled how he devised breathing techniques to avoid detection over the next month or so. Finally, it was at the Camp X training site that he was able to be in her presence without losing his breath.

"*Matthew Seiberling Kane...*didn't anyone ever teach you to duck when somebody is shooting at you?" the female cajoled as she strolled up to the bench.

Matt, jolted out of his trance, immediately recognized the voice, and rose to meet his visitor.

"I did duck, but I'm apparently not as agile as I was ten years ago."

Matt and Marie then embraced affectionately and stood gazing at each other for an interminable minute before speaking.

"How did you know I was here?" he asked.

"I was standing at my window when I saw you walk out of the hotel. I knew something was on your mind at dinner...and I just wanted to see if you are okay after your brush with death. You look troubled. What can I do to help?"

"I'm okay, Marie. I just need some time to work out a puzzle," Matt answered tentatively.

"I know you too well. You're hiding something."

"Perhaps...but it's something I have to figure out for myself. It's been too long since we talked. We need to do better in the future. I tried to call you a couple of weeks ago, but no one at King's College knew where you were."

"I've been teaching languages at Durham University for the past couple of years. When the opportunity arose to move back home to be near my family, I couldn't resist. Mum is not well, and Andrew's leg has gotten worse, so I thought I could help if I was close by."

"How about Edward? How does he feel about moving out of London?" Matt quizzed.

"There is no Edward. We spent some time together at university, and he did ask me to marry him, but we were just too different. I wanted to use my education and he wanted me to support his political career. He's now a conservative member of Parliament."

"I'm sorry it didn't work out. Certainly, you must have other gentlemen friends."

"Not really. I just haven't found the right person yet. I've kept up with you, though. You've had quite a journalistic career...making trouble as always," Marie teased. "How about you? It looks like you found a jewel in Ruth."

"She has literally been a life-saver. We've spent a lot of time together since the shooting and I enjoy her company very much. Where we go from here, I just don't know."

Matt and Marie continued their conversation, gradually getting more personal. They were comfortable together and both knew there was still electricity between them. Neither knew how to handle their rejuvenated relationship. It would take time to sort out their feelings. Circumstances would ultimately resolve the issue.

Meanwhile, James had also noticed that Matt was not himself after the meeting at MI6, and ambled down the hall to check on him. Knock, knock. No answer. James was initially concerned, but figured that Matt was with Ruth and, after giving it some thought, felt obliged to verify his whereabouts.

"Ruth...sorry to bother you, but I just wanted to be sure that Matt is with you?" James inquired after a couple of light taps on her door.

"He's not here, James," responded Ruth as she opened the door. "I told him I would stay with him tonight but he said he just needed some sleep." She was now worried, and she was pretty sure why.

James didn't have a clue, but Ruth was beginning to grasp the bond between Matt and Marie.

Chapter 14

The Covert Operations

James was waiting impatiently at MI6 for his task force colleagues as they arrived at 8:00 a.m. on a cool and drizzly Tuesday. He was anxious to understand the secret operations carried out by the *Special Services Unit* during the war, and the possible connection to the systematic attacks on the Unit's agents. Once everyone was situated in the conference room, he wasted no time with frivolities and immediately launched into the examination of *SSU* clandestine operations.

Before calling on Duncan Giles, the only surviving member of *SSU* Team One, it was noted by General Menzies that secrecy was so vital to the success of the *SSU* that each team's missions were not known to other teams in the group. Therefore, the session would be informative for everyone in the room. He indicated that he did keep detailed records of all operations, which he retrieved from the MI6 archives, to supplement the summaries presented by the former agents.

Colonel Giles began the morning briefing by telling the group that Team One's area of concentration was spy and mole analysis. He explained that all of the *SSU*'s activities were based on *Enigma* intercepts, and that the main task of all *SSU* teams was to ensure that information obtained from the intercepted messages was valid and reliable. The verified information was used to support strategic and tactical operations planned by military leaders. While *SSU* agents were not intended to engage in sabotage or quasi-military encounters like the agents of the

SOE, they were nonetheless combat trained in the event that a direct confrontation with the enemy was unavoidable. His team never had occasion to utilize that training.

The retired Colonel then summarized the three primary sub-operations (Sub-Ops) assigned to his team during the war. He explained that his team's first mission was called Sub-Op *Mousetrap*, which supported the larger **Operation Bodyguard**, and that his team's function was to authenticate double agents being used in the Allied disinformation campaign.

Operation Bodyguard was the code name used by the Allies to mislead Germany about where and when the invasion of the continent was to take place. Its first missions were launched in mid 1943 using captured and turned German spies. Team One's assignment was to verify the veracity of those double agents. Giles explained that German Military Intelligence agents, known as Abwehr, were easily spotted and captured due to *Enigma* intercepts because many were either poorly trained or not strongly committed to the Nazi cause. Amazingly, many of these foreign operatives simply turned themselves in to Allied authorities once they were smuggled into Britain.

Colonel Giles, Andrew Brant and Gale Fraser spent weeks shadowing more than twenty-five double agents throughout Britain, France and the Scandinavian countries, as well as neutral countries such as Spain and Portugal. Sometimes they would befriend their marks or merely monitor their associates and communications. The Colonel revealed that most of these double agents were authenticated, but more than a few were decommissioned and detained.

"As a result of Sub-Op *Mousetrap*," Giles told the assembly, "the deceivers were able to create doubt and wariness in the minds of the Germany High Command about the key elements of the D-Day invasion. Time, location, troop strength, command structure and even a fake army, supposedly commanded by General Patton, were part of **Operation Bodyguard**. A great deal of this trickery was due to convincing messages, manufactured data, and photos conveyed to the Reich by the double agents who were confirmed by our team."

"We believed then...and still do, that SubOp *Mousetrap* was a complete success in safeguarding the execution of the invasion," boasted Colonel Giles. "However, I can't see any connection between *Mousetrap* and the current crusade against the *SSU*."

Team One's second assignment was called *Weasel*, and involved an effort to ferret out possible moles and compromised agents in the *Special Operations Executive*. It seemed a logical extension of the previous mission. While the *SOE* suspected mole activity in the French network, there was no question that subversion was rampant in the Holland organization. The Team was tasked with identifying the counterspies and having them eliminated.

Colonel Giles described the Holland circuit as a 'sticky-wicket', with spies, counterspies, multiple deceptions, and misinformation that was unveiled after the war when Dutch *SOE* operative Hubertus Lauwers was repatriated. Lauwers was dropped into Holland in late 1941 and was captured in the Hague in March 1942.

"The German Abwehr Chief, Hermann Giskes, thought he had turned the *SOE* agent, and permitted him to continue communicating with London. Giskes was aware that *SOE* agents had a security code embedded in each communication, but Lauwers apparently gave a false code and followed his prescribed protocol throughout the war. The *SOE* either missed the signal that their operative had been captured or deliberately ignored the warnings and continued sending additional agents into the country, where almost sixty spies were compromised and, all but five, killed. An outrageous blunder by *SOE* leadership."

Giles referred to his notes and continued. "We were tasked with identifying any defectors or compromised agents in the

Dutch network. We examined as many *Enigma* intercepts as possible and any *SOE* communications we could obtain discretely. Gale Fraser was able to find two revealing telegrams sent by Lauwers, one on March 28, 1942, that began with the letters *ght* and ended with the letters *cau*. In mid-May, another Lauwers telegram contained the complete word *caught* three times. It became clear to us that he had been compromised and that the Germans knew the time and location of every *SOE* agent sent into Holland between March of '42 and early '44."

"We reported our finding to General Menzies and assumed that the appropriate changes were being made in *SOE* communications. Unfortunately, it's still not clear today whether Command knew that Lauwers had been compromised or strategically provided false information. It's a shame that they sacrificed additional agents in order to convince the Germans the invasion would come in the Netherlands," offered Giles apologetically.

"Again, it doesn't seem likely that this mission is connected to the current assassination plan."

Team One's third mission, Sub-Op *Temptation*, was designed to support counter-espionage activities of the newly created American OSS Special Counter-Intelligence Unit known as X-2. Their assignment was to identify Abwehr agents in France, flush them out, and help the X-2 leaders recruit them as double agents.

Colonel Giles explained that his team, using *Enigma* intercepts, was able to pinpoint a Spanish national, Juan Frutos, as an Abwehr agent operating out of Cherbourg in May 1944. Frutos, who had been a trusted German operative since the mid 1930s, was responsible for reporting any Allied activity leading up to the invasion of the continent, and was to stay behind and continue providing troop size, movement, weaponry, and other crucial activity that might be useful to the Germans.

"X-2 operatives captured Frutos in early July and easily turned him into what was called a Controlled Enemy Agent (CEA). He was then vetted by our team before being allowed to resume sending false or vague messages to the German High Command."

"Turning Frutos, whose codename was Dragoman, enabled X-2 to isolate, catch and turn more than a dozen other Abwehr agents throughout France into CEAs. These double agents almost willingly changed sides because they recognized an ultimate Allied victory in the war. These CEAs transmitted deceptive and illusory information throughout the remainder 1944 and the spring of 1945, which gave the Allies major tactical advantages in combat operations, saving lives and hastening the end of the war."

"Only a few people knew of our participation in X-2 activities, so it's unlikely that anyone involved on the German side would have a motive to target the *SSU*. It looks like our Sub-Ops are a dead end. Maybe something can be uncovered from Team Two and Three actions," concluded Colonel Giles regretfully.

After a short break, Agent Rosino called on former Navy Lieutenant Abby Findlay, leader of Team Three, to summarize their wartime missions. He purposely decided to skip Matt Kane's team because his instincts told him that the answer to the lethal attacks on *SSU* agents were rooted in Team Two's undertakings, and he wanted to save them for last. Notwithstanding his personal hunch, he wanted to be sure that all potential triggers were considered.

Abigail Findlay was a rare talent find for the U.S. Naval Communications Security Section based in the United States. She was not only smart, but extremely goal-oriented, focused and resilient. These characteristics allowed her to graduate at the top of her class at MIT, and enabled her to conquer the multiple complexities of both electrical and mechanical engineering. In addition, her military superiors at Op-20-G described her as having 'exceptional leadership skills'. This ultimately led her to the U.S. Naval Computing Machine Laboratory in Dayton, Ohio in 1942, where she worked with National Cash Register Research Director, Joseph Desch, to engineer and supervise the building of the America's version of the British codebreaking electro-mechanical apparatus known as the *bombe*.

"It's nice to see you all again, but I'm truly sorry that it has to be under these circumstances," began Abby. "It's extremely distressing that we're missing Lew Tarquin from our team. He was a true gentleman and friend."

Former Lieutenant Findlay, following Colonel Giles' script, explained that Team Three's operational emphasis was on enemy morale and propaganda, and went on to explain the two major missions they undertook in 1944 and 1945.

Assignment number one was SubOp *Spoof,* in support of the ingenious OSS **Operation Cornflakes**. Findlay described the U.S. spy agency as a wacky, uncouth, creative and degenerate organization led by the master of unorthodoxy, 'Wild Bill' Donovan. Fittingly, the agency's tools and operations were unconventional and bewildering. Agents used every trickery and repulsive antics to confuse, frustrate, anger and dupe the enemy. Two incidents clearly illustrated her point.

"In several actions," Abby explained, "agents urinated in the gas tanks or on the engines of German vehicles, which may or may not have disabled them, but certainly generated a disgusting smell. A second event was the use of a feces-based concoction, called *eau de diarrhea*, which mimicked the smell of a loose bowel movement. It was apparently used most successfully in liquid form in the Pacific Theater when squirted on the uniforms of Japanese soldiers by young children."

This revelation, of course, generated a mixed reaction of laughter and disgust.

"Operation Cornflakes was a bit zany, but simple, clever and effective in deceiving the German postal system into delivering false letters and propaganda materials to the civilian population and military personnel. The OSS Morale Division redesigned the German postal stamp by altering Hitler's image to look like a skeleton, and changed the words on the stamp from 'Deutsches Reich'...German Empire, to 'Futsches Reich'...Ruined Empire. These Dead Head stamps were placed in the envelopes with other anti-Nazi propaganda."

"Propaganda letters were placed in official German postal bags and dropped by special aircraft at the site of bombed mail trains, which were then picked up by clean-up crews and delivered by *Deutsch Reichpost* workers to their intended targets. The project was aided by the chaos in German transportation and communication systems."

"Our role in Sub-Op *Spoof* was to interview German military personnel and ordinary citizens to gather specific information on postal markings, how the postal system worked, and obtain personal information that was used in the fake materials," continued former Lieutenant Findlay. "We combined our data with civilian information from telephone directories in order to create forged letters to real people."

"In order to activate *Spoof*, Hugh, Lewis and I had to be smuggled into Germany and live among the citizenry for several weeks in late 1944. It was tedious and tense work and we had to eliminate several curious German soldiers and more than one meddlesome citizen during the project," she recalled.

"Hugh...do you have anything to add?" asked Findlay.

"Yes, Abby," responded Hugh Kensie. "SubOp *Spoof* was splendid and contributed significantly to **Operation Cornflakes**. The information we gathered by milling with the German public helped the OSS craft believable letters that were effective in lowering civilian morale. The fake materials sent to soldiers implying that wives and girlfriends were being unfaithful were surely successful in lowering their will to fight."

❖❖❖

Abby then proceeded to describe Team Two's second major assignment, Sub-Op *Retrieve*, which preceded the daring **Operation Carthage** in March 1945. The Team was called upon to infiltrate Gestapo headquarters in Copenhagen, Denmark and gather intelligence needed to support a raid on, and ultimate destruction of, the *Shelhus* building, while minimizing collateral damage to the City Centre.

It was known that there were many Danish Resistance members, prominent government leaders, and at least one *SOE* operative being held in the Shell House; all subject to interrogation and torture, as well as being strategically placed as human shields to prevent bombing of the structure. In addition, the Gestapo had detailed dossiers on Allied sympathizers, Danish Resistance workers and operatives, government officials, and the *SOE* network in Denmark.

"Our job was to produce an exact structural layout of the Shell House and surrounding buildings," expounded Abby. "We were tasked with identifying where prisoners were being held, the location of the dossiers, and mapping out a plan that would allow British Mosquito bombers to destroy the building while providing a reasonable chance of prisoner escape. We were able to take photographs and obtain modified structural plans of the building, and learned that the prisoners were being kept in the attic of the building."

"Excuse me, Abby," interrupted Hugh Kensie, "but you're too modest. It was you who insinuated yourself into the confidence of the Gestapo facility and provided most of the inside information. Lew and I did the outside work. Credit given where credit is due," he emphasized.

After a short pause, Abby concluded her summary of *Sub-Op Retrieve* and **Operation Carthage**.

"We were able to complete our mission, and even created a scale model of Copenhagen's City Centre for air commanders and navigators to map out a plan of attack that would minimize the loss of life in the building and collateral damage to other buildings. We learned later that the mission was a complete success...many prisoners escaped, the intelligence materials were destroyed, and key Gestapo members were killed in the bombing raid."

"We also found out that one of the Mosquito bombers in the first wave apparently clipped a streetlamp and crashed into a French Catholic school, igniting a fire that confused pilots in the second wave. As a result, some of pilots drop bombs on the school, killing almost a hundred children and wounding many more. Sadly, while we did our job, we felt we were at least somewhat responsible for the tragedy. It still haunts me to this day."

"Unless there are Danes trying to kill us, however, I can't see how Sub-Op *Retrieve* plays a role in this conspiracy against the *SSU*."

After Abby completed her briefing, James recognized the deflated mood in the room, and acknowledged the need for a break in the session. He was particularly concerned with the troubled look on Ruth's face. Everyone else in the room had first-hand wartime experience, but the hard details of their involvement were clearly unsettling to her. He now openly wondered if he had been hasty in adding her to the task force.

He would have to tend to that issue immediately, and asked her to remain for a few minutes as he dismissed the group for lunch, anticipating that the interlude would be helpful in renewing the team's spirits.

Chapter 15

The Daisy Compound

As the former *SSU* operatives and guardians left the room and departed for The Red Lion Tavern on Parliament Street, MI6 Chief, General Sinclair, entered his car with two guards and instructed the driver to take him to 10 Downing Street to see the Prime Minister. He would rejoin the team after briefing Winston Churchill on the threats against former World War II leaders and operators and the apparent reemergence of the Nazi Party.

The route from MI6 Headquarters to 10 Downing Street takes the Albert Embankment north for half a mile, through the roundabout west across the Lambeth Bridge and River Thames, through the east roundabout to Milbank Street, and north for another half-mile, winding around Parliament Square another quarter-mile to Downing Street. A leisurely ten-minute jaunt. The vehicle would never reach its destination.

A shot rang out just as the General's car was entering the south ring of the Milbank roundabout, hitting the left front tire and causing the vehicle to veer left and come to a stop on the traffic island. Thinking that it was a blown-out tire, the driver and guards left the vehicle to inspect the damage. The would-be assassin, believing that one of the men was General Sinclair, immediately fired two more rifle shots in succession, catching one of the guards in the right thigh and missing the other man completely. The General quickly recognized that they were under attack and sprang into action to remove the wounded guard from the line of fire. He also grasped that he, too, was part of the budding Neo-Nazi conspiracy.

Uwe Fromme, the twenty-one-year-old neophyte German operative on his first assignment, panicked and began running south through the wooded park toward a waiting boat on the river's edge. As fortune would have it, the Thames River Police were approaching the empty powerboat as Fromme arrived. Seeing them, he dropped his **StG 44** assault rifle and turned east toward Milbank Street.   Once he reached the motorway, he hurried across the road and mingled with the men and women on their way into the large white building known as the Thames House, headquarters of Imperial Chemical Industries.

Having been one of the United Kingdom's prominent and effective war materials producers and nuclear research facilities, ICI remained ultra-security conscious in the 1950s. It was now particularly vigilant due to its proprietary research in plastics and pharmaceuticals. It only took a few minutes to identify the young German as an unauthorized intruder in the building. Security personnel quickly corralled and detained him before he could leave the facility.

Upon questioning Fromme, it was apparent that he was out of his element and was unable to provide a plausible explanation for his presence in the building. The ICI Security Chief promptly called the Metropolitan Police to take custody of the suspicious young foreigner. The police, already on the scene of the assassination attempt, arrived within minutes and took the young man into custody. Just over an hour after the attempt on General Sinclair, Uwe Fromme was captured, triaged by London police, and transferred to MI6 Headquarters for interrogation by Sinclair, FBI Agent James Rosino, and Minneapolis Detective Rich Johnson.

Lunch at the Red Lion was amiable and uplifting, and Rosino's talk with Ruth was productive. Yes, Ruth was disturbed by the cold-bloodedness of the enemy and ongoing risk to Matt and other former members of the *SSU*, but she assured James that she was resilient enough to handle any crisis that might arise in the quest to find Matt's shooter and expose the larger conspiracy.

James had been called immediately after the ambush of General Sinclair, and quickly left the group to go to the scene of the attack. Once he assessed the situation, he sent word for the remainder of the team to be spirited back to MI6 under the utmost of caution. The central question at that moment was whether this was a single sniper attack or part of a coordinated effort to kill the entire unit. One thing was now certain...events were developing rapidly, and time was of the essence. The source of the conspiracy and the depth of the plot needed to be uncovered before the situation became untenable.

Uwe Fromme, while alone and frightened, had no intention of revealing anything. He sat quietly while waiting for the interrogation to begin. James deferred to Rich Johnson because the detective was experienced and clever in interrogating criminal suspects.

"Young man, I'm sure you know that you're in a great deal of trouble," declared Johnson.

Fromme sat mute.

"We know you're traveling on a Belgian passport, and that Uwe Fromme is not your real name. Tell us your name and where you came from."

No response.

"Did you come alone or are there others with you?"

No response.

"Are you a member of the new Nazi Party?"

No reaction.

It became clear to Rich that the young zealot was not going to answer any of his questions, but he had an idea about how they might glean some information from his body language. He turned to the General and James and motioned them to the corner of the room, where he suggested that they bring in Matt to question the fledgling operative in his suspected native tongue, German. Having detected both distress and resoluteness in the young man, he was convinced that Matt would be able to elicit some non-verbal responses that could prove enlightening. Both men agreed, and James went to the conference room to get Matt.

"Mein name ist Matt. Wie heißen Sie?"

Fromme looked up, but said nothing. His response confirmed that he spoke German.

"Warum hast du auf General Sinclair geschossen?"

The prisoner reacted with a faint smirk, but again did not speak.

"Wer hat dich hierher geschickt ... und wer ist mit dir gekommen?

"Wir werden Vergeltung dafür erhalten, was Sie uns angetan haben!" replied the insurgent defiantly.

"In English little boy," shot back Matt heatedly.

"We will get revenge for what you did to us!" the prisoner repeated without thinking.

"Do you know Giselle Houlé? How about Clare...?"

"Ja, ja...she will kill all of you," he thundered rebelliously. Then, realizing he had been baited by his interrogator, went mute.

Matt smiled and turned to his mates. They, indeed, had learned a great deal. James suggested that they take a short break to assess what they knew and decide how to proceed. The three men ushered in a marshal to watch the prisoner and left the room to talk in private.

No one noticed during the change of guards that the pretend Uwe Fromme had reached down in his belt buckle, pulled out a cyanide pill and swallowed it. He was dead in seconds.

Sinclair was furious with his officer, but was calmed down by the American trio. Yes, there was more they wanted from him, but they had enough to put them on an appropriate path to full discovery. The Hugo Boss labels in his ashen wool pants with the uniquely German outward-facing pleats, the charcoal tartan sport coat, along with his greyish Josef Siebel chukka boots, were a dead giveaway that he was German. The Wehrmacht **Sturmgewehr 44** assault rifle found by the Thames River officers also implied that the attack on General Sinclair most likely emanated from Germany.

The youthful appearance of the lifeless assassin, along with the knowledge that Matt's attacker Giselle Houlé/Clare Lyon was in her early twenties, sparked a thought that he was anxious to pursue with the complete team. Matt convinced his colleagues that they should shift the focus from the departed Uwe Fromme to one of Team Two's missions.

Upon returning to the conference room, Matt took center stage with his now strong theory concerning the campaign against the former *SSU* and reincarnation of the Nazi regime spearheaded by former *SS* officers.

"Given the events of the past year, culminating with this morning's ambush, I believe I know who's behind the new Nazi organization," Matt began. "I'm convinced that it is the result of Team Two's Sub-Operation known as *Replace*. More on that in a few minutes. Let me first brief you on our other two missions and tell you why they don't appear to be noteworthy."

"Sub-Op *Thrust*, which supported **Operation Dragoon** does not seem to be relevant. Our first assignment in *Thrust* was to seek out and engage Resistance leaders in Marseille and Toulon in May 1944 to provide intelligence on German activity in those ports in advance of the planned August landings by General Patch's Seventh Army in Southern France. Our second priority was to help those leaders organize the nearly seventy-five thousand Resistance fighters in the area to conduct commando raids prior to the landings to confuse the enemy and scatter their forces. We never contacted the Germans directly so it doesn't appear reasonable that we could be targeted from that Sub-Op."

"Our final Sub-Op was called *Screen*, and began in late Spring of 1945. When it was clear that the Allies were going to be victorious, representatives of the British, U.S., French and the Soviet governments met to establish a framework for criminal trials once the war was over. Our assignment was to collect information on possible suspects, do some initial screening of the likely offenders, categorize the defendants, and make recommendations to the court coordinators regarding which individuals should be tried in the Major War Crimes Court, Judges Court, Doctors Court, Industrial Court and Military Atrocities Court. While we did have face-to-face contact with a few of these individuals, most of our work was on paper or in interviews with individuals who had firsthand knowledge. We probably exonerated more suspects than we included so, again, it just doesn't appear likely that our involvement in *Screen* could be the motivation for our elimination."

Matt then continued with a lengthy and exhaustive narration of Sub-Op *Replace*.

"Marie, Pat Kendall and I were tasked with following a lead provided by a series of Bletchley intercepts in May and June 1944 that referred to *Die Nachfolgerregierung*, which translates as *The Successor Government*. Hitler explicitly stated many times that he intended for the Third Reich to last for a thousand years, but these intercepts were the first hard evidence that a plan was actually in motion and that the next Chancellor of the Reich might already have been chosen. This obviously caused great alarm in London and Washington."

"Since we had been successful in Sub-Op *Thrust*, General Menzies assigned us to pursue those leads and identify the designated inheritors of the Nazi realm. We were instructed to notify MI6 once we located the headquarters and leadership group, and General Eisenhower would then assign a commando team to capture or eliminate them before the new organization could be mobilized."

"A common thread in the communications we studied centered around the town of Liège, Belgium with constant references to *die Gänseblümchenverbindung,* or *the Daisy Compound,* so we strongly suspected that headquarters of the Successor Government was located somewhere in the region. We were parachuted into Belgium in early August ahead of the U.S. First Army's campaign to liberate the country, and began to carefully scan the area for any signs of a clandestine *SS* presence. After a week of combing the area, Pat Kendall came upon *L'Académie des Elus,* a boarding school on the south bank of the Meuse River that was unusually heavily guarded. The name translates to *The Academy of the Chosen,* so we were convinced that we had found the successor headquarters, particularly because the schoolyard was bordered by large patches of flowers. Daisies, of course. We just needed to confirm our hunch."

"The property, which we estimated to be about ten acres, stretched from the Meuse River to the main road, and was probably two-hundred meters wide. The entire estate was concealed by three-meter corrugated iron fencing set in heavy oak frames. The only direct view of the complex was the five-meter decorative gate in the front. The fencing also ran along the banks of the river, but had no visible opening."

"We observed the activities of the school for a day and evidence grew stronger due to the presence of a dozen or so men continually moving systematically throughout the school grounds. They were dressed in civilian clothes but appeared to have a high degree of military bearing. Security personnel carrying semi-concealed side-arms seemed too extreme for a boarding school. We briefly considered the possibility that it was just overzealous vigilance for the safety of the children during wartime, but knew there was more at play when a Volkswagen 'tub car' approached and one of the guards snapped to attention and waived the vehicle on to the school grounds."

His energy level now high, Matt passionately continued his riveting story.

"We were unable to see the driver clearly before the vehicle disappeared around the primary building so we decided that we would need to get inside the structure to confirm that the school was indeed a cover for a military compound. Pat repositioned to the south side of the complex and explored options for scaling the fence while I moved to the north side to look for entry options there. Meanwhile, Marie made her way toward the river to see how entrance might be gained and found a gate camouflaged by thick Honeysuckle vines. She also determined that it was secured by an armed guard in an *SS* uniform. It took a couple of hours to complete our assessment, so it was late in the day before we regrouped to devise an infiltration plan."

"We retreated to a café on the river a couple of kilometers from the school and concluded that our best chance to breach the compound was by water. Accordingly, we quietly acquired a small boat that Marie used to lure the guard outside the gate. She dropped us off on shore about twenty meters from the gate and rowed down-stream before crying out several times in distress. It only took a minute or so for the guard to open the gate to see what was happening. Pat and I immediately subdued the sentry and injected him with a barbiturate, sodium amytal, to put him to sleep. Since we didn't want the enemy to know we had penetrated the facility, we force-fed him some Swiss chocolate laced with lysergic acid diethylamide. Since LSD was known to cause confusion, hallucinations and memory loss, we knew the sentinel wouldn't be able to remember the incident the next day."

Marie smiled broadly as she relived the encounter, while the rest of the team was mesmerized by Matt's account. Ruth was impressed with their creativity and boldness, James was amused, and Rich Johnson reflected on similar stories he had heard in the Pacific Theater during the war. They were anxious for Matt to continue his account.

"Once inside the fence, we had no idea what we might find or who we might confront, so we proceeded cautiously up a dirt path for about ten meters before we reached another steel door, which of course was locked. I went back to the guard and retrieved his keys and we moved into the compound. It was a labyrinth of long hallways, elaborate living and sleeping spaces, a large pantry and food storage area, a complete armory with weapons, grenades and several other types of explosives. This would be important later. In addition, the bunker had thirty lavishly furnished offices, a large fully functional command center with advanced communications equipment and abundant audiovisual capabilities. We were impressed at the size and elegance of this virtual underground city."

"Since no one was present in the complex, we were able to spend more than an hour exploring every room and examining some of the documents contained in the offices. We also found a stairway leading up to the school and student living quarters. We didn't try to explore the above-ground facility because there were guards at entry points to the dormitory and classroom areas."

Matt paused for a minute to collect his thoughts and control his emotions before he continued his narrative. The room remained transfixed, but would erupt in dismay when Matt resumed his story.

"The documents revealed that this was indeed the *Daisy Compound* and headquarters of the successor Nazi Government, as well as an *SS* school for high-ranking Nazi officers' children. And given the name of the school, a training ground for the children chosen to rule the Empire in subsequent generations. The offices and command center were full of government papers and a myriad of planning documents that minutely detailed Nazi plans for the colonization of Europe, Africa, parts of Asia, and North America."

"Germania, as the worldwide kingdom was to be called, would be strictly regulated. Fear and obedience would be the hallmarks of the dominion, and education would be denied to anyone not precisely fitting traditional Aryan criteria. Millions of 'sub-humans' would be used as slave labor to build elaborate buildings and provide needed infrastructure support. When they were no longer useful, they would be killed. Country designations would be eliminated and puppet governments established in each colony. Large populations with Slavic or African backgrounds would be relocated to Siberia and systematically starved. I could go on and on, but I suspect you now grasp what we may now be facing."

"Matt, you forgot a couple of other key elements," interjected Marie. "Hitler also planned to completely raze and burn New York, as well as other major U.S. cities and rebuild them in his Germanic image. Furthermore, he would provide two women for each worthy Aryan man to procreate an unspoiled populace, and would forbid the newly created automatons from eating meat, smoking or consuming alcohol. In short, a robotic society that would share the world sphere of influence with Japan and Italy."

"What we found in that compound was staggering," responded Matt. "We knew we needed to report our findings to General Eisenhower immediately. We meticulously left things as we found them, replaced the keys back in the unconscious guard's pocket, and retreated to our safe house to communicate with London and wait for further instructions."

"We arrived at our safe house well after midnight and awakened our Resistance host, *Clarence*. We relayed our urgency to him and he immediately put his network into action so we could contact London by radio. Knowing that the Wehrmacht used radio vans to track wireless communications, *Clarence* had devised his own mobile radio network that called for several coded messages to be sent concurrently while on the move in cars or horse carts, and even in fixed locations like trees or buildings."

"As many as three false messages would be sent at the same time by the stationary agents, and would be less than three minutes in length. The senders would then leave the area. One fabricated and one authentic message would be sent at the same time while on the move. Accordingly, the Germans would have to contend with three simultaneous transmissions at the same time, which confused the enemy long enough to allow us to transmit our findings to London without interference."

"Command responded in mid-morning and instructed us to continue to surveil the *Daisy Compound* and notify them when the appointed Reich rulers were on site. They would then send in American Rangers within twenty-four hours to capture them if at all possible."

"We had no way of knowing if or when the eventual leaders would arrive at the complex so we just returned to the forest near the school and established a primitive camp site about two kilometers from the complex with a week's worth of food, water and some bedding. We crafted a watch plan that would allow two of us to sleep while the other one kept vigil."

"There was no perceptible change in activity for three days until a multi-purpose transport truck arrived in the early afternoon with two dozen uniformed *SS* troops. Since we were convinced the designated government successors were near, all three of us took up our original positions around the school."

"It was dusk when Marie spotted a German E-Boat approaching from the east. It pulled up to the riverbank and at least twenty men dressed in civilian clothes exited the vessel, entered the gate, and went into the compound. They were followed by four porters who carried several trunks that Marie presumed contained their clothing and toiletries. This indicated to us that the future leaders were going to spend some extended time in the complex. Pat immediately went back to the safe house to have *Clarence* alert London to send in the Rangers."

It was a picture-perfect August 20th with a high temperature of 75° as *SSU* Team Two continued to observe the compound and wait for the Rangers to arrive on the scene. They were to brief the paratroopers on the layout of the complex, security measures, and the children's activity schedule, and then return to the safehouse and wait for the advancing U.S. First Army as they approached the Belgian border.

By all accounts, it was a normal school day where the nearly two-hundred Nazi progeny took turns marching, going through their typical classroom indoctrination, and undergoing rigorous physical training sessions. The day had been unremarkable with no unusual activity. Suddenly, as the sun fell below the horizon, the evening sky erupted in fire, gas and debris as a series of massive explosions shook the earth and rocked the compound.

Chapter 16

Die Nachfolgerregierung

The success of the Normandy landings in June 1944 and subsequent assassination attempt on Adolph Hitler in July convinced many members of the German military that the war was all but lost. Consequently, many officers and enlisted men, particularly from the Gestapo and *Waffen SS*, began planning for German capitulation and their own personal escape from justice.

Some officers intended to flee to South America or the Middle East, while others expected to hide in plain sight with new names while working in menial occupations. At the same time, the more fanatical *SS* contingent were maneuvering themselves into place to go underground and reemerge later to reawaken the German Empire and perpetuate the conspiracy to colonize, purify and master the European continent and beyond.

The most passionate and shrewd of these men recognized the power vacuum that was developing as the Allies closed in on the homeland, and anticipated that anarchy would ensue when Germany ultimately surrendered. They looked for opportunities to cultivate a more robust Nazi government in order to continue the quest for world domination.

The twenty-three men in the *Daisy Compound* were among the most fervent and dedicated Nazis and had been selected by Adolph Hitler as *Die Nachfolgerregierung*, or the leaders of the Successor Government. Accordingly, they were afforded all the resources and protection necessary to assume power when Hitler decided to relinquish his supremacy, which he still believed was two decades away.

The next *Führer* of Nazi Germany was to be *SS-Oberst-Gruppenführer* Karl Ulrich Hoffman, a thirty-five-year-old prodigy who had distinguished himself on the battlefield in the early years of the war, and later as a faithful and resourceful deputy to *Reichsführer* Heinrich Himmler in 1944. What set him apart from other possible candidates was his steadfast dedication to Adolph Hitler and his hegemony, as well as his political acumen and unfailing personal charm.

Hoffman first came into prominence as a fearless tank commander for the 3rd Panzer Division in the victorious Battle of Tomaszów Lubelski, Poland in September 1939, and Battle of Hannut in Belgium in May 1940. In the fall of 1940, he was transferred to the *Waffen-SS* Special Forces and elevated to the rank of *Sturmbanführer*, equivalent to a colonel in the British Army, where he trained as a paratrooper. Hoffman's command presence in the Special Forces earned him progressively more leadership opportunities in the next two years, which included a series of successful actions against the Chetniks and Partisans in Yugoslavia in 1941 and 1942.

His *coup de grace* was the courage and boldness he displayed during the Gran Sasso raid in the Apennine mountains on the Campo Hotel Imperatore in September 1943 that rescued Benito Mussolini from captivity. He was rewarded with his final promotion to *SS-Oberst-Gruppenführer* and transferred directly to Himmler's staff in Berlin, where he was carefully observed by Hitler before being chosen as the *Führer-Benennen*, or Leader-Designate.

Hoffman's personally hand-picked second in command was *Reichsführer*-Designate Otto Wenger, a thirty-seven-year-old lawyer in the Reich Ministry of Public Enlightenment and Propaganda. As a member of the growing German Worker's Party, Wenger was an ardent supporter of Adolph Hitler as the organization morphed into the National Socialist Worker's Party.

His allegiance to Hitler and his role in the Munich Beer Hall Putsch earned him an influential position as Deputy to Joseph Goebbels in late 1933.

Shrewd and ruthless, Wenger quickly gained prominence through his design and implementation of campaigns against Jews, homosexuals, sub-human populations, liberalism, and The Treaty of Versailles. His crowning successes came through the formulation of propaganda films glorifying Nazi Germany and vilifying Britain and the United States. Hitler was so pleased that he was elevated to *Reichsführer*-Designate in the summer of 1944.

Next in the line of succession was the President of the reconstituted Reichstag, the ersatz parliamentary arm of the Nazi Realm. The legislature was to include five-hundred-and-four Reichskommissars, or Reich Commissioners, who represented carefully drawn territorial boundaries in each of the conquered countries. The group would meet four times annually and would present the status of their domain to the Reichstag President for transmission to the *Führer*. The supreme leader would then evaluate the observations and issue operating edicts, which were to be unanimously rubber-stamped by the Reichstag.

Fourteen Reich Minister-Designates were also included in the *Daisy Compound* assembly, each of whom would have operational agencies to administer and enforce Germania policies.

The Reich Minister of Subjugated Colonies would have direct authority over the Reichskommissars and would monitor administrative effectiveness in political indoctrination, social training, racial cleansing, population relocation, industrial and agricultural productivity, and infrastructure development and maintenance.

The Reich Minister of Economics would have direct responsibility and authority for Empire economic policy development and implementation, natural resource development, utilization and efficiency, as well as import/export control.

All fiscal affairs would be under the control of the Reich Minister of Banking and Finance, including budget preparation and monitoring, taxation, and property dispute adjudication. He would coordinate financial relations between colonies and districts within each colony, as well as supervise the Reich Bank, Treasury and Labor Offices.

The Reich Minister of Justice would create and modify laws and regulations in accordance with the orders of the *Führer*, and direct all legal activities in the Domain, including colony, district and local courts. All judges would be hand selected by the *Führer*.

Other members of the Successor Government in the Compound were Reich Ministers of Planning, Design and Construction; Public Enlightenment and Propaganda; Security and Policing; Transportation; Postal Services; Education and Culture; Nutrition and Agriculture; Labor; Weapons, Munitions and Armament; Ecclesiastical Affairs; Chief of the Supreme Command of the Armed Forces; and the Commanders-in-Chief of the Army, Navy, Air Force, Intelligence Services and the *Waffen SS*.

The convocation of power leaders was their third gathering at the *Daisy Compound*. The air of urgency that permeated the bunker was palpable, and there was an abiding need to move quickly to finalize the strategic plan and advance the timetable for assuming authority over the Reich. While *Führer-Benennen* Karl Hoffman was a devoted disciple of Adolph Hitler, he had observed the increasingly unrealistic and erratic behavior of the *Führer* and was astute enough to realize that the Empire as presently constituted would soon be crushed by the invading Allied armies.

It was time to act. Hoffman intended to initiate his blueprint for ascension to power, but would warn the assembly that the plan would take time and extraordinary patience. The members of the new Nazi government would need to immediately implement their dispersal plan and reconvene periodically for at least a year after the present government succumbed to the Allies. An inconspicuous rise back to power might take five years.

It was just after nine o'clock on a peaceful August night, as the group was finishing their plentiful dinner, when the dreams of Karl Hoffman and his cadre of power brokers came to a calamitous end. No one survived the blast.

Chapter 17

The Cataclysm

Marie watched in shock as the riverbank disintegrated, water flooded the underground bunker, and the school building crumbled as the earth shook and flames engulfed the structure. Matt recounted the experience with intense passion.

"Pat and I were horrified as we watched children fleeing the area in fear of their lives. We were shocked and dismayed that the American Rangers could have taken such drastic action without conferring with us. Time stood still as we froze for what seemed like an eternity. It wasn't until we saw Marie racing away from the gushing river that we regained our senses."

"Chaos ensued as water engulfed the underground bunker and gas and smoke billowed from the ground below the school. Children ran screaming from the burning building as the surreal calamity unfolded. Nazi or not, Marie insisted that we save the children, so we each scaled the fence and ran toward the collapsing building to rescue as many children as we could."

James, Rich and the former *SSU* team members remained transfixed by the narrative. Generals Sinclair and Menzies sat mute. They had read the operations report years ago and understood the gravity and implications of the event. Marie quietly wiped her eyes and tears streamed down Ruth's cheek. Her tears were not only for the children, but also because the incident drew up intense memories of her brother Robbie's fiery death when his plane was shot down in 1943. She regained her composure quickly as Matt continued his account.

"We didn't have a clear picture of how the school was laid out but as we approached the disintegrating structure it looked like the bunker had been directly under the school itself, and the dormitory and dining areas were offset and spared much of the catastrophic damage done to the two-story school building. Nonetheless, children of all ages were running in every direction and we tried to corral them and spirit as many as possible to the far end of the property."

"As I recall, Marie stayed with the children, tried to comfort them, and address their wounds as best she could. Fortunately, she was fluent in both French and German, so communication wasn't a problem. Most of the young children were in their night-clothes so Pat raced into the smoke-filled sleeping quarters and retrieved towels for cuts and bruises, and blankets to cover them. He then continued to collect children on the grounds and either carry or direct them to Marie."

"I heard panic screams from the second floor of the dormitory and hurried up the stairs toward the cries when I encountered a strong-willed teenage girl who was ushering at least a dozen primary school aged children toward the emergency exit at the end of the hall. She stopped abruptly, and in a commanding voice challenged me to identify myself. I responded that I was here to help, but she insisted that I give her a name before she would release the children to my custody."

"I told her in German that my name was Matt. She responded in French that her name was Karla. She gave me a hard stare and finally relented. I led her and her charges to the stairs and quickly returned to look for other trapped or injured children. There were four wings in the building, and I saw signs in both French and German that signified groupings by age...six to eight, nine to eleven, twelve to fourteen, and fifteen to seventeen."

"The smoke was heavy and breathing was difficult so I found a sink and soaked a towel that I put over my nose and mouth. As I reached the corridor closest to the explosion, I found several older teens that were dead...some with blast injuries and a few that had likely been overcome by the fumes. There was also a gaping hole in the common wall between the school and dorm, and a fifteen-foot break in the hallway floor. I looked down to see several male and female adult bodies, but hurriedly left the area because of the fire and noxious gasses that were billowing through the ruptured space."

"When I was convinced that there were no more survivors, I retreated to the exit where I was met by a guard with a gun. We struggled briefly, but since I was much bigger, I was able to turn the weapon on him. At that point, I knew we needed to leave the compound and return to the safehouse."

When Matt faded for a moment to catch his breath and quiet his emotions, Ruth scrambled from her chair to render aid before allowing him to continue his distressing story. Marie observed the scene with a mixture of anguish, and to her surprise, jealousy.

The embankment on the Meuse River was two meters high and the entrance to the compound was approximately fifteen meters from the water. Because of the proximity of the river to the bunker, Nazi engineers had built a foundation barrier made of reinforced concrete to prevent the river from invading the structure. There was a wide concrete walkway that descended from the foundation barrier to the door of the *Daisy Compound*, which was several meters below ground level. The ceiling of the compound provided the floor for the school above it. To achieve a complete protective seal of the compound, the designers had rigged a mobile protective gate at the beginning of the walkway for use in an emergency. The gate was open on this evening.

The first explosion came from the riverbank near the back gate. The second emanated from outer door to the bunker. The two blasts allowed the Meuse River to surge through the walkway like a funnel into the underground structure bashing everything in its path.

The third, and most violent, eruption came from the armory just inside the compound on the right side of the hallway, piercing the concrete ceiling and sending exploding ammunition through the school and high into the evening sky. At the same time, intense flames melted concrete, steel and people. The fortunate victims drowned, while others came to a more gruesome end.

Shrieks of agony rang out as seismic waves from the thundering sound reverberated throughout the self-contained underground bunker, while the intense pressure sucked the air out of lungs and disintegrated internal organs instantly. Individuals closest to the armory had their bodies ripped apart or simply imploded.

While explosions four and five were at the top of the east and west stairs that led to the school and blocked any means of escape for the bunker occupants, the detonation was so rapid that there was never a chance for escape anyway. In a mere three minutes, water filled the cavity and began launching like a geyser out through the collapsed roof of the school. Within half an hour the flames were extinguished and nothing was left of the bunker and school except smoke and rubble. The dormitory building, while severely damaged, remained.

After steadying himself, Matt resumed his account of the situation.

"It took probably twenty minutes to secure all the surviving children and remove them from harm's way. As we were tending to the injured, we saw at least two Opal Blitz trucks approach the front gate. We watched as *SS* troops streamed from the vehicles and head toward the compound. Since there was no one to open the gate, it took a little time for the commander to order the lead truck to crash the iron fence. This gave us time to scale the wall and escape into the woods."

"It was after curfew and we had to avoid contact with security personnel, so it took us a couple of hours to make the ten-kilometer trek back to the safehouse. Exhausted, we retired and slept until daylight. We compared notes in our morning briefing and realized that we had not seen any British Commandos or American Rangers before or after the explosion. It seemed strange that they didn't contact us before the attack, and wouldn't have at least completed an after-action survey of the damage to ensure that the occupants of the bunker were all dead."

"*Clarence* suggested that we postpone our communication with London until some of his network contacts had a chance to inspect the compound area and assess the current situation. We agreed. It was just after noon when one of his female operators returned to the safehouse with news that the area was completely encircled by a mass of *SS* soldiers. In addition, *SS-Gruppenführer* Eggert Reeder, District President of Belgium and Northern France, was seen on the premises. She also reported that there was no mistaking the rage and angst among those present. Conspicuously absent were any signs of Allied Commandos or Rangers."

After having carefully formulating *SSU* Team Two's status report and readying *Clarence*'s communication system for transmission to London, a knock at the door changed everything. The visitor was U.S. Army Ranger, Major Bradley Pugh. He was there to gather intelligence on the *Daisy Compound* and discuss alternative strategies for capturing the designated future leaders of the Nazi Government. Reality struck. The attack on the bunker was an inside job!

Chapter 18
The Assassin

Karla Hoffman became an orphan at age fourteen when her father was killed in the explosion at the *Daisy Compound* on the outskirts of Liège, Belgium. Her mother died thirteen months earlier, just after midnight on July 28, 1943, when almost eight hundred RAF bombers dropped 2,400 tons of blockbuster and incendiary bombs on Hamburg, Germany, igniting the largest tornadic firestorm of World War II.

The bombing attack was part of **Operation Gomorrah**, the campaign to cripple German industry, including oil refineries and shipyards, and to scatter the labor pool in the city. The result of the raid was the loss of more than forty thousand civilian lives, many as a result of the whirling vortex of fire that reached 1,400 degrees, triggering an updraft that consumed all of the oxygen in the central city, producing mass suffocation. Another one hundred-twenty-five thousand German citizens received debilitating injuries in the conflagration.

Karl Hoffman was in training for the Gran Sasso raid at the time of Kate Hoffman's death, and was later told that her body was found with another female huddled in a stall in a public toilet. She had apparently soaked a blanket in water and placed it over herself and her sister to dissipate the smoke and retard the fire. Notwithstanding her quick thinking and evasive action, she and her younger sister died of asphyxiation.

Karla Hoffman, while strong-willed and resilient, was nonetheless devastated by the death of her parents. With the loss of her mother in an air raid, and her father in the *Daisy Compound,* she vowed to exact retribution on the Americans, especially Matt Kane, who she was sure had triggered the explosion. She remembered his face and name from that fateful night a decade earlier when the *Daisy Compound* disintegrated.

The female assassin was born in Hamburg at 10:49 a.m. on a cloudy, windy and cold January 25, 1930. Karl Hoffman had been a young law student at Universität Hamburg when his girlfriend Kate became pregnant. They immediately married to avoid the social stigma attached to illegitimacy and their child being labeled as a bastard. Ambitious and well-heeled, he also needed to protect his professional reputation. The young Hoffman's ambition and growing affinity for the National Socialist Worker's Party required that he remain untainted in order to ultimately achieve upper level status in the soon-to-be Nazi government. He finished law school and officially became a member of the Nazi Party in 1933, where he served as a prosecutor for two years before joining the Wehrmacht in 1935.

As a result of Karl Hoffman's obsessive attraction to Hitler and the Party, his daughter's tutelage and education were privileged. Karla was trained in Nazi principles and ideology by her parents until she was admitted to an elite government school at age six, where each class began with the 'Heil Hitler' salute and singing of the Nazi National Anthem, '*Die Fahne hoch*'.

Students were generally separated by gender in most German schools because the emphasis in male and female curricula was very different. However, the elite schools also tried to prepare girls for higher education rather than simple motherhood. Instead of stressing instruction in domestic sciences, gardening and preparation for menial work, Karla's curriculum included tutoring in English, French, Latin and the sciences to prepare her for university study. All students were heavily indoctrinated in racial purity.

Adolph Hitler had strong opinions regarding women. He demanded female obedience and disliked women with strong social or political views, and forbade them from smoking or wearing makeup. Only the most advantaged girls were allowed to seek higher education or occupy command level positions within the Reich. Karla was a good candidate for leadership due to her strong Aryan characteristics, ideological fervor, and almost complete lack of interest in feminine pursuits.

At age ten, Karla Hoffman was inducted into the Bund Deutscher Mädel, the female equivalent of the Hitler Youth, and was sent to *L'Académie des Elus* in Belgium. By the time she was fourteen, she was the undisputed leader of her BDM unit. As faithful servants of the Nazi state, Karla and her classmates were trained in living a spartan existence. The females dressed simply, their hair was braided or in a bun, they used no cosmetics, and generally subsisted on simple rations. These chosen ones were being prepared for important positions in the Reich while less privileged German girls were to be relegated to familial subservience.

Notwithstanding their intense disciplinary training, however, most of the startled Nazi children panicked when the *Daisy Compound* and *The Academy of the Chosen* exploded. Karla was a notable exception. Unfortunately for her and her male and female contemporaries, their dreams of a university education, German leadership, and a privileged life vanished at the moment of the explosion. Most were to ultimately become pawns of an evolving clandestine government. Within a decade, they would be an expendable part of a youthful team of assassins...groomed by former *Obergruppenführer* Hans Vogel.

The fugitive assassin, using her third alias, Christa Osen, deplaned at Heathrow Airport just after 7:30 a.m. on Sunday, August 1st. To her surprise, she had slept restfully for most of the flight from Montreal to London. The BOAC staff had been courteous, but had little interaction with the patrons. *Almost like a military operation*, she thought. *Efficient and professional.* She was impressed but eager to head back to the continent and her homeland where she could again be Karla Hoffman.

Christa Osen immediately checked the London train schedule and found that the Golden Arrow 'Boat Train' departed from Victoria Station to the English coast at 11:00 a.m. She knew it would be faster by taxi, but since she was low on money, she opted for the train. Christa converted her American dollars to British Pounds and found her way to the Underground Station in Terminal Three, boarded the Tube, and stood patiently in the crowded car during the forty-minute ride to Central London.

At a few minutes to 11:00 a.m., the calculating female stepped aboard the Golden Arrow for its one-hour run to Dover, where the passenger and freight cars would be loaded onto the Channel ferry. Once in Calais, Christa cleared customs with no difficulty, re-boarded her train car, now attached to the Paris Express, and settled in for the three-hour trip to the French capital. She arrived at Gare du Nord Station and disembarked at 5:40 p.m. Finally, in familiar surroundings, she sighed a long-awaited breath of relief. Once again, she was on holiday as just another European traveler, Karla Hoffman from Aachen, Germany.

The tall blonde was comfortable in 'The City of Lights', having spent many enjoyable weeks there in the last two years as part of her socialization training. Innately stiff and socially awkward, her mentor had instructed her on societal values, behavioral norms and communication skills. In short, she learned how to interact effectively in a civilized post-war world. These were the necessary skills that allow an assassin to move inconspicuously as she stalked her prey.

Karla's first order of business was to call Ruby LeMaire, her friend and fellow conspirator at Voyages Internationaux Français, the cabal's travel agency. She often stayed with Ruby when she was in Paris, and since she was almost out of money, this was her best option as she awaited the morning train to Frankfurt. Ruby graciously picked up Karla at the station and the pair went straight to their favorite bistro, Le Quincy, on Avenue Ledru-Rollin. As usual, the stew was rich and plentiful.

After more than two hours of catch-up conversation, the teammates returned to Ruby's flat fifteen minutes away, just off the Boulevard Diderot in the bustling 11th Arrondissement. Karla slept well and left Ruby's apartment early in the morning on Le métro de Paris for the Gare du Nord Railroad station where she awaited the 7:06 a.m. Paris-to-Frankfurt train. The only interruption in her voyage was a brief border check upon entering Germany. The train then proceeded directly to the Frankfurt Hauphtbahnof Station.

Upon arrival in the still rebuilding city on the Main River, Karla quickly caught the connecting train to Aachen, a trip of two hundred kilometers. The two-hour ride through her still scarred homeland was both satisfying and exasperating. She understood that it would take time to repair her country's damaged landscape and restore its cities to their former grandeur, but it was painful to see how much effort must yet be expended. The divided country was being ruled by the puppet governments installed by the Americans, British and French from the West, and the Soviet Union from the East. Friction and political upheaval plagued the vanquished country, and recovery was too slow to suit her. She was eager to complete her mission so Deutschland could reestablish its dominant world position. *The Fourth Reich is almost at hand*, she thought hopefully.

After almost two exhausting weeks, she was home again. It was time to revise her attack schemes and timetables. She had eliminated four of her nine targets but time was short. Preparations were now almost complete and the initial phases of the conspiracy to reawaken the Reich were in process. Her task was to make quick work of the remaining five former *SSU* members and avenge the death of her father in Belgium. Her top target continued to be the elusive Major Matt Kane.

Karla left the train station and walked the half-mile north to Rademacher's Motorwerkstatt where she stored her 1951 BMW R51/3 motorcycle when she traveled.

"Guten Tag, Peter," she greeted the shop owner casually as she marched past him toward her parking stall. There was little time for pleasantries. She unlocked the gate, meticulously inspected the machine, walked the vehicle out of the garage, donned her helmet, cranked the engine, and was on her way to her domiciliary. She felt free and in charge again as she put her frustrating and wearisome two-week excursion to America behind her.

It only took twenty minutes for Karla to cover the five-and-a-half-kilometer jaunt down Maria-Theresia-Allee, Ronheider Berg and Karlshöher Talweg motorways to the headquarters house in the Aachen Forest. The old estate was owned by a wealthy Jewish industrialist until abandoned just after the *Kristallnacht* attacks in November 1938. The property fell into disrepair until discovered by *Obergruppenführer* Hans Vogel in 1943. He quietly appropriated the house and twenty-nine acres of beech, oak and pine forest and began his secret campaign to take power in Germany.

Karla's first duty was to report to her handler, Herr Doctor Vogel, and explain her failure to kill Matt Kane and Abigail Findlay. The former Nazi officer was annoyed and unrelenting with his key operative, harshly chastising her for being ill prepared and careless in carrying out her mission in the United States. He pointed out flaws in her attack on Matt Kane in Minnesota, as well as her bungled attempt to eliminate her three trackers in New Mexico.

While Vogel acknowledged Karla's resourcefulness in eluding American law enforcement, he berated her for creating the situation herself by panicking and leaving the Commons Park in Minneapolis before ensuring that Matt Kane was actually dead. All of the following reverberations would never have occurred if she had paid closer attention to details in the beginning. He angrily reprimanded her for jeopardizing the plan for the revitalization of the German Reich. Initial stages of the plot were underway and precise timing was crucial to the plan's success. She must take out *SSU* agents Duncan Giles, Abigale Findlay, Hugh Kensie, Marie Spenser and Matt Kane within two weeks to keep the plan on schedule.

In addition to Karla's *SSU* mission, other surviving *Daisy Compound* children, having been thoroughly brainwashed and converted into a network of information gatherers or coldblooded killers, were beginning the process of quietly eliminating known *SOE* and *OSS* agents, their commanders, and other prominent World War II military and civilian leaders before the new blitzkrieg was to begin on December 7, 1954.

Submissive and defiant at the same time, the dishonored Karla Hoffman felt shamed and enraged, and swore to finish her assignments quickly. She knew that only the most successful and efficient of the unit's operatives would be allowed to participate in future planned attacks, and she desperately wanted to be a part of the most important missions.

The next several days were spent communicating with the vast network of Nazi offspring in Europe and the U.S. to locate her *SSU* targets. Karla was informed that Marie Spenser was in Durham, England and should be her first kill.

Voyages Internationaux Français would arrange for her new identity in a week and the assassin could begin her journey as Linette Chamberlin on Friday, August 13th. She would take the 9:23 a.m. train from Aachen to Brussels, catch the one-and-a-half-hour mid-day flight on Sabena Airlines to Manchester, England, and complete her trek to Durham by train, arriving just before 3:00 p.m. A Royal Enfield Bullet motorcycle would be waiting for her at the station. She would ride to the hills overlooking the country road and catch her objective on the way home from University just after 5:00 p.m. This time she would have her own German made **Sturmgewehr 44** assault rifle.

After dispensing with Marie Spenser, the newly created Linette Chamberlin would drive back to the Durham station, load her two-wheel vehicle onto the train and calmly settle in for the six-hour ride to Cardiff, Wales. There she would find her next quarry, British Major Hugh Kensie, now a Director for the Welsh Regional Health System in the UK's National Health Service. She was scheduled to spend the night in London at the Royal Hotel on St. Mary's street, a mere hundred meters from Cardiff Central Train Station.

Kensie typically went to his agency for half a day on Saturday. His office was only a short distance from his flat near Cardiff Bay, so he walked to and from his workplace each day. Linette could easily ambush him from the top of one of the buildings on his morning route the next day. Within minutes, she would catch the 10:18 a.m. Great Western Railway train for the two hour ride to London.

From King's Cross station, the assassin would bike to the small town of Radlett, where she would attend to her final British antagonist, retired Colonel Duncan Giles. The Colonel lived in a heavily wooded neighborhood at the end of Church Close Street. An avid gardener, he spent virtually every Sunday morning tending to his flowers and shrubs. Her plan was to catch Giles as he worked in his garden behind his stately home. Linette would have easy access through the woods behind the house. Once she silenced her adversary, she would retrieve her motorcycle on Watling Street and make the forty-five-minute ride southeast to Heathrow Airport.

After parking her bike in a spot designated by her contact in London, Linette would catch the noon Pan American World Airways flight to Logan Airport in Boston to pursue the elusive Lieutenant Findlay. Initially, her network had not been able to locate her, but after discretely questioning neighbors they found out she and her family often vacationed in Bar Harbor, Maine.

After two days of inquiry, her network proxy was able to verify that former Lieutenant Findlay and her family were staying at the Bar Harbor Inn on Frenchman Bay, and seemed to have established a pattern of hiking in Acadia National Park on a daily basis, normally beginning on the trail to Cadillac Mountain. The contact also found out that the family was scheduled to be at the Inn for another week.

The overnight train trip from Boston to the Maine resort area would take Linette eight hours on the Bar Harbor Express, but the pursuer could travel in a sleeper compartment and be rested and ready to stalk her prey on Mount Desert Island upon arrival on Tuesday, August 17th. She would follow the family along the trail and kill them all when the opportunity presented itself. She would then proceed to the train depot for the return trip to Boston, and finally make her way to Minnesota by airplane to eliminate her primary adversary, Matt Kane.

As Giselle Houlé in late May, Karla Hoffman was levelheaded and calculating. She meticulously planned and staged her attack on Matt Kane with military precision. She confronted him personally because she wanted him to know his assassin. It had worked perfectly...except he didn't die! This time would be different. Linette Chamberlin would be more detached and simply perch behind a tree next to his house where her alter-ego had observed him three months prior. From there she would pump several rounds from her **StG 44** rifle into his wretched body. There would be no mistakes this time.

On Wednesday, August 25, 1954, Karla Hoffman would end the crusade to eradicate her *Special Services Unit* adversaries, and Major Matthew Kane would be decisively purged. *Finally, retribution would be hers.*

Chapter 19

The Pursuit

The newly fabricated Linette Chamberlin, rested and fully equipped, dutifully boarded the train to Brussels on Friday the Thirteenth and arrived in Durham, England according to plan around 3:00 p.m. It was a crystal-clear day with a temperature of sixty-six degrees, low humidity, and a manageable westerly wind of nine miles an hour. A great day to bike and shoot. Unfortunately, this is where her plot went awry. There was no motorcycle waiting for her at the train station.

Erich Krause, another schoolboy survivor of the explosion at *The Academy of the Chosen* in Belgium, had been assigned the task of purchasing a sturdy, resilient and maneuverable Royal Enfield Bullet motorcycle and placing it at the Durham train station for his unknown associate.

Krause was a tall, studious and somewhat shy young man of twenty. While thoroughly indoctrinated by his Nazi teachers and staunchly behind the movement to recreate the Reich, he was judged to be too guarded and circumspect to be a skilled executioner. He, like many of his classmates, was assigned to play a supporting role by gathering information and acquiring tools for the assassins.

As ordered, the cautious Erich purchased the motorcycle in Leeds and rode the hundred and forty kilometers to the Durham Railway Station, where he parked and chained the vehicle to the fence in a designated spot next to the long row of bicycle racks. He left the keys in the compartment under the seat. That's when the trouble began.

A gregarious assistant stationmaster innocently approached the young man and attempted to engage him in friendly conversation by inquiring where he was going and when he intended to return to retrieve his motorcycle. This caught Erich by surprise and he responded in a manner that seemed odd to the railway manager. When the official began to probe further, Erich bolted and ran out of the station, not knowing where he was going. The stationmaster called the Durham Constabulary and the fleeing Nazi disciple was captured within half an hour. The motorcycle was removed from the station and taken to an impound facility near the police station.

Linette's first reaction was anger. She had carefully scripted her next week and one incompetent lackey had upset her timetable. *I'll wait for an hour*, she thought. *Maybe the trip from Leeds has taken longer than anticipated.* She paced for a few minutes and decided that she couldn't wait any longer because she couldn't afford to miss her initial target. She must dispatch Marie Spenser today. The quick-thinking female rose, casually meandered to the bicycle storage racks, discretely checked for an unsecured bike, and calmly removed one and wheeled it out of the station.

While athletic and tenacious, the seven-kilometer ride past Durham University across the river and over to Sherburn Hill was taxing. The trip also took longer than expected. The executioner located a convenient ambush spot along the way on Durham Lane, roughly twenty meters from the road. She unpacked and reassembled her rifle and waited. She could easily kill Lieutenant Spenser and make her way back to the train station for her trip to Cardiff, Wales.

Linette was in place by 4:30 p.m. and patiently waited until the appointed hour of 5:20 p.m. Nothing. 5:45 p.m. Nothing. At 6:00 p.m. the predator experienced her second major irritation of the day. It appeared that she had missed her quarry.

Somehow, Marie Spenser's predictable travel pattern must have been broken. What she didn't know was that Marie had been summoned to London by MI6, and left the university early to pack and have dinner before departing for London. Little did she know that, by sheer coincidence, her target would actually be traveling on the same train to London later in the evening.

The exasperated hunter retreated to her bicycle and pedaled another two kilometers southwest to Marie's house, leaned her bicycle and gun against a tree across the street, and cautiously approached the dwelling to survey the area for activity. She could see Marie's mother and father moving about the house but saw no sign of her prey. The frustrated Linette contemplated killing them but realized it would only alert her quarry and disrupt her two-week agenda.

Then, two minutes later, at precisely at 6:23 p.m., the family's 1950 cream-colored Vauxhall Velox appeared in the drive and Marie exited the house, hurriedly opened the back door, deposited her bag, and jumped into the front passenger seat. As the assassin scurried back to her bike to retrieve her rifle, Marie's brother pulled out of the drive and headed toward Durham. In less than a minute the car was gone.

Totally exasperated, Linette Chamberlin jumped on the two-wheeled vehicle and pushed herself back toward the railway station to catch the 7:02 p.m. train to London where she would change trains and proceed to Cardiff. *Should I track Marie Spenser and kill her or follow the prearranged plan and find her again after I finish with Major Kensie and Colonel Giles*, she pondered as she labored her way to the station? *I must remain on schedule,* she reasoned. *I can find Lieutenant Spenser later and still maintain my timeline.*

The drained and irritated hunter arrived just in time to catch the British Railway steam locomotive as it was pulling out of the station. She jumped aboard the last car and settled into her seat as the train picked up speed for its three-and-a-half hour run to London. She had plenty of time to reassess her strategy and calculate where Lieutenant Spenser was going. She decided that London was the most likely destination. But why? If she knew the purpose of the trip it would be easy to find her.

Meanwhile, Marie was comfortably seated three passenger cars ahead of her stalker, completely unaware of the impending danger. *Why after all these years did MI6 command her appearance,* she wondered? *And what was so important that time was of the essence?* She would find out soon enough. She put her thoughts aside and opened her advance copy of C. S. Lewis' new book, *The Horse and His Boy*, which had been given to her by the author himself upon his most recent visit to Durham University for a speaking engagement.

For Marie, the trip was leisurely and enjoyable. For Linette, it was interminable, annoying and fidgety. Her first five assignments, including the ambush of Matt Kane, had been carried out without any difficulty, but since her confrontation with the three pursuers in the American desert, she had experienced a continuous string of problems or delays. She was anxious for another success to settle her nerves and restore her confidence. *Killing Major Kensie will get me back on track,* she told herself.

The train pulled into the Paddington Station at 10:38 p.m. Linette sat for a minute trying to decide if she should proceed as planned to Cardiff or spend the night in London. Deep in thought, she glanced out the window and saw Marie Spenser on the platform walking to the taxi stand. *I can get her now,* she calculated excitedly. She jumped up, snatched her two bags and exited the train. Her plan was to take the same taxi to her prey's hotel, follow her to her room, and shoot her with the same **Walther P.38** pistol she used on Major Kane.

Already dressed in her attack clothing from earlier in the day, Linette stopped briefly in a small alcove to put on her black wig. Another miscalculation as Friday the Thirteen was coming to an end. By the time she reached the taxi stand, Marie had entered the vehicle and it was on its way to who knows where.

It will be better tomorrow, Linette told herself. It was time to improvise. The foiled female looked around and saw the Great Western Royal Hotel just a few steps away and decided to stay in London overnight if they had a room. She was finally in luck. She would sleep for six hours and catch the 5:46 a.m. train to the Cardiff Central Train Station and hire a taxi to get to the bay near Major Kensie's flat. She was sure she could be there by 8:30 a.m. and catch him just after 9:00 a.m. as he took his normal Saturday morning walk to work.

Before retiring, Linette called her emergency telephone number in London and arranged for a support associate to have another Royal Enfield motorcycle waiting for her at King's Cross Station by noon the next day. After dispatching Kensie, Linette would be back on schedule. She would board the 10:18 a.m. train back to London, pick up her bike, find Marie Spenser, kill her, and head to Radlett to eliminate Colonel Giles on Sunday morning. Then she would be off to the United States to take care of Abigail Findlay and the previously indestructible Matt Kane.

Saturday, August 14th, was no better for the young assassin. She slept well, caught her train to Wales, taxied to Cardiff Bay, took her place on a roof not far from Hugh Kensie's flat, and waited for her mark to appear. He never materialized. Her intelligence notes told her that he had not missed a Saturday morning walk to the health care agency office a single time in the six weeks he had been observed. Although irked and vexed, Karla Hoffman, aka Linette Chamberlin, was still insightful and shrewd. *Something is wrong*, she thought. *I must find out what has happened.*

Linette took off her wig, changed clothes into a stylish royal blue dress, and walked the few blocks to the Welsh Regional Health System building. There she discretely inquired about Director Kensie and was told that he left for London the previous day. *Can it be that all of my objectives are in London*, she thought?

Energized at the possible turnaround in her luck, Linette decided to follow the original plan and go to Radlett and verify her suspicions. While she was not scheduled to execute Colonel Duncan Giles until the next morning, she figured that if he was there, she could advance her timetable and take him out that afternoon. If not, she believed he and the others were likely together in London, probably at MI6. Linette immediately had an idea about how to eliminate them all at the same time, and if she was right, she would contact Herr Vogel for approval to attack the entire group at the same time.

Linette Chamberlin was now completely invigorated. She hurried back to the Cardiff Train Depot and sat impatiently until she boarded the train back to London. She bounded off the railroad car at King's Cross Station and immediately spotted the new Royal Enfield Bullet in the designated spot. She approached the vehicle, reached under the seat, retrieved keys to the lock and ignition, and put on her helmet. In minutes she was on the road to Radlett.

The ride through the countryside breathed new life into the young woman, although she had not eaten since the train ride from Durham twenty hours ago. That could wait until her suspicions were confirmed. If Vogel approved her plan, she could end the crusade to eliminate all vestiges of the *Special Services Unit* within a day or two and avoid having to return to America.

Linette parked her motorcycle next to the church near the corner of Watling Street and Loom Lane and carefully made her way through the trees to the back of Colonel Giles house. She quietly observed the house for almost two hours. All she saw was her adversary's wife. There was no sign of the Colonel. *They know about our plans and must be together at MI6*, she reasoned. *I must get back to London and talk with Herr Vogel.*

"Hallo," answered Hans Vogel.

"Ich glaube, sie kennen unsere Pläne," blurted out the eager Linette Chamberlin.

"Are you still in England?" he questioned.

"Ja."

"Then you must speak English."

"I believe they know about our plans," she repeated.

"What makes you think that?" queried her superior.

"I know Lieutenant Spenser and Major Kensie went to London on Friday. I followed Spenser and a sekretärin in Kensie's office told me that he was there. Also, I went to Colonel Giles' house and he was not there. I think they are all at MI6."

Vogel thought for a moment and continued to probe his top operative.

"Why do you think they know our plans?"

"Each of them has broken their normal daily schedules and are all in London at the same time. Where else would they go together except to British Intelligence? Particularly after all this time. We need to attack them before they have time to counter our operation. I have a plan to finish this phase of the action in the next two or three days, but I need your help."

"If you are wrong, we will lose the element of surprise for our final operation in December," the master emphasized. "We are not quite ready yet!"

"Herr Kommandant, we must attack them before they can react," insisted a firmly resolute aka Linette Chamberlin. "I know they are there. Just listen to my plan."

Linette methodically laid out her attack scenario. Vogel was impressed with her creativity and agreed to the plan if it could be proven that the former *SSU* agents were indeed at MI6. He would arrange for his underground agent in London to confirm her suspicions. He would also advance his ambush on the head of the British Secret Intelligence Service, General John

Sinclair, on his way to his normal weekly briefing with Prime Minister Churchill.

Vogel hung up the telephone and called one of his best novice marksmen and ordered him to London. Uwe Fromme was on the next plane to Heathrow Airport. He would initiate Phase Two of the Operation on Tuesday, August 17th.

Chapter 20

The Strategy

As afternoon began to stretch into evening, James Rosino and the exhausted former *SSU* colleagues in the conference room at MI6 now displayed a genuine sense of urgency.

"General Sinclair has briefed the Prime Minister on the situation," informed Rosino. "He's anxious for us to get to the bottom of this threat as soon as possible and will give us whatever resources we need. Also, the guard that was hit in the thigh is out of surgery at Westminster Hospital and should fully recover. The prime question now is, where do we go from here? We're in full alert mode and must act quickly. Time is critical."

"You're right, James. We have to assume there will be more attacks, particularly since we're all together," added Matt. "We certainly can't return to the hotel since we don't know how many agents they have, and if and when they will try again. But make no mistake, they will persist."

"We have to assume they know we've been staying at the St. James Hotel and have been traveling back and forth by bus. If I were them, I'd bomb the bus. Since we can't go back to the hotel, we just need to sequester ourselves here until we've sorted out our options and developed a plan of action."

"Sorry to interrupt, Matt, but I think we really need to understand the enemy's end game and anticipate their strategy and tactics before we construct a response," intervened a calm and analytic Rich Johnson. "Is there really a conspiracy to re-establish a militaristic German Empire? Is there any credible evidence or is this just rumor? If there's some kind of plot, who's behind it? How big a following do they have? What kind of resources? Are they planning some kind of military action?

When? Against whom? If so, what kind of weapons do they have? Rockets...ballistic missiles...nuclear bombs? These are the kinds of questions we asked about the Japanese in the Pacific during the war. We need to address these issues and develop our counter strategies before we can ferret out the conspirators."

"Detective Johnson is absolutely correct. Let's start by organizing our thoughts and listing the facts as we know them right now," retorted Abby Findlay. "First, based on convincing evidence we have from MI6 and the U.S. National Security Agency, there *is* some kind of Nazi rekindling that's been underway for a while. How big is the organization? We don't know, but since there seems to be a concerted effort to kill us and the head of MI6, it's logical to assume they have a large enough network of operatives and resources to wage a meaningful campaign against the world. Second, as for who's behind the conspiracy, we simply need to follow the clues they've provided."

"Abby," responded Rosino showing his growing impatience. "Organization and analysis are necessary, but first things first. That's the safety of the individuals in this room. We just need to quickly move to a secure location where we can address these questions and formulate our fact-finding strategy. We can't do that if you're all dead!"

"I suggest that we simply stay here, James," insisted Matt.

While James was the ranking member of the group, he was astute enough to recognize that not only was Matt an experience intelligence officer and interrogator, but he was also the informal leader who commanded the room. He could see that the former *SSU* agents looked to Matt for direction. As a result, he deferred to Matt and asked for his thoughts on a security plan and investigative process.

"We have to think like our adversary," resumed Matt. "My gut tells me they know we're aware of their plot to take over Germany again. And perhaps beyond, which seems likely. We know things about them that could thwart their plans. Otherwise, why would they try to kill us?"

"I'm confident that they have people following us. The woman who killed Lew Tarquin and tried to kill me is the *key* to uncovering the conspiracy. She's probably in London. Likely with a squad of goons who are watching us right now. Our immediate priority is to track down and catch this Giselle Houlé/Clare Lyon or whoever she is. She's vital to uncovering the plot, and when we find her, I think she'll lead us to the top. In my opinion, staying here until we have a plan is the safest course of action."

"It's time to take a break anyway. We have some space here that can sleep a dozen or so people and I'll arrange for meals to be sent in," General Menzies responded as he hurried out of the room.

"Collect your thoughts and compare notes and we'll get back to work in the morning," declared James. "With all of the brainpower and experience here, I think we can get our act together in a day and begin our search for the mystery woman on Thursday."

General Menzies arranged for a generous portion of salad, pasta, bread and, of course, hot tea, to be picked up by a marshal from Olivelli restaurant on Store Street, a short distance from MI6. Matt, James, Ruth and Marie gathered together around the table and engaged in somewhat uneasy small talk throughout dinner. It was clear that Ruth now viewed Marie as a rival. Marie, though still drawn to Matt, expected that his future was with Ruth. James sensed that Matt was uncomfortable but attributed it to rib pain that he was suppressing.

Matt was in a quandary. He had developed a deep affection for Ruth but couldn't shake his feelings for Marie. He excused himself early and went to the men's sleep room to get some much-needed rest. He tried to convince himself that he was almost fully healed, but he knew better. Still, he wanted to end the frantic game and get on with his life, maybe married to Ruth. He quickly drifted off to sleep.

The group spent the next morning outlining what was known of Matt's assailant and her movements. It was established that:

- She was almost assuredly German.
- She was known to have used at least two different passports, one as Giselle Houlé, and the other as Clare Lyon.
- Since the last sighting of her was in New Mexico, she likely used another name and passport to exit the United States.
- Most of her travel and hotel reservations were made by Voyages Internationaux Français, a travel agency in Paris.
- Travel arrangements were made by telephone from someone in Aachen, Germany.
- She wore grey pants, a black leather jacket, and some kind of boots in Minneapolis, Flagstaff and Albuquerque.
- It appeared that she wears a dark wig to conceal her blonde hair.
- She was taller than average and in her mid-twenties.
- She appeared to be an expert motorcyclist.
- She had some kind of support team helping her.

By noon on Wednesday, the motivated group was ready to break out of their confinement and begin the search for the elusive female antagonist.

General Menzies and Colonel Kensie had earlier been tasked with tracking down former *SOE* agents and making them aware of possible danger from the re-emerging Nazi organization. MI6 staff had been gathering data since Monday afternoon and were keeping a tally of any of those individuals who may have died under suspicious circumstances. The results were startling. Nearly half of the known *Special Operations Executive* agents had either died or gone missing since the end of the war. Many as a result of accidents or sudden illnesses. Some from gun violence. This confirmed that there was indeed an uprising in progress.

Abby and Marie were assigned to go to Paris and interrogate the staff at Voyages Internationaux Français to find out how much they knew about Giselle Houlé and Clare Lyon, whether she had other passports, and if and when they had made travel arrangements for anyone else from Germany. Marie was highly suspicious that the travel agency was part of the conspiracy. Therefore, they would conduct their inquiry with ample skepticism.

"Rich, Duncan and I will proceed to Aachen to see if we can find the headquarters of the conspiracy and determine how widespread and viable this Neo-Nazi organization is," instructed Agent Rosino.

"Not without me!" protested Matt.

"You're going to remain right here and coordinate the information we gather, Matt. We may have to move fast and there may be some trouble...and you're not yet physically up to it," James retaliated. "You may be willing, but we've seen a couple of occurrences in the last two days that tell me you're not ready for any vigorous physical activity. I won't give in this time. You will stay here."

Matt's face turned red with a mixture of embarrassment and agitation, but he knew James was right. He took a deep breath and responded inaudibly. "Okay, James. You win."

"And you, *Miss Chessman*, are going back to Minnesota," commanded Rosino. "And there will be no protest from you either. These people are being stalked by at least one killer and I won't allow you to become a target too. They have no choice, but you do. We'll see that you get safely to Heathrow this afternoon and I'll catch up with you when this is all over."

"I'm going to stay here and take care of Matt," Ruth declared. "If he's too disabled to travel, he needs a nurse. I'm staying here and you can't stop me!"

"I'll carry you myself if I have to," James snapped.

"Just try it," she shot back.

The room erupted in laughter. Even Matt broke into a smile.

Chapter 21

The Confrontation

Abby Findlay, Marie Spenser, Colonel Duncan Giles, FBI Agent James Rosino and Minneapolis Detective Rich Johnson were individually spirited out of MI6 headquarters at different times throughout the afternoon. They were driven to Gatwick Airport to catch privately chartered aircraft for their trips to Paris, France and Aachen, Germany. At Rosino's request, General Sinclair arranged for two marshals to personally escort Ruth Chessman to Heathrow Airport for a return trip to New York and subsequent flight back to Minneapolis. Matt, Hugh Kensie and Stuart Menzies remained at MI6.

Linette Chamberlin returned to the Great Western Royal Hotel next to Paddington Station to make arrangements to initiate her attack plan. She again called her London maintenance telephone number, and the contact gave her the names and addresses of two key communist organizers and labor leaders in the city. She would get them together and engage them to initiate her plan. With money, of course. And lots of it.

The early 1950s was a challenging time for labor and the demographics of the United Kingdom. The war had decimated both housing availability and industrial production, and England was in dire need of both skilled and unskilled labor. To address the problem, Parliament passed the British Nationality Act in 1948, which gave citizenship to all peoples in the colonies and allowed unrestrained immigration into the country. Many of the immigrants were from the West Indies, India, Pakistan, Uganda,

Nigeria and Kenya, leading to a substantial rise in the non-white population. This caused social unrest, which labor leaders capitalized on to foment discontent among workers. Seventy percent of available jobs were manual labor, the workweek was typically forty-eight hours, pay was low, and working conditions in many mills and factories were abysmal. Resentment and anger were widespread.

There was also an expanding and active communist party presence in London in the post-war period, and more than a few main labor leaders were politically active in developing the party. These elements combined to provide tinder for a labor rebellion, and Linette's plan was to use the politically ambitious and restless workers to provide cover for an ambush of the *SSU* bus. The attack would take place on Thursday morning, August 19th as the lorry made its way along the route between the St. James Hotel and MI6 Headquarters.

Hans Vogel had assigned one of his London agents to surveil MI6 since the Saturday afternoon telephone call with his intrepid female operative. He observed on Monday and Tuesday that the pickup of former *SSU* agents occurred promptly at 8:00 a.m., and the lorry took a leisurely fifteen-minute drive around Buckingham Palace, the Victoria Memorial and St. James Park toward MI6. Linette intended to have the communist leaders arrange a demonstration by rank-and-file workers that would bring traffic to a halt in the roundabout at Spur Road next to the Park. She would then have an explosives expert negotiate his way through the crowd and attach a powerful RDX type plastic explosive bomb to the bottom of the bus as it was stopped. It would detonate two minutes later.

Protest organizers would not be told about the bombing. It was anticipated that the explosion would not only kill the intended victims but also some workers, causing confusion and panic among both the protesters and police. Ultimately, each side would blame the other for the violence and the Nazi plot would be preserved. The plan was inspired...but it never happened. By Thursday, Karla Hoffman and Herr Doctor Hans Vogel would become the hunted.

The MI6 marshals shepherded Ruth to her TWA flight and left as she moved down the stairs toward the aircraft. Once she saw them leave, she secretly returned to the gate and requested that they remove her luggage. It took nearly half-an-hour to retrieve her suitcases and change her ticket for another flight on September 1st. She calculated that she could call her supervisor at Minneapolis General Hospital and wangle a one-week extension on her leave.

Ruth studied her options. She wanted to be convenient enough to MI6 to be useful to Matt, but not close enough to be spotted by MI6 marshals. She also figured that it would be helpful to be near inexpensive public transportation. Paddington Station and the Great Western Royal Hotel would work out just fine. By dinner time, the crafty Minneapolis nurse was checked in and ready to play amateur spy.

Wednesday evening was a restless one for Ruth. She wanted to be near Matt and wrestled with herself about whether or not to let him know she was still in London. In an attempt to calm her nerves after dinner, she walked a few blocks toward Hyde Park but was warned by a Bobbie that the Park was too dangerous for a female after dark. Frustrated, she just returned to her room and paced until going to bed after midnight. She arose early and decided she would have breakfast and muster up the courage to call Matt.

Ruth's predicament was resolved as she entered the elevator on the third floor of the hotel. There was one other person in the elevator. The young female was wearing gray pants, stylish gray boots, and a black leather jacket. She also had dark hair, but Ruth detected a couple of strands of blonde filtering out of the back. She was obviously in a hurry.

"This is Ruth Chessman. I need to speak with Mr. Matthew Kane immediately!"

"I think he and the others are still asleep, miss."

"Wake him. This is an emergency. I have information about the woman they're looking for. Hurry before she gets away."

It seemed like an eternity before she heard Matt's calming voice.

"Ruth, are you home?" he queried.

"No, Matt. I'm in London and I saw her!" she shouted.

"What do mean you saw her? Saw who?"

"The woman who tried to kill you!"

"Ruth...that's a bit dramatic, don't you think?" Matt asked unemotionally. "You don't even know what she looks like."

"Well, I know now," she responded. "I got on the elevator with her at the Great Western Royal Hotel less than ten minutes ago. How about gray pants, a black leather jacket, boots...and a black wig?"

Now Matt was interested. And almost convinced. "Where is she now?" he asked.

"I followed her out the door and she got on a motorcycle and took off in the direction of Buckingham Palace. Come and get me, Matt. We've got to find her."

The former *SSU* agent roused Generals Sinclair and Menzies, as well as Major Kensie, and quickly briefed them as he dressed. In fifteen minutes, he and two marshals were on their way to pick up Ruth. General Sinclair would alert the police, describe the fugitive's clothing, and have them on the lookout for the female fugitive.

As the MI6 vehicle approached the Victoria Memorial, a crowd was gathering on the edge of St. James Park. That's where he saw her.

"Stop! She's right there," he roared.

Matt couldn't believe his eyes. Ruth was absolutely right. His attacker was indeed dressed in her battle attire. He quickly deduced that this was to be the ambush point. *That's what I'd do*, he reasoned. *Create a diversion and bomb the bus. I've got her now*, he thought excitedly.

Matt instructed the driver to go to the hotel and pick up Ruth and call Sinclair to let him know where to meet him. He and the other marshal exited the car and cautiously moved toward the woman. They decided not to confront her until all avenues of escape were covered. They would simply watch her until help arrived.

The elusive female had a bulge in her jacket that he was sure was a weapon. They would ultimately have to approach her with care. She didn't have a bag of any kind, so Matt surmised she had a co-conspirator to plant the bomb. He scanned the growing crowd and saw a square-jawed, intense looking young man in work clothes carrying a metal lunch pail. *Why would a protester carry his lunch to a demonstration*, he questioned? *He must be the accomplice. It must be C4 type explosive.*

It was a few minutes after 8:00 a.m. and the mob was growing but still somewhat restrained. Police were arriving and tension was rising as the protesters began swarming into the street shouting about better pay and working conditions. A few protesters threw bottles and rocks and police were responding. It was only a matter of time before the demonstration turned into a full riot.

8:15 a.m. came and went and there was no bus. Traffic was snarled, but Linette became irritated because the bus had not arrived. *What happened*, she thought. *Why are they late?* By 8:30 a.m., she realized the coach was not coming. *Did the driver hear about the protest and alter his course*, she asked herself? *Did one of the labor leaders tip off the authorities? How, and why*, she pondered?

As the fuming female executioner considered her options, she failed to notice the increasing presence of law enforcement around her and the approaching former American *Special Services Unit* agent.

"*Remember me?*" Matt queried his soon-to-be captive.

"I believe we met in a park in Excelsior, Minnesota," he jabbed.

Karla Hoffman immediately spun around to run but was grabbed by two London policemen. Almost simultaneously, her associate with the lunch box was taken to the ground by a policeman and MI6 marshal. The marshal, as a bomb specialist, carefully examined the container and gently opened it. Sure enough, it was full of plastique explosives attached to a timer set for two minutes.

The master assassin said nothing as she and her comrade were transported to MI6 Headquarters for interrogation by Matt, Hugh Kensie and Stuart Menzies. She had no idea that she had been discovered by a chance encounter in a hotel elevator by an American nurse turned amateur sleuth.

"Do you prefer German, French or English?" Matt began his interrogation in all three languages.

The young female, no longer wearing her black wig, sat mute.

"Okay...English it is. We're aware of the new Nazi plot and have already rounded up many of your associates," Matt bluffed convincingly. "What I don't know is why you confronted me personally instead of killing me like you did Lewis Tarquin in Arizona. That was a mistake. It has to be something personal. What is it?"

She sat quietly but her face betrayed her as she turned bright red. Sweat also became visible on her upper lip. Matt was sure he was making progress.

While the woman had no identification on her when she was apprehended, a quick-thinking Ruth had rushed to the desk clerk in the hotel, identified herself as an MI6 agent, and demanded to look through the guest register. The bewildered clerk granted her access and it only took a moment for Ruth to identify the mystery woman as Linette Chamberlin.

"We know you've used several aliases...Giselle Houlé, Clare Lyon, and now you're here as Linette Chamberlin. We've been tailing you all along. We know a lot about you and your gang of young thugs, so you might as well talk to me," Matt pressed forcefully.

The expert interrogator paused for a moment to let the woman contemplate her fate. Still flushed and sweating, the highly trained antagonist still refused to speak. As Matt examined her closely, the obvious hit him like lightning. *Why hadn't I thought of it before*, he asked himself.

"You're Karla from *Die Akademie der Auserwählten!*" Matt gushed. "Why would you want to kill me? I helped save a lot of your classmates."

"You bombed us and murdered my father!" Karla screeched.

"We didn't bomb anybody," he responded firmly.

"You are a liar," she shot back. "They told us you would deny it, but we saw the evidence. You killed important German people and many children. You murdered my father. You do not deserve to live. That is why you must die, and when I get out of here, I will kill you," she ranted.

Matt was astounded at her complete misinformation and rage. *Now I have an avenue to facilitate a meaningful dialogue*, he thought. *I can show her some action reports and let her know it was an inside job. In the process, I should be able to finesse her into giving us more information on the conspiracy.*

"I'll show you some documents that prove the Allies had nothing to do with the explosion at your school," Matt offered. "I'll have someone get them out of storage and then we can talk some more. It may take a while. In the meantime, do you remember seeing any Allied soldiers in the compound? No. There were none. Only the three of us who were watching the school and underground compound. Our job was to report on what we saw. Nothing more. The explosion surprised us just like it did you."

"Do you remember the female member of our group? She gathered all the children and kept them together until help arrived. The other man, Pat, rushed into the burning building and gathered towels, sheets and blankets to cover up the children and bandage their wounds. I don't know what evidence you think you saw, but our records are clear. Your school was blown up by a group of disgruntled German officers."

Matt then artfully changed tone and approach. "I'll bet you're hungry. What would you like to eat?"

"I do not care," Karla responded as she calmed down. *I must not give in to his tactics*, she thought. *What he said cannot be true. He is lying to get me to talk.*

Matt smiled and left the room comfortable that there would be no repeat of the earlier Uwe Fromme suicide. Karla had been thoroughly searched before being taken to the interrogation room. Unfortunately, he was in for another surprise.

Even though Karla was handcuffed to the chair, a marshal was stationed in the room to make sure she couldn't harm herself. Less than three minutes after Matt exited the room, a former *SOE* operative who joined MI6 after the war knocked on the door. The marshal turned, opened the door and was greeted by the butt of a pistol to the head. He fell to the floor unconscious. The woman quickly retrieved the keys to the handcuffs and hurried toward the prisoner.

The rescuer uttered her code word, *Engel*, twice as she approached Karla. "Wir müssen schnell gehen," she said. "Wir müssen dich zurück nach Deutschland bringen."

"Not before I kill Major Kane," Karla retorted in English.

"There is no time. You are too important to the plan. We must go now," the rescuer insisted.

The pair made their way down the back stairs and left the building within five minutes. They waited for a short time before moving to the street, where they climbed into a waiting taxi driven by another London-based Neo-Nazi collaborator. Their plan was to make their way to the English coast where they would board a small boat to take them back to the continent. The double-agent's nine years with MI6 had now come to an abrupt end. However, there were still two others in place within the agency to carry on the mission.

The liberator was born and raised in Marseille, became a Nazi sympathizer like many others in the coastal city, and quickly became a staunch advocate for the Vichy Government. She was sent to England in 1942 to infiltrate the *SOE*, and after several months of training was dispatched back to Paris to collect and transmit vital information to London. She provided a great deal of valuable material to her German handlers throughout the war, and enough operational intelligence to the Allies that she remained free of suspicion. Hans Vogel recruited her at war's end to spy on the British Intelligence Agency. She was subsequently invited to join MI6 in late 1945 and had provided a strong inside presence for the Neo-Nazi Party.

On his way to get food for his captive, Matt stopped to call James and Rich in Aachen to inform them that they had the German fugitive in custody. He instructed Ruth to call Marie and Abby in Paris.

Matt and General Menzies returned with a hearty breakfast plate that included an omelet with potatoes, cheese, bacon and ham; a large Belgian waffle with brandied Apricot butter; a small bowl of strawberries and bananas; and a glass of apple juice. They were stunned when they opened the door and found the semi-conscious marshal with a copious amount of blood streaming down his face.

The General summoned Ruth to tend to the marshal's wound, and while she worked on him, he was informed that the assailant was MI6 agent, Martha Decard.

"*I knew it!*" exclaimed Matt. "They couldn't have known we were here or had Karla without someone on the inside. General...the Neo-Nazi network is bigger and more pervasive than we could have imagined."

Abby and Marie were on their way out of the Lutetia Hotel when Ruth called to let them know that Matt's attacker had been caught and that her real name was Karla. This would be helpful as they questioned the staff at Voyages Internationaux Français.

It was almost noon on a comfortable but cloudy summer day when Abby entered the small travel agency on Rue de Sèvres, just a short walk from the hotel. She could see two male and three female staff members and approached the nearest agent and questioned her in perfect French regarding a possible trip to the United States. Whether it was fate or luck, the woman was Ruby LeMaire.

The affable agent asked Abby if she had ever been to the U.S. and, of course, she replied no. Then the adept American NSA officer asked if she could have the same itinerary that her friend Karla took in May.

"Karla Hoffman?" replied Ruby cautiously.

"Oh, je veux dire Giselle Houlé," Abby responded.

"Certainement," the agent responded knowingly. Obviously, the patron was another of the many Nazi disciples that Voyages Internationaux Français had served for the past few years. Her compatriot was presumably trying to finish the mission that Karla was unable to complete.

Once a rapport had been established, Abby continued to engage the naïve Ruby LeMaire in a dialogue that convinced her that the agency was a Nazi front that coordinated the movements of dozens of spies. They would need to shut the travel agency down and confiscate their records, but not quite yet. There was still much to learn from the staff.

While Abby was engaged with Ruby, Marie entered the office and approached one of the male employees for assistance.

"Sprichst du Deutsch?" Marie inquired.

"Ja," came the immediate reply.

Marie asked the man to arrange transportation to Aachen, including a vehicle to take her to headquarters. The agent was startled with the open use of German and direct reference to headquarters. When he hesitated, Marie heatedly insisted that it was vital to the plan that she get back to Command to report on the capture of a key operative in London. The man capitulated and within twenty minutes Marie had a direct route to the leadership of the Neo-Nazi conspiracy.

"Danke. *It is over soon*," she added in expressive German as she turned and exited the shop.

Abby continued her conversation with Ruby for a couple of minutes and left. Once they were back at the hotel, they exchanged information and placed a call to Matt at MI6. Finally, they felt like they were ready to tighten the noose around the new Nazi faction. As always, however, they would find out that it wouldn't be that easy.

Chapter 22
The Breakthrough

"We need to know where she's going," Matt stressed to Marie on the telephone. "I'm convinced that she's going to Aachen, but where specifically?"

"I don't think it's a good idea to shut down Voyages Internationaux Français yet," Marie insisted. "We need to let the situation play out for another day or so to see how they react. If we rush in now, they may be able to tip-off the leaders in Aachen and we'll lose them."

"I'm afraid that's a chance we're going to have to take. James, Rich and Duncan are in Aachen, but don't have any reasonable place to start their hunt for the nerve center. The only way to narrow the possibilities is to get the exact telephone number in Aachen. The travel agency has it and the only way to get it is to shut the place down."

"I know time is of the essence," she responded, "but I still don't like it. I fear that all we'll do is scatter the leaders and prolong the operation. If you insist that this is the only way, Abby and I will get in touch with French authorities immediately and try to get them to secure the agency and detain the staff. Give us a few hours and hopefully we'll be able to get back to you with the telephone number."

"Thanks, *Rose*. You're a jewel!" Matt answered warmly.

Marie appreciated the sound of her World War II code name.

James, Rich and Colonel Giles reached Hotel Benelux near the recovering Central Zone of Aachen on Wednesday evening and planned to begin their search the next morning. But from where? The call from Matt was welcome news, but they still needed a place to launch their investigation.

Although Duncan Giles was the only one of the three trackers who spoke German, albeit awkwardly, they decided to split up and simply canvas the area as best they could to look for a meaningful starting point. Duncan would seek out any military authorities he could find, Rich would consult with local law enforcement, and James would attempt to make contact with borderline criminal elements by prowling the alleyways and backstreets of the central city.

Typically, the underworld has a feel for any clandestine activity, and although it's always dangerous to poke around in their territory, James was confident he could glean some worthwhile information without suffering any physical damage. And as his experience had unfailingly demonstrated, he knew that money always helped.

While their Paris and Aachen colleagues were pursuing leads on the ground, General Menzies and Matt went to the deceased Pat Kendall's office to examine documents related to his investigation of the budding Nazi conspiracy. In particular, they were looking for a detailed dossier that Pat had compiled on former *SS* personnel who were possibly involved in a new Nazi plot. They wanted to find out if any of his persons-of-interest had connections to Aachen. They believed that identifying a specific leader in the German city would provide another data point for James, Rich and Duncan as they searched for the headquarters of the Neo-Nazi alliance.

General Menzies looked puzzled as he rifled through the file cabinet. "There's nothing here but some trivial paperwork," he pronounced to Matt. "General Sinclair told me he ordered the room sealed and undisturbed until further notice when we heard of Pat's death."

"Maybe he released the materials later so they could be used by another agent," Matt offered. "Let's check with the head of the documents section. She should know something."

The Documents Section Chief told the pair that no one in her department had received a release authorization. All materials, including the dossier, should still be in Pat's office. Now it made sense. The double-agent who freed Karla took them.

Having failed to gain any useful information at MI6 headquarters, Menzies decided he could be more useful in Paris in coordinating the raid on Voyages Internationaux Français. Accordingly, he quickly arranged for a British Air Force plane to take him to the French Capital.

"The motorcycle angle makes some sense. We'll keep our eyes open for Karla Hoffman," James responded in his second call of the day from Matt. "But we won't see her for a day or two. It would be a lot easier if we knew where the phone calls originated from and had a couple of names we could explore," he asserted.

"I've asked Abby and Marie to have the travel agency seized as soon as possible by the French Directorate of Territorial Security," informed Matt. "And General Menzies is headed to Paris to supervise the operation."

"Good. Maybe they can retrieve the number and get it to us before the day is out. By the way, you didn't tell me how you located Karla Hoffman in our last call?"

"You really don't want to know. You won't be happy. Ruth never got on the airplane and returned to a hotel in central London. This morning she actually got on the elevator with her and called me."

"*What!* Wait till I get my hands on that reckless little..." James reacted. He admired her tenacity but was alarmed at her lack of caution.

"In any event, she's safely here with me...and I'll keep an eye on her. You take care and don't do anything outrageous yourself," Matt ended with a chuckle.

Shortly after 6:30 p.m., nine fully armed officers of the French DST and the venerable General Stuart Menzies entered Voyages Internationaux Français and arrested all of the travel agency staff, or so they thought. A sixth agent slipped out a side door into the adjoining antique store and skillfully strolled out the front without being noticed. He stopped at a tavern two blocks away, purchased a token from the bartender, and stood in line for the public telephone, located just outside the doors to the public toilet.

After having breathed the stench from the privy for almost ten minutes, the telephone was free and the escapee quickly dialed the Aachen telephone number, extended the code word, and informed the voice on the other end that the Nazi facade had been raided. The call lasted less than a minute and an emergency alert was triggered. Marie was right, catching the fugitives would now be more difficult and time-consuming.

Meanwhile, Abby and Marie joined the French officers a few minutes later and began combing through files looking for records of any transactions involving Giselle Houlé or Clare Lyon. It took fifteen minutes to find what they were looking for. A full transportation and housing itinerary taking the female assassin from Aachen to Paris, New York, Chicago and Minneapolis had been arranged on May 20th. They also found the Aachen telephone number, which traced to the Hotel Kron, a few hundred meters northeast of the central city zone of Aachen.

Perhaps even more important than the immediate intelligence regarding Karla Hoffman, the former *SSU* agents uncovered an abundance of material detailing travel arrangements made from the same Aachen telephone number. While it would take time to convert aliases to real names, the sheer volume of agents increased the likelihood of uncovering vital details about the organization and pinpointing the epicenter of activity. It also confirmed that the conspiracy was much wider than the killing of a few former Allied agents and leaders.

"This is General Menzies. Put me through to Major Kane."

"Yes sir," responded the telephone operator as she dialed the extension number.

"Matt, we have the telephone number in Aachen. We also found hundreds of travel transactions that should help us catch other Nazi agents. We'll work on that when I get back to London."

"Thanks, General. Give me the number and I'll pass it along to James."

"I'll stay here with Marie and Abby so we can interrogate the travel staff and find out how much they know and how connected they are to the insurrection. It may be Saturday before we return. In the meantime, I'll have someone send you a few names to check out."

"I'll take care of it," Matt responded somewhat troubled.

While the slightly disgruntled former intelligence officer knew he should pass the telephone number on to James in Aachen, Matt decided to call the number himself. He simply didn't want to be tied to a desk and left out of the proceedings. This was a way to inject himself into the action.

"Hotel Kron," answered the gentleman politely in German. "How can we help you?"

"I do not speak German well," responded Matt in broken Deutsch. Do you speak French?"

"Yes, sir," answered the proprietor.

"This is Mathieu King from Voyages Internationaux Français in Paris. I have a question about a travel registration for a Clare Lyon. Can you help me?" Matt quizzed.

The hotel owner was silent for a few seconds before responding.

"I am sorry sir. I am not sure I understood your question. Can you repeat it for me?"

Matt immediately knew he had struck a nerve...and he knew why. There was obviously a code word that he failed to use.

"I wanted to verify a travel date for Mademoiselle Clare Lyon. Can you give me the beginning date?"

"No sir. We don't make travel requests," came the answer guardedly. "May I help you will anything else?"

"Non, merci," responded Matt as he hung up the phone.

Matt immediately dialed the Hotel Benelux to relate his telephone call to James. There was no answer. He pondered leaving a message but decided to go to Aachen and tell him in person. He also wanted to be part of the interrogation of the Kron Hotel manager.

Matt went straight to General Sinclair and convinced him that a major breakthrough in the situation was imminent and that he needed air transportation to Aachen as soon as possible. Not aware that the former *SSU* agent had been ordered to remain at MI6, the General made a telephone call to Gatwick Airport and quickly arranged for a plane to take Matt to Germany the next morning.

Matt left London at 9:14 a.m. Greenwich Mean Time on Friday and arrived at the small Beek Airfield in southeast Netherlands at 11:48 a.m. Central European Time. The four hundred-twelve-kilometer flight and ensuing twenty-seven-kilometer drive to the Hotel Benelux took just over two hours. Notwithstanding his aching ribs, Matt was revitalized.

Chapter 23

The Leads

"*Not you too?*" grumbled James when he saw Matt standing in the lobby. "You didn't bring Ruth, did you? You and your friends obviously never learned to follow instructions!" he added in frustration.

"No, Ruth's safe and sound at MI6...and not happy that I left her in the custody of two female marshals," Matt responded gleefully. He was strengthened to be back in the fight.

"There are some important developments," Matt reported. "I got the telephone number from Menzies last night and called it. As it turns out, the number was in the manager's office of the Hotel Kron. I identified myself as an employee of the Paris travel agency and inquired about reservations for Clare Lyon. I got stonewalled, probably because I failed to use a code word. We need to get over there immediately. Where's Rich and Duncan? It wouldn't hurt to have them with us in case we have any trouble."

"We agreed to meet here at 1:00 p.m. and compare notes so they should be back at any time," answered James, still irritated at Matt's failure to stay in London. "As soon as they arrive, we'll get over to the Kron."

"In the meantime," he continued, "I had an interesting foray into the Aachen underworld this morning. I found a local who spoke English and engaged him as a translator. We roamed the city looking for shady characters and found some who were quite willing to take a few deutsche marks to talk with us."

"One street gang member told me there's been some Nazi talk floating around, but nothing concrete. He did say, however, that much of the gossip has been about a Werewolf camp somewhere in the Hürtgen or Aachen Forests. He also explained that the West German authorities aren't particularly interested in former Nazis, and that there are several high-ranking *SS* or Gestapo members still walking freely around the country."

Matt was intrigued, not so much by the apparent lack of interest in the known Nazis who were being ignored, but by the Werewolf congregation who he considered to be extremely dangerous. He remembered that the German resistance group was formed in late 1944 by Heinrich Himmler to operate behind Allied lines and create havoc for invading American and Soviet troops. They were largely made up of students and young zealots who were trained in hit-and-run tactics and savagery.

Werewolves stayed behind Allied lines and harassed invading columns, disrupted supply lines, and generally sowed fear among soldiers by ambushing lone individuals or small groups when they strayed from their columns or camps. While the Werewolf movement was unsuccessful in actually slowing down the American advance, it did strike fear in both soldiers and the civilian population because of its supposed link to the occult. No tactic was off limits.

Matt drifted into thought as James continued to brief him on what he learned during his excursion. *Did the movement simply go dark while it was recruiting and training new members? Is this group part the new Nazi military? How many of them are there? What kind of...*

Within a few minutes, Rich and Duncan bounded into the hotel lobby and reawakened Matt.

"Who let you out of your cage?" questioned Rich dispassionately. "You're supposed to be in protective custody."

"Never mind that, we have some good leads to follow and time is wasting. We need to get to the Hotel Kron. That's where the telephone calls came from," Matt replied.

"Slow down, Matt," responded Rich casually. "Let's have lunch and then check out the hotel. I doubt that the bad guys are gonna get away in the next hour."

While the group was having lunch at the café next door to the Benelux Hotel, James used the time to debrief Rich and Duncan regarding their morning activities.

"Did you two find out anything useful?" asked James.

"Possibly," responded Duncan. "I talked with Mayor Heusch and he believes there's a large gathering of ruffians in the forests around the area, possibly former Nazi Werewolves. He believes they're up to something but he's not sure what, and the local police aren't anxious to go into the jungle after them. As far as he knows, they haven't broken any laws yet."

"That mirrors what I found out in the streets today," confirmed James.

"How about you, Rich? Did you get anything from the local police?" James asked.

"Duncan's right," explained Rich in his typical *just-the-facts* manner. "There's definitely suspicious activity in the hills between Belgium and Germany. While the coffee smuggling rings have largely been eradicated, the authorities still believe there's a significant crime trail between the countries. Monitoring the forests is only haphazard and is quite dangerous according to the Chief Inspector. They've also heard rumors of a Neo-Nazi gathering in the Hürtgen area, but haven't attempted to investigate since they don't have the resources to challenge them. They're clearly either disinterested or intimidated."

"Law enforcement is complicated because of border disputes between the neighboring countries, the resettlement of refugees that's taken place since the war, and overall confusion due to the continuous activity surrounding the rebuilding of the city. They told me that the population of Aachen was only around four thousand people at the end of the war. It's now over a hundred-and-fifty thousand and growing. They sincerely apologized that they couldn't offer us any help in locating the Nazi hideout. They're concerned, but don't know how to handle it."

"Okay...we know the headquarters is here in the area somewhere," stressed Matt convincingly. "We also have a direct lead at the Hotel Kron. We need to get there now before the masterminds scatter."

It took the determined crew-of-four less than twenty minutes to reach the Kron. Matt took the lead, identified the group as international law-enforcement officials, and ordered the desk clerk to find the proprietor. The clerk dialed the hotel owner's number and informed him that some policemen wanted to see him. He then warily guided the men to the proprietor's office where a fiftyish looking man with thinning grey hair awaited them. Matt and Rich glanced at each other and nodded. This docile looking businessman was clearly not a leader in the Nazi uprising.

Matt, James and Rich took turns grilling the nervous hotel owner. He swore he knew nothing about Nazis or a conspiracy. However, he readily told his interrogators that a forceful and threatening man had approached him late in 1950 with a proposal to permanently lease a room in a lightly traveled area of the newly reopened hotel. He agreed to pay five times the normal rate and would not need janitorial or maintenance services. He simply required complete privacy and ordered that all phone calls requesting to speak with Herr Engel be routed through the manager's office. Calls not specifically requesting Herr Engel should be terminated and the room sentinel notified immediately.

The rattled manager thought the man was either a government agent or criminal, and he didn't want to be too inquisitive. His wartime experience with the Gestapo taught him not to question authority. He reluctantly agreed to the arrangement because the income equivalent to five room rentals in a lodge with only sixty-four rooms was substantial for a recovering business.

The manager reported that his tenant had caused no trouble and paid faithfully over the past three and a half years. The only problem was that the volume of telephone calls had begun to rise substantially in the past few months and the proprietor thought about asking for more money.

"Do you know if anyone is in the room right now?" asked Matt.

"I think someone is there all the time," came the reply.

"You need to take us to the room," demanded James vigorously.

The frightened owner took the four investigators up the back stairs to the top floor and turned to walk away when Duncan Giles restrained him.

"Knock on the door," ordered James quietly. "Tell him you need to speak to him about increasing the rent because of the number of telephone calls."

The little man looked horrified. Duncan pulled the proprietor a few feet down the deserted hallway and made it plain that he had more to fear from him than the chap in the room. The terrified owner slowly moved back to the apartment and knocked on the door as instructed.

"Who is it?" came the response in militaristic German.

"It is Mr. Schuster ...the hotel owner."

"What do you want?"

"I need to talk to you about rent."

"Do you have a key?" asked the occupant suspiciously.

"Ja."

"Use your key and come in."

As instructed, the reticent business owner unlocked and opened the door. He paid with his life. Because contact protocol had been breached, the former *SS Oberscharführer* anticipated that this was a ruse and was prepared to react as trained. He sat behind the desk and fired his pistol as soon as he caught a glimpse of James behind the fearful Schuster. The shocked innkeeper never grasped what was happening.

Rich instinctively pushed James out of the way as a bullet grazed the FBI agent's shoulder and fired three shots into the former Nazi Sergeant. It was over in an instant.

"*That went well,*" Matt observed sarcastically to no one in particular.

"I didn't see that coming," pronounced James as he scrambled to his feet wiping blood off his left shoulder.

"That's exactly why I told you to stay in London. How would I explain your death in Germany to Director Hoover?" he barked at Matt.

"Well, *you* didn't fare so well yourself!" Matt barked back. "Rich just saved your life."

"He did at that," James admitted uncomfortably as he nodded to his friend.

"That's enough, you two," Rich decreed. "We still have work to do."

Duncan simply watched in amusement, completely unaffected by the violent confrontation. In fact, he wished he'd fired the shots that killed the Nazi bastard.

James regained his composure as he looked at the bloody mess and two dead bodies. "He was definitely military and anticipated us. He must have been warned by somebody. Maybe Herr Schuster failed to use a code word again. We need to keep this as quiet as possible for the time being. Maybe we still have an opportunity to grab his replacement and gather intelligence before the rest of the pack gets scared off."

"Let's get Schuster's body out of the hall and mop up the blood as best we can before someone comes along and creates a panic," advised Rich.

It took a several minutes to restore the hallway, cover the bodies, and formulate a strategy for handling the situation. Notwithstanding Matt's interaction with the hotel operator the previous day, he spoke fluent German and was assigned to the hotel owner's office to answer telephone calls. Duncan spoke passable German, so he volunteered to stay in the secret room to take any calls. He also had an ulterior motive. He wanted to be the one to greet the replacement telephone attendant.

Rich used the hotel telephone in the room to call the Aachen Chief Inspector to inform him of the incident and asked for an eight-hour delay in any police response. He requested that the bodies be taken out quietly after midnight to maintain secrecy. In the meantime, he would keep watch in the lobby area.

As they were tending to the dead and cleaning up the room, James located the WWII **Amtsanschliesser 44** field telephone that was being used to communicate with headquarters and other Nazi outposts. The room was clearly being used as a communications hub and clearinghouse for the developing Nazi revolt. Apparently, the SS communications expert had coupled the field phone with the Kron's telephone wiring such that it left no identifiable footprint. Calls from the **Am 44** could not be traced.

On the floor, they found a telephone log with incoming caller names and times. The names were coded, but if they could capture one of the room attendants, they figured they could squeeze out some useful intelligence. James would station himself in the office with Matt to make use of his military knowledge and language expertise but would move around the lobby and check in with Duncan Giles periodically throughout the evening.

The half-eaten plate of Wiener Schnitzel, salad and bread on the floor was cold, indicating this had been the lunch meal, and that either a quartermaster or the replacement telephone screener would be coming soon. It was almost 6:00 p.m. when everything was in place. Sure enough, half-an-hour later, Rich spotted a stout middle-aged man hastily making his way through the lobby toward the stairs at the end of the hallway. He carried a bag that the detective surmised was a meal of some kind. He also carried a drink.

Rich rushed to the hotel manager's office and summoned James, who promptly ordered Matt to call Duncan and remain at the telephone while he and Rich slipped up to the third-floor room to aid their compatriot. The capture went off without a hitch.

The replacement monitor used his key to enter the room and was greeted by Duncan Giles with a pistol aimed at him. In just over a minute, Rich and James, guns in hand, joined their partner.

They were now on their way...or so they thought.

Chapter 24
The Misfires

Matt was sitting at the manager's desk steaming at his exclusion from the operation when the night clerk entered the office to check in with Herr Schuster before going on duty. The young man was surprised at the sight of the stranger and wanted to know where his Direktor was. Matt explained that Herr Schuster would be away for a few days and that he would be in charge until the proprietor returned. The clerk was suspicious and demanded to speak with his superior.

Matt uncharacteristically rose from the chair and walked menacingly over to the diminutive employee, who immediately backed away from the aggressor. At six-feet-two, Matt towered over the minion and sternly directed him to sit down and answer his questions. The young man, totally intimidated by the outsider, complied without protest.

For the next few minutes, the frustrated investigator took the initiative and questioned the clerk about his duties and how he handled telephone calls. Matt learned that the clerk answered requests for Herr Engel and transferred the calls to the 'secret' room. Clearly frightened, the employee admitted that he had been curious about the strange arrangement and actually listened briefly a few times. The room attendant always answered with Herr *Engel*, and the response would always be a strange name like *Dachs, Eber, Viper* or *Raubtier*.

The clerk told Matt that his line would then go dead, but he could still hear muffled voices like a party-line call. None of it made sense to him so he kept his anxiety to himself. It seemed too much like the Gestapo schemes he observed as a boy during the war, and it upset him. Matt informed him that he would take all Herr *Engel* calls until further notice and dismissed the relieved clerk to return to the front desk.

After nearly twenty minutes, the former intelligence officer's impatience got the best of him. He abandoned his post and hiked up to the third floor to get in on the action. Once again, James was not pleased, but quickly realized that Matt's language and interviewing skills were needed since they hadn't made meaningful progress in the inquiry.

The skillful interrogator once again worked his magic on the captured room attendant. Matt's experience taught him that sometimes it's not what you actually know, but what the prisoner thinks you know that matters. Within an hour, the soldier revealed that he had been a senior non-commissioned officer in the *SS* and a communications controller during the war.

Matt also used what limited knowledge he had of the conspiracy to bluff the captive into inadvertently confirming that the hotel was simply a screening location, and that the real headquarters was in the surrounding forest. The question was where, but it was evident that the Nazi conspirator would never reveal the location. Matt did, however, uncover the prisoner and his dead combatant's code names, which would later prove to be valuable in tracking down other Neo-Nazi operatives.

As requested, the Aachen police appeared at the hotel at 1:21 a.m. on Saturday morning. The hotel was quiet and the heavy rain proved to be excellent camouflage for the body extraction and investigation by the Chief Inspector and his police. Secrecy had been maintained. Once again, he apologized for not being able to help in the forest search but did commit to assist the investigation in the hotel and hold any detainees for questioning.

Late on Saturday afternoon, Abby and Marie arrived on the scene. After a good night's sleep, their immediate task was to station themselves at the Hotel Kron with Matt to sort through the log of telephone calls and match them with names from the travel agency records. Matt parked himself on a couch and dozed on and off throughout the night. The telephone was silent.

It only took a short time for Matt and the two former female agents to begin assembling the puzzle on Sunday morning. They found several code names that corresponded with the names used on passports and travel documents. They were quickly able to track the movements of several operatives throughout Europe in the past three years. Within a few days, they expected to be able to determine if these individuals were involved in the suspicious deaths of political figures or former *SOE* agents.

By late morning, a definite pattern was developing, and Matt and his colleagues were beginning to realize that *SSU* members were only a small fraction of a huge plot to wipe out any vestiges of the World War II intelligence community and anyone who had knowledge of Nazi strategy or tactics. Assassinations of some political leaders in Belgium, The Netherlands, France, Poland and West Germany, coupled with the recent attempt on General Sinclair, seemed to indicate that the Neo-Nazi movement was attempting to destabilize several European governments. Something was happening...and soon.

Matt had staffed the Kron Hotel proprietor's office for almost thirty-six hours. There were no calls. This led him to believe their presence had been discovered. Marie knew him too well. She recognized that he was agitated and restless and was trying to settle him down when the telephone rang. Matt sprang to the phone.

"Hotel Kron," answered Matt in his best German articulation. "How can we help you?"

"I want to speak to Herr *Engel*," instructed the determined female.

Matt knew in an instant. It was Karla Hoffman.

He was on the verge of asking her where she was when he heard a train whistle and arrival announcement in French. Karla was in Paris. He simply complied and forwarded the call to Duncan Giles.

"Herr *Engel*."

"This is *Raubtier*," Karla replied. "Get me Herr Vogel...quickly."

Both caller and responder slipped up in their brief exchange. The telephone line went dead. The assassin mistakenly used Vogel's real name instead of his code name, and the Colonel incorrectly phrased his response. Karla instantly realized that the communications hub had been compromised. She was on her own.

Matt was annoyed by the communications mix-up, but Marie and Abby tried to coax him into looking at the positive side. The call confirmed where she was and that she was on her way to the area. More importantly, they now knew her code name was *Predator*, and that her superior was a Herr Vogel. They were much closer to finding the headquarters and identifying the leadership. It didn't help. He was sure she would find a way to alert her co-conspirators and they would leave the area.

"Let's notify the police and have them watch out for her," advised Abby.

"I'll go get Rich and have him contact the Chief Inspector," added Marie.

James and Rich spent Sunday morning arranging for support from NATO and the U.S. Army to conduct their search of the forests between Aachen, Monschau and Düren. American Rangers arrived at the rallying point near Mayen at 1:42 p.m. James, Rich and Duncan appeared thirty minutes later. Before they left, Rich informed the Chief Inspector of the situation and gave him a description of the female fugitive. While the three men were out in the field, the police would keep watch for Karla Hoffman. The Hauphtbahnof Rail Depot would get special attention.

Each of the men was accompanied by a squad of American soldiers from the Wiesbaden Army Garrison near Frankfurt as they ventured into the Hürtgen Forest to seek out the suspected encampment of the Nazi Werewolves. Each group consisted of an officer, an NCO, and ten Rangers trained in jungle warfare. Their mission was to reconnoiter the area and capture some alleged guerrillas for interrogation. However, their intent was to be cautious and avoid armed conflict, if possible, because the size of the clandestine group was unknown.

James' unit went east in the forest toward the town of Hürtgen; Rich's team moved slightly southeast in the direction of Vossenack; and Duncan's forces trekked their way a little further southeastward to the city of Schmidt, the site of fierce fighting during the war. If their initial foray was unsuccessful in locating the Neo-Nazi base camp, they would fan out north, south and west through the Hürtgen Forest.

The retired British Colonel Giles was sure he had the answer. To him, it was obvious. The area around the town of Schmidt was a stronghold of German forces late in WWII, and it only made sense that they would recreate that haven. He reasoned that the complex network of visible mountain tops, deep wooded ravines and Roer River tributaries near Schmidt provided an excellent defensive obstacle for possible intruders. Just as important, the mountaintops afforded a clear view of the surrounding valleys such that they could observe any interlopers and react as needed. Overall, the area provided a formidable strategic base for the cluster of revolutionaries. Quite possibly, it even housed the primary headquarters of the entire Neo-Nazi movement.

The slog through the mountainous terrain was taxing and slow, reminding the Rangers of the difficulties faced by the American First and Ninth Armies in October and November of

1944. The claustrophobic wall of trees, thick underbrush, and muddy ground made the hike challenging for James and Rich, but they were grateful they didn't have to contend with snow and cold as the American invaders did ten years prior. Duncan, twenty years their senior, however, enjoyed the excursion immensely. He was in his element.

By nightfall, the two American lawmen concluded that the Werewolf compound was not in their sectors. They prepared to move north toward Duren and west toward the Belgian border the next morning. James and Rich's forces stopped to make camp just before sunset at 7:36 p.m. Duncan's group continued until dusk. He then convinced his American Captain to send two men another mile up to the ridge to see if they could detect any activity.

Bingo. The dogged British Colonel proved to be right. The two scouts were able to see significant light from campfires two hilltops away. They had found the Werewolf redoubt. The three-mile hike would take six hours or longer to reach the compound, depending on the weather the next day. Another deluge was expected, but Duncan thought it might work to their advantage. His experience told him that the lookouts would be more interested in staying dry than watching for unwanted visitors.

Captain Paul Martin radioed his counterparts to the north and south just after 10:00 p.m. and informed them they had found the Werewolf hideout. They agreed to coordinate their arrival and converge on the compound from three directions on Monday night. This would allow Duncan's unit an opportunity to reconnoiter the area and afford James and Rich's forces enough time to link up with them and construct a plan to quietly take four or five prisoners.

Captains Martin, Griggs and Wilson, along with Duncan, James and Rich, assembled roughly a hundred yards on the west side of the compound at 9:27 p.m. on Monday. It rained heavily much of the day and the guards were indeed lax. Martin's Rangers probed the camp perimeter throughout the afternoon and estimated the Werewolf strength at five-hundred or so. Too large to confront without more men and heavier weapons. They did find a weak spot on the northwest side where they believed they could slip into the camp without being discovered.

It was still cloudy after midnight, which obscured the slight crescent moon, as six teams of five Rangers moved quietly into the encampment in search of high value prisoners. Each group was assigned a specific objective. Two groups targeted rank-and-file troops, two teams aimed for mid-level combatants, and two groups focused on high-ranking leaders.

The first two teams made quick work of the incursion, taking out two guards near the entrance of the complex. The remaining four teams silently made their way through the bevy of tents looking for signs of rank. Team three located a single occupant tent that housed a former *SS* assault squad leader, expertly subdued and muzzled him, and spirited him out of the camp in less than the allocated ten minutes for the mission. Team four struck out.

Teams five and six sighted a collection of four wooden buildings at the far west edge of the compound, which they assumed contained the highest-ranking officers. They peered through the windows of each structure and found one that contained two individuals. They silently entered the building and adeptly overpowered the two officers and dragged them out of the west side of the camp. It took twenty-two minutes for the entire band of Rangers to assemble at the collection point and begin the hike back to the previous night's camp site. It proved to be a long but productive night.

As the three squads of Rangers and the three civilians began their strategic withdrawal, Captain Martin radioed Wiesbaden Army Headquarters and requested a battalion of NATO troops to assault the mountaintop hideout in the morning and purge the forest of the Neo-Nazi paramilitaries. James intended to have their captives taken back to Aachen for interrogation by late Tuesday.

Meanwhile, on Monday morning, Matt and his two female colleagues experienced another stroke of luck. At 9:12 a.m., a policeman at the train station noticed the attractive young woman in a black leather jacket hastily leaving the area and making her way north toward the central city. He followed her to Rademacher's Motorwerkstatt and notified the Landespolizei headquarters. Within a few minutes he observed her leaving the shop on a motorcycle headed southwest on Zollamstrasse. The Chief Inspector had been asked to track but not apprehend her. Following their instructions, the police monitored her as she again made her way down Maria-Theresia-Allee, Ronheider Berg and Karlshöher Talweg motorways into the Aachen Forest, less than ten kilometers from the train station.

Just after 10:00 a.m., the Aachen Police Inspector called Matt at the Kron Hotel and informed him that his fugitive's destination was a school for disabled children on a large estate southwest of town. Matt was sure this was the conspiracy headquarters. While he knew he should wait for James and Rich, it could be a day or two before they returned from their mission and would likely be preoccupied interrogating Werewolf captives. He once again reasoned that time was short and decided to pursue his quarry. Abby and Marie were just as eager to enter the chase.

Within minutes, a policeman arrived and transported Matt, Abby and Marie to *Die Kinderschule*. The grounds were immaculate, and the stately house, adjoining school building, and dormitory were in excellent condition. There were six matrons outside supervising several younger children with a variety of physical maladies, while the light and airy classroom inside appeared to be bustling with older children. By all accounts, this was just as it appeared, an extraordinary school for the disabled.

"I'll go in and see what I can find out," volunteered Abby. "They may recognize you two, but I haven't had any contact with anybody yet so they might not know who I am."

"Okay," responded Marie. "But be careful. It looks innocent enough, but Karla came here for a reason. Get in and out as quickly as you can. We can always back away and call for reinforcements."

Abby casually made her way up the hill and in the front door of the main estate. Once inside, she was met by an amiable woman in her late twenties.

"Guten Morgen. How can I help you?" the receptionist asked in polite German.

Abby responded in French that she understood some German but was more comfortable with French. The hostess promptly re-directed her greeting in the preferred language.

Abby explained that she and her family were moving from Liège to Aachen and that she had a ten-year-old daughter who was in a wheelchair due to a bout with Polio. Abby inquired if she could talk with the headmaster about enrolling her daughter in the school.

The concierge politely informed Abby that Herr Vogel...*uh* Herr Walter, had left earlier in the day on a trip out of the country and would not be back for several days. *She's nervous. This, indeed, is the Nazi headquarters*, thought Abby. *We'll need to call in the international authorities and cordon off the area as soon as possible.* She thanked the woman and briskly walked back down the hill.

When the truck arrived at the driveway entrance to the school, the driver had stopped the vehicle, exited the truck, and opened the door for Abby. He remained outside to smoke a cigarette, leaving Matt and Marie alone for several minutes.

"Matt...how are you really doing?" Marie asked after a few awkward moments. "You've been pallid and restless for most of the last week. I'm worried about you."

"I'm okay, Marie." I'm still recovering and just not getting better as fast as I'd like. It's quite annoying. I know I've been a bit edgy. I'll try to handle my frustrations a little better."

"Hopefully, we'll get to the bottom of the conspiracy soon and you and Ruth can get back to your lives," Marie offered as she gently touched his hand.

Matt tenderly glanced over at Marie, and she responded with her own affectionate look. *If only...*she thought, as the policemen opened the door.

Chapter 25

The Ghost Trail

Abby returned to the vehicle and confirmed that *Die Kinderschule* was likely a cover for the Nazi nerve center.

"Herr Vogel, who is also going by the name Herr Walter, is the headmaster, and appears to be the leader of the movement. He left in a hurry this morning and told the staff he would be out of the country for the foreseeable future."

"We need to call the Bundespolizei and have them surround the school as soon as we can. Karla's in there somewhere, and there may also be some useful documents that will help us determine who Vogel is and where he might be headed."

"I'm still concerned that many of the Federal Police could actually be a part of the conspiracy," Matt responded. "I think we should call the Secretary General of the ICPC, Marcel Sicot, in Lyon and get his advice on how to proceed. If he says the German Bundespolizei are okay, we can engage them. If he can't vouch for them, we should call in the American Army."

"Just call Wiesbaden now and have some NATO troops sent down here immediately before Karla and her confederates destroy all the evidence and get away," advised Marie. "Whatever we do, we need to be sure the children are out of harm's way and properly cared for."

"We share your concern," Matt assured Marie. "We'll just watch and wait until the troops arrive and we'll make sure the children are well protected when they get here."

The driver radioed the Aachen Chief Inspector and asked for additional police to surround and observe the school until the Allied troops arrive. The Chief Inspector initially balked, but finally agreed to send two officers with strict instructions not to engage with anyone at the school. He was afraid of endangering the children and didn't want to be involved in what he saw as a developing international conflict.

Abby and Marie stayed out of sight observing the handicapped children's complex while the driver took Matt back to the Aachen police station to call the commanding general at Wiesbaden. Matt briefed him on the situation in the Aachen Forest and requested that he send a company of soldiers to assist in securing the suspected Neo-Nazi headquarters. The general readily agreed to dispatch the requested two-hundred troops immediately and indicated that the soldiers would be in Aachen within a couple of hours. He also informed Matt that he would have someone call and give him a status report as soon as he received any communication from the Hürtgen Forest operation.

Matt then placed a call to ICPC Secretary General Sicot and updated him on the past week's developments and questioned him about the loyalties of the Bundespolizei. Sicot responded that he was confident that the German Federal Police were loyal and reliable, although some may have been German soldiers during the war. Matt thanked the Secretary General for his honest assessment and overall support of the investigation, but was still somewhat uneasy about involving the Bundespolizei.

It was late on Monday afternoon when American troops arrived and began systematically executing a peaceful, non-threatening incursion into the school. It was too late. Karla and several of her former classmates from the Liège school in Belgium had already cleared out the underground compound and made their way through an escape tunnel into the wooded hills northwest of the school. A dead end...maybe.

It was early evening as Matt, Marie and Abby began interviewing each of the remaining thirty-three staff members.

Within three hours the interrogations were complete, and they were able to gather enough information about the school and its staff to begin to understand the underlying structure of the growing Neo-Nazi machine.

The four-hundred and thirty-two children were all offspring of former Nazi, Gestapo or Wehrmacht soldiers, many born during the war. These undesirables had to be shielded from fellow soldiers, the public or the government because of Adolph Hitler's Children's Euthanasia Program. Vogel's special schools were not only a godsend for parents, but they were also an excellent recruiting strategy for his planned reincarnation of the Nazi Reich.

Just like Karla's escapees, most of the remaining fifty-six staff members had also been students at the Liège school. They ranged in age from eighteen to twenty-seven, and Matt and Marie had helped save many of them after the devastating explosion at the *Daisy Compound*. While Marie didn't readily recognize most of them, they certainly remembered her. She had been protective and comforting to them during the ordeal, and many were quite willing to talk freely with her about their journey over the last ten years.

Matt and Abby had some success, but Marie's kindness a decade prior paid big dividends. They learned that virtually all of the staff members of *Die Kinderschule* had been orphaned but were rescued, sheltered and educated by *Obergruppenführer* Hans Vogel and his deputies from late 1944 through the end of the war and beyond. Once they finished their formal schooling, they were either sent to university or employed in various jobs at several enterprises throughout Europe owned and administered by Herr Doctor Vogel.

After the devastating events at the *Daisy Compound*, the parentless children had been relocated to a small private school on the outskirts of the safe city of Konstanz, Germany on the Swiss border. The facility was situated in the southeast corner of the city near the Grillplatz Wasserwerk in a heavily wooded area on Lake Constance. The school was shuttered in the summer of 1946 and the children were then moved to the present complex in the Aachen Forest.

Marie was told that the stronger boys and a select few of the sturdier girls were sent out for additional training of some sort when they finished school at age eighteen. The remaining females became teachers or matrons at *Die Kinderschule* as more disabled children were admitted to the school. While some of the specially trained students returned after their training and now have a permanent residence in the estate, they are generally secretive and come-and-go regularly.

It was apparent to the three former *SSU* agents that the youthful staff members were extremely loyal to Vogel and his ideology and believed that a new dominant Germany was at hand. It was equally evident that they had little knowledge of the violence that had been perpetrated by their contemporaries. Vogel and his deputies observed, categorized and segregated their disciples by personality traits, relegating the less bold and confident to clerical and administrative support roles. The more gifted and resolute contingent were groomed as assassins, combatants or potential military/administrative leaders.

Matt and Abby inquired about Karla Hoffman and hit a stone wall. No one wanted to talk about their former classmate or what role she played in Herr Vogel's organization. They got the feeling that Karla was alternately admired and feared. Marie was able to find out that she was a prominent member of the operation who was nice and charming most of the time, but hard and ruthless when disobeyed or challenged. The remaining Vogel devotees wouldn't share any information about Karla, even with Marie.

While the three investigators conducted their interviews, the detachment of American soldiers meticulously searched all the rooms in the main estate, school building and dormitory looking for Karla and other possible operatives. They found nothing except evidence that the occupants had left in a hurry.

After completing their interviews, the drained agents were debriefed by Army Lieutenant Colonel Warren Wright. He indicated that his soldiers would quarantine the staff and safeguard the students overnight and await further instructions from Wiesbaden on Tuesday. One of Colonel Wright's men then transported Abby, Matt and Marie back to the Hotel Benelux for the night.

It was early in the morning when a lightning bolt hit Matt. *Why didn't I think of it last night,* he thought? *There's a bunker under the estate. Karla's hiding under the main building! We've got to get back there right now.* He sat up and called Marie.

"She's in a bunker under the building, Marie," declared Matt, as she answered the phone.

"What time is it?"

"It's just after five, but that doesn't matter. We need to get there as soon as we can."

"Why don't you call Colonel Wright and have him do a more detailed sweep of the buildings?"

"I don't have his number handy, and besides, he isn't going to know where to look. I can find the entrance once I see the complete layout of the campus."

"Okay, I'll wake Abby and we'll see you in the lobby in a few minutes. I don't think we can call the Chief Inspector at this hour, so we'll need to take a taxi."

"I'll call for one right now," Matt assured her as he hastily hung up the telephone.

Lieutenant Colonel Wright was surprised to see the three trackers before six o'clock in the morning. Matt explained the urgency of the situation and the commander quickly ordered a squad of men to accompany him into the main building. Abby and Marie insisted that no soldiers come with them as they examine the school rooms or dormitory to avoid frightening the children. The colonel concurred.

Matt was confident that the bunker entrance was in the administrative building and he knew exactly where to start. He went straight to Vogel's office and began to probe the walls and floor for a hidden door. After thoroughly examining the room and finding nothing, he was about to move on to the next office when he stopped to take one more look.

If I was Vogel, I'd want to put my escape hatch in the least likely place intruders would look for it, and I'd want it readily accessible so I can exit quickly in the event of a raid, Matt reflected. His eyes were instantly drawn to the fireplace in the corner of the room.

"Lend me a hand," Matt requested of two soldiers standing next to him. "Let's see if this monstrosity moves."

"Yes sir," they responded in unison.

Matt and his assistants pushed, pulled and tugged on the structure to no avail. Then one of the men decided to see what would happen if he stepped on the hearth. It dipped slightly. He stepped off and it rebounded by perhaps an eighth of an inch. He repeated the process. They were now convinced the fireplace was movable and vigorously began looking for a key to unlock and move the stone apparatus.

"It's mechanical," declared Matt. "There's probably a lever or button located close by so he can get out quickly. Look around for anything in here that might serve as a knob or pedal. I'll check the desk."

It took under a minute for Matt to find a button located on the underside of the desktop in the center drawer of Vogel's desk. He pushed it and the two-hundred and forty-seven-pound hydraulic device quietly lifted out of the floor and swung open, revealing a set of stairs leading to an underground bunker.

It was totally dark. Sergeant O'Callaghan fumbled around on the wall until he located a small round switch. Matt gave him a nod and when he carefully turned the dial, a subtle light came on and unveiled a stairway descending at least seven meters. With weapons raised and ready, Matt and his troops proceeded cautiously into the unknown. There were no signs of activity.

When they reached the bottom of the stairs, O'Callaghan found a series of knobs, which he immediately turned, revealing a generously furnished circular antechamber suitable for twenty or more occupants. There were eleven doors in the lounge wall arranged in a semi-circle. Matt systematically opened each door, ten of which opened into spacious two-person bedrooms. The middle door led to a hallway with two doors on the right, one of which opened into a community shower room and several toilet stalls. The second door was locked. Across the hall on the left side was a complete kitchen, pantry, and large eating area.

Matt sent one of the soldiers back to Colonel Wright to request some equipment to dislodge the bolted door. Corporal Wilensky returned with two sledgehammers and handed one of the bludgeons to Private Crowe. The two soldiers then took turns battering the steel door until it unhinged and fell into a large lavish apartment, complete with sleeping quarters, an office, a private toilet, and bathing facilities. This obviously belonged to Nazi *Obergruppenführer* Hans Vogel.

After inspecting the space, the point man, Sergeant O'Callaghan, took a few steps beyond Vogel's suite and found another dial that, of course, he couldn't wait to turn. He, Matt and the entire squad were astonished at what they saw when a long line of sconces lit up. The dim lights revealed a corridor that stretched as far as the eye could see. For an instant, Matt was taken back to the entry to the *Daisy Compound* in Liège. That passageway was perhaps fifteen meters. This escape route was at least fifty meters.

Matt and his unit moved guardedly down the tunnel, looking for possible booby traps along the way. They found none. They did notice that the pathway floor rose gradually by perhaps ten centimeters per meter and as a result, the end of the tunnel proved to be four to five meters higher than the beginning. The steel reinforced concrete corridor ended suddenly at a ladder attached to the wall, which spanned three meters or so.

Sergeant O'Callaghan adroitly climbed the steps and once again found a round knob which he turned. The hallway went dark. He quickly turned the dial again, much to the relief of Matt and the squad. O'Callaghan also found a lever and pulled it, expecting the steel doors to open. He was right. The motorized doors swung open up into the heavy underbrush on top of a hill.

The men took turns scrambling up the ladder into the forest and fresh air. They looked back and could barely see the estate through the trees and vegetation. The rain of the past two days had also covered up any trace of activity.

Matt was at a dead end. Marie and Abby also struck out. Karla was again in the wind. All was not lost, however. They learned a great deal about *Die Kinderschule* and its staff, and their investigation revealed how Vogel brainwashed and groomed children of the former Nazi regime as acolytes for his looming Fourth Reich.

James and his exhausted companions returned to the Landespolizei headquarters just after 4:00 p.m. where they deposited their captives. After returning to the Benelux Hotel to shower and change into civilian clothes, he called Matt at the Kron and asked him to meet them at the police station so they could properly interrogate the prisoners.

Upon arriving at the Chief Inspector's office, Abby, Matt and Marie gave James, Rich and Duncan a lengthy account of their incursion into *The Children's School* and what they learned about the Neo-Nazi organization. Duncan returned the favor by giving an enthusiastic blow-by-blow description of their assault on the Werewolf compound in the Hürtgen Forest.

While the rag-tag group of former German soldiers and self-proclaimed Nazi followers had not yet actively engaged in any overt operations, their compound full of weapons and explosives clearly violated Allied occupation laws and made them subject to dispersal and arrest. Even though law enforcement in the area was aware of the Werewolf presence, until now no one had dared to challenge them, quite likely because of fear of recriminations from the Nazi faction.

The assassination of Aachen Mayor Franz Oppenhoff in March 1945 by Werewolves clearly still weighed heavily on the minds of local officials. Incredibly, it took two gunshots in a small Minnesota park to initiate any meaningful action against the growing Neo-Nazi army.

Each of the five captives was grilled in turn by James, Rich and Matt. The two foot soldiers were of little help. All they knew was that their numbers were growing and that a major operation was planned. The battle hardened *SS* squad leader would only give his name, Otto Beck; rank, *Oberscharführer;* and *SS* number, 109332.

Most of the interrogation centered on the two men who appeared to be the highest ranking captives, both former Captains in the Wehrmacht. They, like many other former German officers, were disillusioned by the harshness of the occupation, and proved to be easy converts to Vogel's crusade to establish a Fourth Reich. *Hauptsturmführers* Bauer and Kerch were as steadfast as Beck. They were resolute Neo-Nazi believers who divulged nothing to their interrogators. It was obvious, however, that they knew a great deal, and their arrogance spoke volumes. Something was happening soon, but where, when, and how big?

After a less than fruitful night of questioning, Matt and his companions released the prisoners to Lieutenant Colonel Wright for transport to Wiesbaden Army Base for incarceration and trial. While much had been learned in the past week about the conspiracy, specific details about the size, scope and complexity of the new Nazi organization were still unknown. Perhaps more troubling was the fact that Karla Hoffman had eluded them again, and Herr Vogel, or Walter, was still a ghost.

Strike three came when the battalion of Army forces reached the Werewolf base camp in the Hürtgen Forest. The camp was empty.

Chapter 26

The Ghost

Doctor Hans Vogel was a short, bespectacled man with essentially no sense of humor. Generally intolerant, he expected perfection from himself and everyone else. His military bearing was sharp, and his appearance was always impeccable. He demanded nothing less from his associates. Those who failed to live up to expectations were quickly expunged.

Born into a noble family in Klosterneuburg, Austria, the third son of Peter and Lina Vogel, Hans was recognized as a wunderkind as early as age four. Because he was such a prodigy, his parents had him examined and tested by a team of psychologists, who calculated the boy's IQ at somewhere between 192 and 204. By then he was reading and writing fluently and was engrossed in engineering and science textbooks by age seven. He couldn't attend regular schools and had to be tutored at home by professors from the University of Vienna. By the age of ten he was smarter than his teachers. He had a photographic memory and easily recited book passages by page number and paragraph when challenged. His intricate architectural renderings were regarded as brilliant by the time he was twelve.

Notwithstanding his intellectual ability and cleverness, Vogel's childhood was challenging. While his two older brothers were not mentally gifted, they were bigger and more physically imposing, and constantly teased and bullied him. His mother and father were of little help. As a result, he became a loner and found creative ways to avoid contact with his parents and siblings as much as possible until he was sent to the newly opened elite *Schule Schloss Boarding School* in the southern German city of Salem. It was there at age thirteen that he was introduced to the serenity and sanctuary of Lake Constance. A place he would return to throughout his life.

By his late teens, Hans Vogel was well aware that he was always the smartest person in the room, and his egotism was a problem. He had few friends...but many followers because of his scholarly prowess. His classmates disliked his arrogance, but he curried their favor by tutoring them in engineering, natural sciences and English. He quickly learned how to control people and command his environment and became so skilled at manipulation that he was elected school president in his last year at the school.

Vogel's experience at *Schule Schloss Salem* taught him that his ultimate success in life depended on more than his visible intellectual skills and raw ability to exploit people. By his late teens, he realized he needed to be more diplomatic and display his brainpower strategically in order to effectively influence people to do his bidding over a long term. He honed his political acumen as he pursued his undergraduate degree in both engineering and psychology at the University of Paris.

At age eighteen, Vogel returned to the University of Vienna, where he earned Doctorates in both engineering and mathematics. He also began his steadfast interest in the evolving Nazi Party and its fundamental theme of creating a master Aryan race to dominate the world. Vogel watched from afar as Adolph Hitler exploited the public through the 1920s, while the budding mastermind was establishing himself as a thriving entrepreneur in the field of engineering. It was through his business that a chance encounter with an undistinguished tool maker changed the course of his life.

On October 25, 1928, while managing the construction of an iron and steel mill, Hans Vogel met Karl Rahm, who was born on the same day in the same hospital as Vogel. Although Rahm came from a working-class Viennese family, he was brash and cynical, which intrigued Vogel. He cautiously engaged Rahm and within a few weeks the meticulous and erudite Vogel and the complex and volatile Rahm formed an unlikely friendship that lasted until the end of 1945. Rahm prompted Vogel into joining the Austrian National Socialist German Workers Party and introduced him to Austrian *SS* leadership.

It took little time for Ernst Kaltenbrunner to embrace Hans Vogel. Kaltenbrunner, the top official in the underground Austrian *SS*, possessed a doctorate in Law, and was at least in Vogel's intellectual range. By late 1933, the eminent Nazi legal consultant was actively working with Adolph Hitler and Heinrich Himmler to plan for the annexation of Austria into the Third Reich. Kaltenbrunner introduced Vogel to Himmler during one of his sessions in early 1935.

Himmler took an immediate liking to Hans Vogel, perhaps because of the striking resemblance between the two men. Himmler was seven years older and four inches taller, but facially and physically they looked as if they could be brothers. Both men had childhood issues though, but for different reasons.

The *Reichsführer-SS* came from a stable middle class family and was treated well, but always craved more attention and praise than his mother or father gave him. He, like Vogel, was clumsy and athletically pathetic. Unlike Vogel, however, Himmler was not a good all-around student. His passion was history and religion, where he excelled. Perhaps the traits that especially wove them together were their extreme detail orientation, pursuit of perfection, and brazen ambition.

Although Heinrich Himmler was somewhat anti-Semitic before joining the Nazi Party, his original strategy for growing the master race was to segregate the superior Aryans from Jews and other sub-races through regulation. His position gradually progressed through the strong demands of Adolph Hitler and his deep-seated need for personal approval. After a few meetings with the *Reichsführer-SS*, Vogel recognized Himmler's enduring need for achievement and praise, and found simple ways to parlay that understanding into advice that could enhance Himmler's status in the Reich.

Almost from the time they met, Himmler implored Vogel to join the military and become his personal aide in Berlin. He did so immediately after Germany's annexation of Austria and Hitler's fiery speech in front of the Hofburg Palace in Vienna on March 15, 1938. Doctor Hans Vogel, now at the seat of power, began to formulate his covert plan for succeeding Adolph Hitler.

While Vogel believed strongly in Germanic domination of the European continent, he found Adolph Hitler's master plan to be too ambitious, and his behavior too crude and erratic. As the leader of the Reich, Vogel's approach would be more cerebral and calculated. He would strike hard and fast with advanced technological and chemical weapons to break the will of the former Allied powers, then outsmart the rest of the continent and take control through economic and social programs. Prolonged war and sheer power would only be used as a last resort. Initially, however, as a key aide to Himmler, Vogel held his tongue.

Hitler recognized Vogel's intelligence and commended Himmler for his discovery of such great Austrian talent. Increasingly, Vogel became a fixture in Berlin as part of the advisory group to the *Führer* and experienced a meteoric rise in military grade until he reached the four-star rank of *Obergruppenführer* in 1942. While initially enamored by Hitler, Vogel became increasingly frustrated and exasperated at the *Führer*'s habit of berating anyone who disagreed with him, as well as his imprudent decision-making.

Vogel advised the *Führer* to conclude a non-aggression pact with Stalin, which he did in 1939, only to violate the agreement and attack the Soviet Union less than a year later. He thought it foolish to establish a second front against a tyrannical leader with almost unlimited manpower and complete lack of regard for his own soldiers' lives. He also advised Hitler not to declare war on the United States after the Japanese attack on Pearl Harbor, reasoning that Germany could not successfully compete with America's industrial might.

One recommendation that the *Führer* did embrace, however, was the concept that the supreme leader should establish a succession plan if he intended the Third Reich to last a thousand years. He convinced Hitler that he could ensure his legacy by fashioning future governments in his own image. In less than six months Adolph Hitler did indeed select his successor government. The problem was that Hans Vogel was not chosen as the future *Führer*. That prize went to *SS-Oberst-Gruppenführer* Karl Hoffman, a stately, confident military hero who Vogel detested.

Hans Vogel was raised in an intensely anti-Semitic country but agreed with Himmler that segregation was preferable to liquidation. He supported the relocation of Jews to less desirable locations, which he believed would be supported by most of the world. However, he thought they should be allowed to own property and conduct commerce within their isolated society. He advised the *Führer* accordingly, but was strongly rebuffed. He warned Hitler that a Holocaust would become a major rallying point for the Allies if they were to learn of mass exterminations of Jews.

Not long after his promotion to *Obergruppenführer*, Vogel began to speak his mind more freely, particularly to Heinrich Himmler. He criticized Hitler's meddling in military operations and general distrust in his generals in the field, and expressed that the *Führer* relied too much on his own instincts and personal whims. His frustrations erupted in early 1943 in a strategy meeting at Berchtesgaden when he aired complaints about the lack of preparedness for the resistance movement, poor use of intelligence, the complexity of many operational plans, and too much micromanagement from the top. Vogel was banished from Himmler's staff within a week and sent to work with Albert Speer in the Reich Department of Armaments and War Production.

The demotion proved to be a strategic victory for *Obergruppenführer* Vogel. He was back in his element as a chief architect and engineer in charge of bunker construction throughout the Third Reich. He now had command of the manpower to build his own empire and the status to move about freely without supervision. As long as Speer's projects were accomplished, no one challenged Vogel's activities.

Chapter 27

The Conspiracy

Ironically, the first engineering assignment given to the discredited Hans Vogel was the design and construction of the *Daisy Compound*. He was tasked with finding a secluded and impregnable location for the Successor Government's operational headquarters and personally supervise its construction. His experience with the project essentially became a blueprint for his personal empire building over the next decade. One that he used very effectively.

Vogel reasoned that the Allies would concentrate their search activities in remote locations like forested areas or caves, or perhaps even in urban factories. He preferred to build secure bunkers in plain sight and disguise them with legitimate activities like schools, hospitals, or libraries. He also favored locations on or near bodies of water when possible because ingress and egress would be convenient, unassuming and inconspicuous.

The large acreage on the east bank of the Meuse River in Liège offered the perfect location for the *Daisy Compound*. In spite of Hitler's banishment of Vogel from his post in the Reich Chancellery, Hitler was quite pleased with the engineer's choice of a private school for *SS* children as a shield for the future Nazi leaders' headquarters. The design and efficient construction of the bunker reflected positively on Albert Speer, enhancing Vogel's standing in the Department of Armaments.

Having designed and built the bunker, the discontented four-star general knew the vulnerable areas where strategically placed explosives could effectively obliterate the underground structure and school while largely preserving the dormitory. The surviving three or four hundred children would become his minions and would form a clandestine army of intelligence agents, business operators, soldiers and assassins.

Concurrent with his work on the *Daisy Compound*, Vogel secretly acquired the abandoned estate in the Aachen Forest with funds appropriated from Jews and other German detainees scheduled to be sent to concentration camps. In return, he had them assigned to his construction crews where he treated them with compassion. They responded by working industriously on his soon-to-be headquarters and school for the unfortunates. His strategy worked very well. When they were no longer needed, he had them sent to the death camps.

Once the aspiring *Führer's* headquarters and *Children's School* were completed, he turned his attention to the area around the venerated Lake Constance for his major communications center. He split his time between his Konstanz project and construction of the **La Coupole** V-2 rocket complex in the forested area near Saint-Omer in northern France. During this time he recruited a dozen or so carefully selected *SS* and Wehrmacht officers and men and stationed them in his new communications base. He had them listed as killed in action on official records. These men thereby became his first faithful aides.

In early 1944, Hans Vogel concluded that time was running out for the Third Reich as it was presently constituted, and that he had to be more efficient in implementing his long term plan for a revitalized German Empire. Cleverly, while he was supervising work on the massive **B8 Bergkristall** Messerschmitt jet fighter complex near St. Georgen an der Gusen in northern Austria, he began working on his own secret bunker project.

The emboldened Nazi officer discretely diverted slave labor from the nearby Mauthausen concentration camp to work on his massive underground Technology, Weapons and Science facility, accessible from the Danube River. Vogel took mostly Polish, Hungarian and Soviet internees from Mauthausen sub-camps to do the manual labor on the secret project and groomed the more erudite Jewish and Italian prisoners from the main Mauthausen facility for intellectual activities. Surprisingly, he was able to find several highly trained and skilled mechanical and electrical engineers, chemists, scientists and mathematicians to help organize and manage the construction of his fortress. He was even able to secure an aerospace engineer who had worked with the preeminent German rocketry and jet propulsion engineer Wernher von Braun.

Once again, Vogel was civil to his conscripts, which improved both efficiency and productivity. He shared his vision for the future with a select number of the most talented and pliable thinkers, most of whom eventually joined his developing Neo-Nazi operation. The shrewd leader cared more about intelligence and commitment than race or ethnicity so some of his new aides were even Jewish. He quietly disposed of those elites who he deemed to be untrustworthy, as well as common laborers when they were no longer needed, explaining that they had been transferred to additional critical projects. While hundreds of thousands of prisoners died working on other Nazi projects, he fed his menials well, only worked them on ten hour shifts, and actually paid them a token wage, perpetuating the ruse that he was charitable and fair. He confiscated their cash and valuables when they were sent to the gas.

While the **B8 Bergkristall** underground factory nineteen kilometers away was discovered and heavily bombed by the Allies in late 1944 and 1945, Vogel's underground weapons site was overlooked and, after nearly a year-long hiatus, resumed its work throughout the next decade. The occupation forces were too fixated on the Mauthausen and Gusen concentration camps to notice the cavernous construction project on the nearby banks of the Danube River.

As the war was coming to an end in the late spring of 1945, Vogel slipped away from the jet factory project, discarded his military uniform, changed his name, and assumed the role of innocuous headmaster of *The Children's School* in Aachen. Before he disappeared, however, he had one more mission to accomplish...procuring gold, diamonds, and other precious jewels from the Reichsbank's hidden Nazi stash in Merkers, Germany. In late March, barely a week before General Patton's Third Army took the town, he and his band of recruits raided the potassium mine and escaped with over nine hundred and eighty million American dollars of gold and marketable assets.

Headmaster Hans Walter spent the next seven years patiently creating the image of a hard-working, intelligent and charitable educator in both Aachen and Konstanz as his young malleable charges in both *Children's Schools* matured into instruments of his Neo-Nazi realm. At the same time, he and three of his converted lieutenants began probing for former *SS* and Wehrmacht soldiers eager to revive the German Reich. Predictably, finding unhappy former military men and women was an easy task, mostly because of the wrath foisted upon them by German citizens for losing the war and causing the complete annihilation of the homeland.

Political upheaval, tension in Allied governance, and the general chaos of rebuilding the German infrastructure and economy during the late 1940s provided the ideal environment for the former *SS-Obergruppenführer* to create and expand his conspiracy to restore German dominance. During these years, Walter funded the growth of the Werewolf movement so he would have a terrorist element to intimidate reticent government officials into supporting his power grab. He also cleverly assembled a classic military organization of over fifty thousand former soldiers and young devotees to occupy and police the subjugated countries after the takeover.

At the same time, the self-appointed Neo-Nazi *Führer* meticulously researched, selected and indoctrinated talented Austrians and Germans for his new administration. Some of these individuals were already in place as government or law enforcement officials and were able to identify others sympathetic to the cause. Many of these chosen elites were housed in the Konstanz area, awaiting the assumption of power. In addition, he stockpiled hundreds of Nazi believers in target countries to join the movement, and groomed them to activate, organize, structure and fill the power vacuum in their national and province governments when the *tour de force* occurred.

The primary logistical issue during the veiled development period was providing employment for those men and women who would eventually produce validation and political advocacy for the new Reich. He addressed the problem by resurrecting old service establishments or creating new ones throughout western Europe, the first of which was *Voyages Internationaux Français.*

In addition to his children's schools, other insulating enterprises included an array of renewed hospitals and bistros, a leather works, a furniture and accessory factory, a clothing manufacturer, and perhaps most importantly, a construction company. Some of these enterprises had underground fortresses that acted as bureaus for conducting official Neo-Nazi business. The ultimate irony was that through a mind-blowing twist of fate, the alias Hans Walter was cunning enough to arrange for many of his new enterprises to be funded by the fifteen billion dollar Marshall Plan enacted by the United States in 1948.

By 1952, the smoldering Fourth Reich had a solid footing in Germany, Belgium, The Netherlands, Luxembourg and France. Walter had built a complete underground economy, a functioning communications network, a vigorous army, and a ready-made government network for his new sovereignty. The only missing component was a stockpile of reengineered V2 rockets with intercontinental range, adequate nuclear warheads, and a reservoir of deadly Sarin gas.

The now de facto *Führer* of the Fourth Reich set the Phase One start date for his European coup for mid 1953. By then his young crew from the *Daisy Compound* were mature enough to carry out their information, supply and assassination assignments. He planted the seed of retribution in the minds of these neophytes by repeatedly harping on the murder of their parents and massacre of innocent German citizens by Allied forces during the war.

Walter continually stressed that the destruction of the Homeland had been fueled by intelligence operatives like the British *Special Operations Executive*, the American *Office of Strategic Services*, and the joint American/British/French *Special Services Unit*. He also decreed that Allied government and agency leaders needed to be systematically eliminated. In short, he instilled a strong personal hatred in each of his charges...especially his star pupil, Karla Hoffman.

Phase Two of the campaign would begin after all or most of the World War II leaders and operatives had been executed, which he calculated would take more than a year. Vogel reasoned that it would likely take that long to complete his weapons repository and missile launching sites. By quietly emasculating the former intelligence community, he anticipated that his target countries and world leaders would be in a state of confusion, eliminating any effective response to his assumption of power.

Hans Vogel, aka Hans Walter, while skillful and clever, became more delusional as his empire developed. Over time, he became more convinced of his mental superiority and considered himself to be the smartest person in the world, even more brilliant than the expatriated eminent German-born physicist, Albert Einstein. By 1953, he was so deluded that he was sure there was no problem he couldn't solve. Afterall, he had continually demonstrated his genius during and after the war.

Hadn't he correctly calculated the course of the war and warned the paranoid Dictator about his obvious mistakes? Didn't he manipulate the ambitious and vain Albert Speer into giving him unrestrained freedom to divert labor for his own cause? Hadn't he ingeniously outwitted both German and Allied forces to snatch a billion dollars of gold and jewels from under their noses? Finally, hadn't he deftly built a new regime without detection? In a few months, he was set to unleash **Operation Destiny**, his fury on his WWII enemies, and realize his birthright as savior of The German Empire.

Vogel's plan was simple. His domain would span the bulk of countries on the European continent and the oil rich countries of North Africa. From Sweden, Norway, Denmark and Finland on the north, to Ireland and the United Kingdom, Spain and Portugal on the west, to Egypt and Saudi Arabia in North Africa on the south, and Turkey and the Baltic countries to the border of the Soviet Union on the east.

The repatriated *Führer* would begin his takeover and send an authoritative message to the world on the symbolic date of December 7, 1954 by launching his newly readied intercontinental V-3 rockets filled with Sarin gas warheads on America's capital, Washington D.C., and its center of commerce, New York. At the same time, he would hurl V-3 rockets east, armed with nuclear warheads, to completely expunge the Soviet capital, Moscow, as well as the old imperial capital, St. Petersburg. He would immediately warn the United States that he had no plans to inflict further damage on the country unless America attempted to interfere in European affairs. Any retaliatory action would result in numerous lethal chemical and nuclear attacks. In his mind, this would completely neutralize the United States.

Once the Soviet government was eliminated, Hans Walter, now openly reverting to Hans Vogel, would assure those attempting to assume power in Russia that he had no territorial designs on their country. He would faithfully pledge to live in peace with them unless the new leaders took aggressive action against his Fourth Reich. He would warn them that any retaliation would result in more devastation to the Soviet people.

Vogel did not judge China or Japan to be credible threats against his new regime, and would simply inform them of his assumption of power over the continent. His relations with them would be cordial and cooperative.

Simultaneous with the missile attacks, the new *Führer* planned to activate his previously appointed government officials to peacefully assume power in the subsumed countries, promising prosperity and equitable treatment for all subjugates. He would also dispatch an armored brigade of fifteen-hundred to two-thousand men to facilitate the takeover of power in each country. The troops would stay on to instruct leaders and provide supervision for each country's military and police forces as they transitioned into the Reich's organizational structure.

Vogel calculated that once the world saw his military capabilities, there would be no need for overt intimidation or a conventional ground war, although resistance leaders would be swiftly punished. He believed that his benevolence to the cooperative citizens of each country would mute any resistance activity and turn most of the population into faithful Reich adherents in a short period of time.

Within a year or two, his colonized governments would explain that particular classes of people were to be civilly resettled to some eastern bloc countries according to race, religion and spoken language. In return for their cooperation, the displaced would be fairly compensated and be allowed to take all of their belongings. Further, the new German Empire would allow them to work freely and own and operate businesses in order to contribute to the Reich economy. The relocated would be assured that there would be no concentration camps or corporal punishment for loyal citizens.

The implacable *Führer* envisioned that within five years the Fourth Reich would be thriving politically, socially and financially and his sovereignty would be assured. There were three critical flaws in his scheme, however.

First, Vogel severely miscalculated the motivation and temperament of his band of co-conspirators. He didn't understand that they were mostly disenfranchised fringe elements of German society before the war and had personal, economic and power motives for joining the insurgence. Many were outrageously cruel to Jews and the common citizens of occupied countries during the war, and he didn't comprehend that he would not be able to control their behavior in the future.

Second, Vogel wildly underestimated the missile defense systems of the U.S. and Russia, who had been preparing for possible attacks by each other. He was completely unaware that they could intercept and destroy his rockets long before they reached their targets.

Finally, the would-be *Führer's* illusion that he could be an admired benevolent Dictator demonstrated a complete lack of understanding of himself. Hans Vogel, while mentally gifted, quick-witted and resourceful, failed to have insight into his own personality. He was stiff by nature and somewhat inconsistent in his behavior. He was generally composed and placid, and especially kind to disadvantaged or bullied children. He was a genial manipulator rather than a browbeater, and at the same time uncompromising and inconspicuously ruthless, quietly eliminating those who were no longer useful to him or the conspiracy. Being amiable and consistent were not natural for him; rather they were a tactic to attract and retain followers.

Objective observers had to wonder if the Machiavellian Hans Vogel's illusory kingdom was ever to be.

Chapter 28

The Reveal

"Hello, sir, we have a person-to-person telephone call for you from a General Stuart Menzies in London. Do you wish me to put the call through?" asked the hotel's cautious switchboard operator.

"Yes, I'll accept the call," responded Matt groggily.

"I know it's early, Matt," blurted out the General, "but we've gathered some good information from the travel agency staff and the ICPC that seems quite urgent."

"That's okay, General. It's almost 7:00 a.m. here. Remember, it's an hour later here than in London. What do you...?"

"It appears that this Herr Walter you wired about yesterday is really a Doctor Hans Vogel, a high level former Nazi SS officer who disappeared from the jet plane factory in upper Austria in March 1945. He had been presumed dead. One of the employees of the travel agency, a scared young French woman named Ruby LeMaire, confessed that she was working for the Nazi underground. She believes that this Vogel chap is the likely leader of a sizeable army planning to retake Germany from the Russia and the western Allies. Apparently soon. Karla Hoffman is one of his assassins."

"How about the ICPC, General?" asked Matt.

"Undersecretary Manfred Emery did some research last night and discovered that Hans Walter is a principal owner in several businesses in Germany, Austria, France, Belgium and Italy. Four of these enterprises are schools. If, in fact, Walter and Vogel are one and the same, we have something. I'll wire the complete ICPC report to you immediately."

"That will help a great deal and give us a good place to start tracking him down," replied Matt sharply. "I'll get everybody together in the next hour or so and we'll work on a search strategy."

"Cheerio, old boy. Keep up the good work and let me know what else you need."

Wednesday, August 25, 1954 was scribbled on the chalkboard in the Benelux Hotel lecture room, and the clock on the wall read 8:02 a.m. as the resolute crew filed into the room to regroup and brainstorm about how to proceed in their search for Vogel and his co-conspirators. They had been so close, yet failed again to apprehend the elusive Karla Hoffman and her controller, former *SS-Obergruppenführer* Vogel.

"Good news, folks," began James. "We're now almost certain that Hans Vogel and Hans Walter are the same person. He has his hands in several ventures in four or five countries. We'll need to engage some help to visit these enterprises and see what they know about this supposed ghost. He was reportedly killed at the end of the war, but apparently has risen from the dead."

Matt jumped in. "I'm particularly interested in the four children's schools among his endeavors; two in Germany, one in Austria and one in England."

"I know where I'd go if my headquarters had been compromised," declared Abby. "Another one of those schools. I'll bet he has bunkers in each of those places, don't you think?"

"Probably," reacted James, "As a matter of fact, the ICPC report we just received indicates that Vogel was born and raised in Vienna, and was later schooled in Salem, Germany on the north side of Lake Constance. One of the children's schools is on the south shore of the lake, and another is in Vienna. They look like a good place to start."

"What about Karla Hoffman?" asked Marie. "She seems to be closely tied to Vogel."

"I suspect she's headed there too," responded Matt.

"Okay...Matt, why don't you and Marie partner with some Bundespolizei and see if you can track Karla Hoffman to the *Children's School* in Konstanz?" James requested.

"Duncan and Abby, how about contacting the Bundespolizei in Vienna and have them help you check out the school in Donaustadt? I'll go back to London and get General Menzies and Hugh Kensie to help me take a look at the *Children's School* in Lambeth."

"We should also engage federal police forces in the other countries to help investigate the legitimacy of the business ventures in each one while we take a look at the other two schools. Rich, as a policeman, you're probably the best person to coordinate the investigation of the other businesses. Are you okay with that?"

"That's reasonable, James," replied Rich. "I'll go to Bonn and meet with the American Occupation High Commissioner, Dr. Conant, and have him provide introductions to the federal police in Germany, Belgium, France, and Italy. General Sinclair knew him during the war and speaks very highly of his intellect and forceful nature."

"Good," responded James. "Before we go looking for Vogel, however, we need to revisit some key questions and see what we actually know about the intent and scope of the conspiracy. How big is his organization? What is he really trying to accomplish? Is he trying to retake Germany, or does he have a more ambitious plan? What kind of weapons does he have? How is the organization financed? Indications are that he's already begun his campaign by targeting former *SOE, SSU, OSS* agents and other former military leaders. Why? How will that further his plan?"

The veteran group of trackers spent almost three hours assessing what they knew and reasoning their way through the conspiracy. They determined that the plan was wider than simply regaining control of Germany. It made no sense that Vogel would establish business ventures in several other countries or try to eliminate former military and intelligence agents or current leaders outside Germany unless he had a more sweeping objective. They concluded that he was well funded, had a large following, and probably had advanced weapons. They left the room realizing that their task was monumental, and while there was a measure of urgency in their pursuit, they couldn't know that they had less than a week to prevent a worldwide apocalypse.

Upon learning that his Kron Hotel communications hub had been compromised, the fuming Hans Vogel decided to rush to Konstanz and meet with members of his government-in-waiting and communications staff in the underground complex below the school. He summoned his driver and hurriedly exited the Aachen children's school on his way to his major command center on the Swiss border. The six and a half hour drive gave the unyielding antagonist time to revise the timetable for launching his rockets on the U.S. and the Soviet Union and initiating government takeovers in the target countries. He, of course, would first travel to the weapons repository and missile complex in Austria to supervise the launch of his rockets, then proceed swiftly to Berlin to assume power.

Operation Destiny would have to be advanced from December 7 to the historic date of September 1, the day the courageous German military overwhelmed Poland and began to exact retribution on the Allies for the humiliating Treaty of Versailles that ended World War I.

The intrepid Karla Hoffman had a nagging feeling that she was being followed from the Hauphtbahnof Train Station and, upon arriving at the school, hastily alerted her counterparts that she suspected an impending raid on the complex. She and four of her *Daisy Compound* contemporaries briskly gathered their belongings, weapons and papers and scurried down the escape tunnel into the Aachen Forest, and headed to a safe house less than ten kilometers away.

Having anticipated the possibility of a raid on the school at some point, Vogel established three small farms as sanctuaries along the Hühnertalweg south of the compound. These twenty hectare adjoining properties produced wheat, barley and sugar beets, and were registered to and operated by some of the more restrained Daisy and Konstanz school graduates. They had hidden stores of food, clothing, weapons and escape vehicles for use by fleeing operatives.

During her journey from London to Aachen, Karla carefully reviewed the files stolen from Patrick Kendall's office at MI6, giving her more insight into **Operation Destiny**. The report contained a warning regarding a growing restlessness among former German military officers and men, and speculated that there was a developing plan to create a Fourth Reich. Kendall suspected that the emerging organization was being led by a former unidentified *SS* officer. He was tracing the whereabouts of several possible leaders of the conspiracy...including a supposedly deceased *SS-Obergruppenführer* Hans Vogel, when he went missing almost a year ago.

One page of the Kendall report unnerved the female assassin. The deceased *SSU* agent turned MI6 spy opined that the *Daisy Compound* explosion was orchestrated by *SS* officers and government officials unhappy with Adolph Hitler and his choices to succeed him. Major Kane had also voiced that fact at MI6 Headquarters and said he could prove it. She dismissed the claim at the time as American propaganda and escaped before her captor had a chance to produce the evidence.

Karla and her companions reached the sugar beet farm after a three hour hike through the hilly forest. They sheltered at the farm overnight, supplied themselves with food and additional clothing, and headed south to Konstanz in a 1952 Volkswagen Transporter Camper. Now becoming more paranoid, the group of fugitives took a circuitous route of back roads toward Konstanz.

While the three male and two female killers were familiar with Konstanz and *The Children's School*, they were completely unaware of the how vast and safeguarded the communications complex and command center was beneath the school. Karla's instincts told her that Vogel would take refuge there if the Aachen school was compromised. She had questions, and she needed to find him for answers.

The plainclothes guards at the gate of the school were reluctant to admit the non-credentialed group of five, citing the need to protect the disabled children. Karla carefully explained who they were and why they had fled the Aachen compound. They had urgent business with Herr Walter. When the two former *SS* enlisted men again refused to let them into the compound, Karla and her counterparts slowly raised their **Walther P.38** semi-automatic pistols in unison, pointed them at the men, and forcefully demanded entrance to the facility. The two sentinels quickly agreed to call headquarters for instructions.

Herr Walter had been at the compound, but left on Monday. His second in command, former *SS-Oberführer* Gerhard Brunner, verified the operatives and instructed the guards to admit them to the grounds. They were told to report directly to him in his office inside the school. Brunner was aware of the activities at *Die Kinderschule* in Aachen and informed the operatives that the timetable for the transformation had been moved up. He advised them to remain in the Konstanz residence bunker and await instructions from Vogel. An ill-fated strategic decision.

❖ ❖ ❖

Still somewhat suspicious of the German Federal Police, Matt placed a call to the Wiesbaden Army Garrison and again requested the support of U.S. forces. He knew they were a day or two behind Karla if she had fled to the southwest city on Lake Constance and needed to make up some of the time gap. He asked for a helicopter to transport him and Marie to Konstanz, along with a squad of Rangers. Within two hours, a newly commissioned Sikorsky CH-34 chopper landed on a strip of land just off Hanbrucher Weg not far from police headquarters.

Due to the limited cruising range of the CH-34, the trackers had to make two refueling stops before proceeding to Konstanz; one in Wiesbaden and a second at the Stuttgart Army Airfield, roughly one-hundred and fifty kilometers from their destination. As a result, the total travel time from Aachen to Konstanz was just over an anxious four hours. Matt was surprised that they were met by four Bundespolizei with a truck to transport them to *The Children's School*.

While James was aware that Matt was wary of the German Federal police, he knew they couldn't operate in the country without their assistance. Consequently, he contacted the Headquarters Division Chief in Potsdam, briefed him on the impending crisis, and requested assistance and cooperation with Occupation forces. The Brigadegeneral was most obliging and pledged support wherever needed in Germany and Austria. Matt promptly found out how valuable his new companions were.

For the second time in two days, the sentries at the gate of Konstanz school were presented with an unmanageable dilemma. They again tried to deny entry to unknown visitors, but were quickly coerced by the German Federal Police into admitting the group to the campus. They were prohibited from alerting the school to the presence of outsiders. One policeman and one Ranger remained at the gate to monitor the guards.

Matt, Marie, Captain Kenneth Anderson, and the German police sergeant entered the main building of the school in search of Headmaster Walter. The reception staff was irritated by the intrusion and demanded that the trespassers leave. Once again, the police staff sergeant exercised his authority and demanded to see the Headmaster. After being informed that Herr Doctor Walter was not at the school, he ordered all administrative staff to report immediately for questioning. The first person to arrive was the Assistant Headmaster, Rona Strobl. A middle-aged former Wehrmacht officer, she was not easily intimidated, and instructed her staff not to obey the intruder's instructions, whereupon Captain Anderson radioed for his squad of men to enter the facility. Panic now ensued.

Strobl became physically abusive to the sergeant and had to be forcibly restrained. The staff began to scatter, turning the inquiry into a military sweep of the school and grounds. As matrons and teachers fled, children screamed in terror and the ambulatory ones ran in all directions. Bedlam ensued. Several wheelchair-bound children were knocked over and the mentally challenged ones attempted to attack the Rangers and German policemen. As the melee ensued, a cadre of armed school guards appeared out of nowhere and shots rang out. It was now a full-fledged firefight.

During the confusion, a vigilant matron alerted Herr Brunner that a breach was taking place. Brunner at once locked down the underground complex to prevent any penetration. He assembled and armed the telecommunications personnel and prepared for an armed confrontation if the compound entrance was detected.

The conflict lasted less than fifteen minutes, but resulted in the death of eleven compound guards, one Ranger, one police officer, four teachers, Rona Strobl, and one eight-year-old girl who swallowed her tongue during an epileptic seizure. It took nearly two hours to restore order. Marie was shaken by the ordeal, but the confrontation confirmed that the school was again a cover for the conspiracy. Matt and company were sure there was an underground bunker, and their next task was to search for an entrance to the fortification.

Hearing the gunfire from above and observing the frenzied activity coming from the communications center, Karla and companions were once again on the run. They decided to exit the compound rather than engage in open warfare with an unknown number of aggressors. They calmly collected their belongings and weapons and went looking for the escape tunnel, not knowing where they were going. The resourceful female suspected that the escape route would be by water, so she guided her team toward the Lake. As they searched for the passageway, however, they passed by at least two dozen offices full of files and drawers. Another fortuitous occurrence for her.

Chapter 29

The Unraveling

The chaos created by the raid on the Konstanz school and compound provided a perfect opportunity for the resolute Karla Hoffman and her comrades to rifle through the offices of the new government leaders looking for clues that would indicate where Vogel had gone. In their haste to leave, Vogel's assistant inadvertently left his cabinet and desk keys sitting on a chair by the door. One of Karla's partners found the keys, unlocked his desk drawer and several cabinets and began to examine each folder. He made a stunning discovery. He found complete files outlining every facet of **Operation Destiny**, the campaign to resurrect the German Empire. While it was a monumental find, it was another folder that captured Karla's attention. She was astonished at what she read in the file entitled *Kinderarmee.*

"Can this really be true?" the young woman growled. "I must find him and get answers."

Marie again wanted to attend to the children after the hostilities, but knew their priority was to find Vogel and his young protégé. In any event, the German police sergeant called for reinforcements during the armed conflict, and also requested several female officers to help take care of the terrified students.

"Matt, we know there's a bunker below and an escape tunnel out of the fortress," Marie stated emphatically. "I'm betting it's by water just like the *Daisy Compound.* Why don't you look for the upstairs access while I take a couple of Rangers and see if I can find the lake entrance?"

"Okay," responded Matt, "but you need to be careful. They'll be a lot of desperate people trying to get out and they'll be armed. You stay out of harm's way and let the Rangers do the fighting if it comes to that."

Marie countered with a mischievous smile. "Don't worry about me...at least I know how to duck!"

"Very funny," Matt replied in mock shame.

His previous experience in Aachen led Matt straight to the Headmaster's office. Sure enough, there was a fireplace, but it was immoveable. He and his complement of Rangers advanced methodically throughout the administrative building probing cabinets, shelves, doors, furniture or anything else that might conceal a secret entrance. Nothing. After a brief moment of reflection, it occurred to the erstwhile intelligence officer that the entrance might actually be in the classroom building or staff living quarters.

Matt reasoned that any hidden entrance would be in a lightly trafficked area, so they began the search at the back of the school building. His eye immediately came to the janitorial closet at the end of the hallway, which was locked. One of the Rangers simply kicked it in. Matt knew immediately where to look. The large structure that contained the cleaning supplies. He vigorously shook the steel shelf and it moved slightly but did not dislodge so he began looking for a lever or button that would activate a mechanical device. After a brief scan of the small room, he located a large bolt on the floor just below the sink that looked out of place. He carefully touched it with his foot and decided that it was a step-switch.

Anticipating that the cabinet would move and reveal a stairway, the group of hunters prepared for another confrontation. Matt carefully stepped on the floor switch and indeed the cabinet quietly opened to unveil nothing but a blank wall with no visible seams. Matt banged on the wall in frustration. It was made of steel. He was sure they had found the entrance and now they had to figure out how it worked.

Matt, addressing no one in particular, mused, "Is this just a sham to deceive intruders, or is this a clever construction feat by Vogel's engineers? Why a steel wall if there's nothing to hide?"

"Sir," responded Captain Anderson. "If he went to all this trouble to disguise an entrance, there's certainly something big down there...*if* there's really an underground facility."

"I assure you there's a bunker, Captain," retorted a determined former Major Kane.

"We're missing something. It just doesn't feel right. Get me something to stand on," he commanded. "I want to see what it looks like where the wall meets the ceiling."

One of the Rangers produced a chair that allowed Matt to get a look at the ceiling joint. Sure enough, he spotted an almost imperceptible crease that ran across the length of the ceiling and down each side wall. The entire structure was definitely mobile.

Whoever designed this was a genius, Matt thought. Then he remembered what he read in the dossier on Hans Vogel. He was an architectural and engineering savant. *Now we just need to find the toggle that opens the mechanical marvel.*

"Okay, guys...this thing moves. Where would you put the device that opens it?"

"Sir, I would want it close to the foot pedal for convenience," offered one of the Rangers. "If you were in a hurry, you wouldn't want to waste time getting out, right?"

"Okay, let's look around the floor close to the sink."

Another Ranger kneeled down and began probing the wall and floor and saw nothing unusual. When he started to get back up, however, he hit his head on the bottom of the sink and instinctively looked up. There they were. Two neatly hidden knobs attached to the sink.

"I think I found something, Major Kane," the Ranger uttered in embarrassment as he rubbed his head.

Matt kneeled down and confirmed the finding. Now they were ready to breach the bunker. The group again prepared for a confrontation as Matt pulled the handles attached to the sink. The wall silently slid straight up into the ceiling revealing a three-meter-wide opening and stairway. As Captain Anderson cautiously moved to the entrance, a hail of gunfire rang out from below causing Matt, the police sergeant and Rangers to recoil.

The resourceful German police sergeant casually collected himself and threw a tear gas canister down the stairway. While tear gas had been banned for use in World War II, it was a legitimate tool of civilian police to control riots or potential acts of terror. Within a minute or so, the bullets stopped and the communications staff in the bunker began to gag and cough.

"We surrender... we surrender...do not shoot," came cries from below in terrified German.

"Drop your guns, raise your hands, and come up the stairs," yelled Matt in a commanding German response.

Following Matt's instructions, more than two dozen dazed and groggy men and women dropped their weapons and filed up the stairs rubbing their eyes, coughing and sputtering. Their leader, Gerhard Brunner, bolted to the escape tunnel.

Once the communications personnel were subdued and treated by a school nurse, Matt and his companions entered the hidden command bunker. It was massive and elaborate, with state-of-the art technology beyond anything he ever imagined. This worried him. It would take time to interrogate all the upstairs and below ground staff. Time he didn't have.

Marie and her Rangers arrived at the north bank of Lake Constance just in time to see Karla and other young men and women board a World War II era German VP-Boat and speed off toward the northeast side of the lake. She quickly radioed Matt.

"Karla's on a boat headed toward a town on the other side of the lake. According to the map, it's probably the town of Meersburg. Can we alert somebody over there to grab them when they land?"

"It's going to be awhile before we get any information from the people we snagged here," Matt replied. "Why don't we just have somebody tail them so we can see where she's going?"

"That makes sense. *Wait...*" she exclaimed, "There's another group of men getting on a second boat."

SS-Oberführer Brunner spotted the Rangers and ordered the sailors to begin firing from the departing craft. The Rangers fired back and thought they hit one or two of the occupants, but the boat quickly moved away without further damage.

"Sergeant, can you notify your colleagues in Meersburg and ask them to follow both groups," Matt asked his new friend.

"Certainly," the Bundespolizei Sergeant responded.

"Also, if you don't mind, we'll let your men question the captives here while we take the helicopter across the lake and try to catch up with the runners."

"Very well, Major Kane."

Duncan and Abby, along with a contingent of Rangers, took a military transport aircraft to Austria on Thursday morning where they were met by a handful of Bundespolizei at Tulln Air Base, roughly thirty kilometers northwest of Vienna. Escorted by a handful of Austrian Federal Policemen, they immediately proceeded to *The Children's School* to question the staff.

In contrast to her approach to the personnel at *Die Kinderschule* in Aachen, Abby's communication with the staff at the Donaustadt school was direct and foreboding. The headmaster was clearly intimidated and was quick to cooperate and answer her questions. Yes, she knew Herr Doctor Vogel, but he rarely visited the school. He was always polite and genial, and there was never any political discussion. She had almost complete freedom to operate the school.

And while there were two security guards at the entrance to the property and two around the school, she never saw any weapons or unusual activity on the two hectare campus. She was quite confident there was no underground bunker, and invited the police to search the buildings and grounds. Her only request was that they not frighten the children by displaying their weapons. A careful examination of the school and grounds indicated that this was nothing more than what it appeared to be, a special school for disabled children. A dead end.

James arrived in London late on Wednesday evening and was met at Gatwick Airport by General Menzies. During a late dinner at the rustic Ye Olde Six Bells pub near the airport, James and the General discussed strategy for investigating *The Children's School* in Lambeth the next day.

"I have a splendid idea, old boy," offered Menzies. "Why don't we use your American friend, Miss Chessman, to discretely probe the school as a visiting nurse? She can examine some of the children, case the buildings, and have access to the entire school without raising any suspicions. I'm confident she will be able to provide bountiful intelligence to help us decide on our next steps."

James stared at Menzies for a few seconds to process what he just heard and collect his thoughts. "General, with all due respect, I think you've lost your mind! Ruth is just what you said...a nurse. Not an investigator. She's not trained or equipped to..."

"She found and alerted us to Karla Hoffman, didn't she?" Menzies interrupted. "She's smart, fearless and determined. I think she's just what we need."

The dumbfounded FBI agent was speechless. What he didn't know was that Ruth had completely charmed Generals Menzies and Sinclair while the task force was in Germany.

James persisted. "She may be all those things, but she has no experience either dealing with spies or violence. If they spot her, they'll kill her. Do you want that on your conscience? Why don't you use one of your own trained agents?"

It was no use. The Generals had already made up their minds and began prepping her for the assignment. During her several days of confinement at MI6, Ruth cajoled Sinclair and Menzies into allowing her to review war documents relating to the *SSU* and intelligence reports on a possible Nazi resurrection. She skillfully reminded them that James had officially appointed her to the Task Force, and she had signed the Official Secrets Act Oath. They found her to be observant, thorough and flexible ...good qualities for a spy.

"Do I detect a bit of proprietary interest in the young lady?" asked Menzies.

"No. She's already spoken for. I just don't want to be responsible for putting an American civilian in harm's way."

"Then it's settled. You can brief her on the latest information in the morning and we'll arrange for her to be transported to the Lambeth school."

This *Children's School* was established in South London in 1948 to house and school war orphans from the United Kingdom and several other European countries. By 1954, there were more than five hundred students, many disabled. In six years, the institution had developed a stellar reputation and became a ray of light in the area so heavily damaged during the war. There was certainly no reason to suspect that it might be a Nazi cover.

Ruth spent a full day at the school, interacting with staff and examining children under the guise of the International Red Cross. She came away satisfied that there was no underground facility, but was suspicious of the administrative personnel, including Headmaster Frances Gibbs.

Gibbs, an attractive woman in her early thirties, seemed too attentive and kept a close eye on Ruth throughout the day.

When the headmaster was not in plain sight, Ruth felt as though she was being surveilled by one or two male assistants. The teachers and matrons were warm and gracious, but the administrative staff were reserved and circumspect. Her intuition told her that something was amiss.

"James, I think you should see what you can find out about Frances Gibbs and an aide named Joseph Lawal," suggested Ruth. "I think they're hiding something."

James was duly impressed by her insight and requested that MI6 follow-up on her suggestion.

"You did a good job, Ruth, but I think you should stick to nursing instead of playing amateur detective," James responded with a mixture of admiration and worry. "If indeed those people are Nazi operatives, you could have gotten yourself killed."

"Maybe, but I had to keep occupied so I wouldn't worry about Matt. Is he okay? No more fainting spells or chest pains?

"As far as I know, he's fine."

By late in the day, MI6 had scoured public records and found that Frances Gibbs was born on April 1, 1923 and went missing after a V-1 rocket attack on June 13, 1944. Ruth was right. The school headmaster was a fraud.

Early on Thursday evening, MI6 arrested Gibbs and three assistants. By Friday afternoon, interrogators were able to determine that the assistants were deceased *SS* officer progeny and were former students at the Konstanz *Children's School*.

Frances Gibbs was actually Francine Gruber, illegitimate daughter of *SS* Colonel Kurt Gruber, creator and first Chairman of the Hitler Youth. He was a rising star who was slated to be in the Successor Government but died of a stroke in December 1943. Her three male assistants had similar backgrounds. While the school was legitimate, Gruber and several administrative personnel were Neo-Nazi spies regularly passing along information to Vogel's communications center in the Konstanz bunker. They knew the revolution was developing but had no knowledge of the scope or timetable for the uprising.

Rich Johnson's sojourn to Bonn, Germany was also very productive. With the support of Dr. Jim Conant, the High Occupation Commissioner, he was able to arrange for the close surveillance of each of Hans Vogel's businesses in the four target countries.

The federal police in Germany took immediate action to begin assessing and monitoring Vogel's holdings in their country, while the authorities in Belgium, France and Italy assured Rich that they would organize and initiate their inspections within a day. Their efforts to impede the conspirators in the Nazi-front businesses would prove to be invaluable as the plot began to unfold.

Chapter 30

The Final Destination

A self-assured and driven Hans Vogel sat in his below-ground office in the Technology, Science and Weapons compound on the Danube River, crafting final instructions to members of his new governments in Berlin, key German cities, and the capitals of soon-to-be subjugated countries. The aspiring *Führer*, however, was unaware that his communications center in Konstanz had been captured.

After the surrender of the communications personnel in Konstanz, veteran interrogators from the German Federal Police were able to segregate the committed Neo-Nazi operatives from the merely proud former Wehrmacht soldiers who supported the rebirth and unification of the country. Those individuals were not looking for world domination; they only joined the Neo-Nazi uprising because they needed a job. Many were eager to cooperate with authorities in exchange for immunity from prosecution.

The investigating officers learned that the specialists had already alerted hundreds of officials throughout Europe that **Operation Destiny** would launch in four days at 12:01 a.m. on September 1, 1954. Further instructions would follow within forty-eight hours. The exact nature of the plan was not known to the communications staff, but it was clear from the interviews that the conspiracy was far-reaching and forceful. More importantly, it was determined that the Konstanz facility was the primary communication hub for the new German Empire and that many new Reich officials lived in Konstanz and worked in businesses or shops in the area. They had been advised to prepare for transport to Berlin at any time.

The officer in charge of the inquisition immediately notified Bundespolizei headquarters in Potsdam, who promptly relayed the message to authorities in Bonn and Berlin. By sheer happenstance, Rich Johnson was in the Berlin office conferring with senior police officials and U.S. Occupation officers at the time. He quickly called James in London to apprise him of the breakthrough, but was unable to reach Matt.

The joint police and occupation forces were put on alert and would be deployed once top Neo-Nazi officials were identified. The unknown wild card, however, was still the strength and location of opposing military personnel or extent of their weaponry.

After examining the. **Operation Destiny** files gathered from Vogel's office in Konstanz, Karla knew exactly where to find her surrogate father. Upon reaching Meersburg, the desperate group of Nazi killers commandeered a faded red Volkswagen bus sitting by the dock and proceeded due east toward the Mauthausen area weapons compound, some five hundred kilometers away. They were in such a hurry, they were oblivious to the police following them.

Gerhard Brunner, four bodyguards and three sailors landed a kilometer north of Karla and her companions in Meersburg. The *Unter Führer* designate, and three bodyguards quickly disembarked and went to the nearby Neues Schloss Castle, where another member of the evolving government was employed as barracks superintendent for the French occupying forces. Three wounded men remained on board and were arrested by local police within fifteen minutes.

Brunner's co-conspirator procured four high-priority train passes to Berlin under the guise of official French business, and provided transportation for Brunner and his comrades to the nearest Meersburg station. The process took less than an hour.

Unfortunately for the fleeing Brunner and his security detail, the next train was not scheduled for almost two hours; plenty of time for authorities to catch up with and track them. The Neues Schloss superintendent was arrested by Federal Police after Brunner's party left the castle.

Meanwhile, James Rosino's FBI Task Force was seemingly making progress by apprehending many lower level players in the plot. They still had no actionable intelligence on the conspiracy, although Rich Johnson suspected that the fleeing Gerhard Brunner was a high ranking officer in the cabal. Otherwise, why would he have bodyguards? He intended to find out once the fugitive reached Berlin.

Upon landing in Meersburg, local authorities escorted Marie and two Rangers to the train station to monitor Brunner on his thirteen-hour journey to Berlin. She and her escorts were instructed to track Brunner to his final destination and alert Rich so he could assemble a strike team to apprehend and interrogate the presumptive senior Nazi official. Once again, fate intervened.

It was just past midnight on Thursday morning when Gerhard Brunner abruptly sat up, screamed in pain, rolled his eyes, and fell to the deck of his sleeper car. He died almost instantly from a brain hemorrhage. At forty-six years old. Hearing the commotion, the Ranger on watch awakened Marie. She rushed to the scene and quickly decided that the bodyguards should be taken into custody for delivery to authorities in Berlin. They wouldn't be as informed as Brunner, but perhaps they could verify who he was and his role in the conspiracy.

Brunner's security detail would not submit easily. Once they realized they were going to be arrested, they drew their weapons and a brief clash between the bodygards and the Rangers ensued. An innocent bystander and one Ranger were slightly wounded, and two bodyguards were killed. Fortunately, the remaining member of the security detail was captured and would later confirm Brunner's status in the new government. He knew nothing else.

Matt was fixated on Karla and vowed to follow her wherever she went. Therefore, while Marie's escapade with Gerhard Brunner was unfolding, he was chasing his would-be killer. The helicopter pilot flew him to Memmingen, just over a hundred kilometers away, where he linked-up with the police who were trailing Karla. They continued tracking her well into the night. He was sure the elusive female would lead him to Vogel but had no idea where his quarry was going or any inkling of what was in store for him when he arrived at his destination in Austria.

The Austrian Technology, Weapons and Science facility, code-named *Die Belladonna-Verbindung*, aka, *The Belladonna Compound*, was likely the most expansive subterranean project ever completed. It took almost ten years and thousands of forced and employed laborers to build. Incredibly, without ever being detected because the above ground cover business was a concrete and steel construction company.

Located two-hundred meters inland from the banks of the Danube River, the underground facility spanned almost two square kilometers and contained over one-million-seven-hundred thousand square meters of space. The compound included a first-class communications center, a chemical-based weapon testing and production station, a science-based research laboratory, an ample nuclear development lab, an enormous manufacturing and rocket assembly plant, a parts and weapons storage repository, and a long conveyor belt leading to the missile staging area.

The *Belladonna Compound* also housed more than two dozen administrative offices, several fully operational kitchens and dining rooms, and enough domiciliary space for dozens of chemists, geologists, physicists, virologists, mechanical and electrical engineers, and rocket technicians. In addition, the facility supplied sleeping quarters and weapons for more than a thousand soldiers who worked as laborers for the construction company.

Having designed and destroyed the *Daisy Compound,* Vogel was careful to position his bunker close enough to the Danube River to allow water access but far enough away to preclude any flooding risk. An innocuous appearing dock with a handful of fishing vessels disguised the access point to the hidden complex. The fishermen on the dock were former elite *SS* soldiers who shielded the property from prying eyes. Well trained and experienced, they presented a formidable obstacle for potential intruders. Their only flaw was that they didn't look like sailors, and their strict military appearance would be obvious to Matt and his Rangers.

If one could actually surprise and neutralize the guards, they would still have to find the hidden tunnel fifty meters away, and traverse another hundred and fifty meters without being detected. An extremely risky task, given that intruders would not know where they were going or any other security measures that might be in place. The only other entrance to the vast complex was through the construction company's main building.

The entire grounds were fenced and shielded by tall Austrian pine trees, interspersed with beautiful but poisonous belladonna bushes. In addition, the number of worker-soldiers and activity level were more than enough security to prevent any encroachment on the hidden bunker system. Also, both entrance points had panic buttons that could sound a siren, alerting everyone in the compound to the threat of a breach.

It was late on Wednesday night when Karla and her fellow fugitives drove their worn-out van up to the entrance of the construction company. Having learned from their experience at the gatehouse in Konstanz, Karla was much more diplomatic in her interactions with the guard and controlled her antagonism. She calmly explained to the suspicious young man that they were part of the *Kinderarmee,* that the Konstanz center had been taken, and that it was critical for them to report to the *Führer* without delay. The guard was completely baffled by their story, but warily directed his two companions to escort the group to the office building where they were to be held until morning before notifying Vogel of their presence.

Matt and his small force of Rangers and federal police parked their truck a safe distance away and observed the interaction between the guard and vehicle occupants. Matt's sixth sense told him that this was the place, and he was again certain there was a concealed bunker on the property.

The obsessed journalist was now fully transformed into his persona as a World War II intelligence officer. He carefully assessed the situation and ordered several of his charges to follow the fence line around the property to see how large the compound was and what it encompassed. It took more than two hours for the Rangers to reconnoiter the area and return to the assembly position in the forest two kilometers away from the construction site. Upon learning that the fenced area extended all the way to the river, Matt knew the compound would have waterside entry. He wanted to personally evaluate that himself.

Matt, Captain Anderson, and the Austrian Federal Police Superintendent made their way along the heavily cloaked border to the Danube riverbank. *This is no Daisy Compound,* Matt thought. *There's a lot of activity for this time of night and those are definitely professional soldiers.*

"We'll have to find a way in through the top," Matt whispered to his two colleagues. "Those guys are clearly former

SS, and we don't know how many there are. Let's get back to our staging spot and talk about tactical alternatives."

It was after 2:00 a.m. on Thursday morning when the three men finished their mission and Matt was in severe need of rest. He was worn out, his surgical sites ached, and he had to admit to himself that he couldn't think clearly. He assigned Rangers and police to establish a rotating schedule to observe the compound from the front and river entrances and report any meaningful activity to him immediately. He grabbed a blanket from the truck and found a tolerable place to sleep against a tree. He urged those not on guard duty to do the same thing.

A stream of light hit Matt's face at 5:19 a.m. and he abruptly jerked awake. One or two Rangers were already active, but most of the troops were still asleep so he quietly rose, picked up his walkie-talkie, trudged a hundred meters toward the construction compound, and called the lookouts at both locations for a report. All was still quiet on this cool morning.

When Matt returned, Captain Anderson and Superintendent Klein's men were now up and eating field meals for breakfast. Matt picked up a C-4 ration box, opened it, retrieved his P-38 can opener, and sliced into a can of peaches. At almost the same time he tore open one of the two cereal bars in the box. He realized that he hadn't eaten in almost twenty hours and devoured the entire contents of the container.

It was just after 6:00 a.m. when Matt and his two military and police leaders began comparing notes and possible approaches to penetrating the compound. They agreed that it must be from land but concluded that significantly more forces would be needed. By 7:00 a.m. there was mounting activity at the construction site, so Captain Anderson called the commander at Wiesbaden and requested a battle-ready battalion with heavy weapons and equipment. General Hoge readily granted the request and indicated that it would take approximately eight hours to muster the troops and equipment and make their way to the Mauthausen area. Superintendent Klein also agreed to provide as many as a hundred police to coordinate with and provide language support for the U.S. Army during the raid.

In the meantime, Matt and his group of less than thirty men would observe the movements of the working crew and try to determine the probable entry point to the suspected bunker. Matt was buoyant that justice was finally at hand.

Chapter 31

The Reckoning

An exhausted and liberated Matt Kane stepped off the Lockheed C-121 Constellation at RAF Lakenheath Air Force Base on Saturday, August 28th at 9:42 a.m. Accompanying him were two Army Rangers, the construction company owner and former Wehrmacht three star General, Hugo Wagner. He was also the Neo-Nazi General of the Army designate. The hundred-and-forty kilometer ride from Lakenheath to MI6 headquarters was traversed in almost complete silence. Thursday and Friday had been long days of conflict and interrogation, and the peace and quiet was a welcome respite for both victor and vanquished.

Matt led his prisoner to the now familiar conference room where Generals Sinclair and Menzies and the entire *SSU* contingent were waiting. Ruth was aghast. Matt looked like he was on the verge of collapse. He was drawn, colorless, and had clearly lost weight since she last saw him almost two weeks ago. Marie was also distressed at the look of her partner. The strain of the final confrontation had clearly taken its toll on him.

At noon, a wide assortment of sandwiches, along with two large containers of potato salad and coleslaw, arrived from the Paul Rothe & Son Deli. While somewhat awkward, General Designate Wagner was allowed to remain with the group through the meal. Matt had learned during his wartime interrogations that high ranking captives were much more likely to cooperate and provide meaningful information when treated with dignity and respect. His instinct was correct. Wagner was able to fill in many gaps in their understanding of **Operation Destiny**.

❖ ❖ ❖

"Splendid job by you all," pronounced General Menzies. "You haven't missed a step in the last decade. Well done! Now it's up to the military and police forces on the continent to ferret out the remaining conspirators and bring them to account."

During the past few days Rich Johnson had coordinated simultaneous police raids on Hans Vogel's business interests in Belgium, France, Italy and Germany. Almost completely without bloodshed. Rich found it telling that the so-called Nazi fanatics capitulated so easily and were generally cooperative with their captors. Perhaps the foundation of the conspiracy was not as solid as Vogel believed.

Through two days of grilling of Francine Gruber and her lieutenants from *The Children's School* in Lambeth, James was able to identify a Nazi spy network in Britain, many of whom had already been rounded up by British police, including two members of the MI6 administrative staff.

Notwithstanding the valuable information gathered by everyone in the entire task force, it was the take-down of the *Belladonna Compound* in Austria that finally collapsed the entire operation.

"Colonel Herrera's battalion of nearly a thousand men arrived just after 5:30 p.m. on Thursday," Matt began slowly. "We rallied about three kilometers from the compound, and I briefed him on the layout and perceived enemy strength. There were several hundred construction workers that we believed were soldiers, but we still had no idea what kind of weaponry they had. Our surveillance hadn't revealed any heavy artillery around the complex, but we couldn't be sure they didn't have cannons or rockets hidden in some buildings. Actually, we did identify what we thought might be a missile launch area, however. That caused great alarm."

"At first there was significant disagreement between Colonel Herrera and Superintendent Klein about the timing of the incursion," Matt continued. "The Colonel wanted to deploy the troops immediately while the Superintendent thought we should wait until dawn on Friday morning. As luck would have it, the winds began to whip up and we could see a large band of clouds approaching, signaling that a heavy rainstorm was on the way. This was the major tactical advantage we needed."

"We positioned the troops and waited for the cloudburst and crashed the gate with very little resistance sometime around 6:00 or 6:30 p.m. Captain Anderson and I directed about a hundred men to the largest building that we surmised was the headquarters and entrance to the bunker. We found maybe twenty workmen-soldiers sheltered in the building and caught them completely by surprise. Only a few shots were fired and two of their men were killed. We sustained no injuries at that time."

"I was right about an underground complex. Unlike the Liège and Konstanz installations, however, the entrance to this bunker was not well hidden. As we cautiously approached the open stairway, all hell broke loose. The ear-piercing sound of the *Aooga* horn alerted the entire complex of our presence, and the steel doors promptly closed in front of us. Almost instantly, we could hear the sound of machine gun fire coming from the other buildings and braced for the counterattack on our position that never came. Then there was a thunderous roar from..."

"What about the other buildings?" interrupted Menzies.

"I was getting to that, General. The roar we heard was a German eighty-eight, stationed behind a false wall about fifty meters away. Almost immediately there was return fire from our 240 mm M1 Howitzer. It hit the German cannon and ignited all its ordinance, setting off a gigantic blaze."

"Smashing!" roared Duncan Giles, which brought chuckles from everyone in the room except the German captive, who sat mute throughout Matt's briefing.

"The battle didn't last long and was pretty one-sided," resumed a re-energized Matt. "Our forces leveled most of the buildings except ours and a couple of smaller ones near us. At least three hundred of the Nazi contingent surrendered within half an hour, but the bunker was sealed tight."

"We still didn't know how large the bunker was, the number of combatants who were in there, or any idea of armaments. Colonel Herrera arrived within a few minutes and was clearly not a patient man. He took little time in ordering his men to blast open the steel door in the main building."

"As we had done in Konstanz, several canisters of tear gas were thrown down the stairs, but with no effect. A squad of men put on gas masks and cautiously began moving down the long stairwell to reconnoiter the area. When they reached the bottom of the stairs, they were met by a hail of machine gun fire and were all killed. We realized at that point it was going to be a pitched battle below ground."

"Where were you during all this, Matt?" asked a worried Ruth.

"I stayed out of their way while the soldiers judiciously worked their way into the bunker. After a few minutes of gunfire and exchange of hand grenades, our guys were able to get a foothold in the complex and I joined them. Both sides suffered a few casualties before a couple of dozen of them surrendered. When I got down there it was a mess, but I could readily see that this compound was much different from the ones we saw in Germany. It was more like the *Daisy Compound*, but bigger...much bigger...and more sophisticated."

"How much bigger, and what kind of sophistication?" asked a curious Marie.

"I can't really describe it adequately, Marie. It was cavernous. As we probed further, we found other steel doors separating laboratories, production facilities, fantastic amounts of weapons and ammunition, living quarters, offices...you name it, they had it. While the *Daisy Compound* occupied maybe ten or fifteen thousand square meters, this one must have had over a million square meters of space."

His colleagues were astonished.

"How could this vast facility be built without anyone knowing about it?" probed a puzzled Marie. "The authorities were either blind or didn't want to know."

"More likely, everyone was absorbed by the horror of the nearby concentration camps and repatriation of the inmates," responded General Menzies.

"This guy Vogel was an architectural genius, and he was clever enough to use the construction company as a perfect cover for the complex," added Matt. "I'm getting ahead of myself though."

"It took nearly two hours to secure all of the sections of the bunker because the complex was a labyrinth of hallways and cavities that were sealed from one another and had armed guards that had to be eliminated. Our troops killed and captured dozens of the enemy but also had many casualties. Finally, we got to the administrative compartment and found Dr. Vogel and General Wagner."

"We understand that Vogel is dead," stated James. "Did you kill him, Matt?"

"No, James. I never saw Hans Vogel alive," replied Matt. "Believe it or not, General Wagner said he was shot three times by Karla Hoffman after a heated exchange. I should let him tell you what happened."

A proud General Hugo Wagner proceeded slowly with an air of professionalism and self-control. He was a defeated enemy, but maintained pride in his country and position in the Neo-Nazi organization. He served honorably in the Wehrmacht during the war and had never been accused of wrongdoing. He had not been a member of the Nazi Party. In short, he was a professional soldier who conducted himself according to the recognized conventions of war.

He joined Vogel's campaign to re-establish Germany as a world leader for two reasons. First, he believed that Vogel was an intelligent and benevolent leader who would govern the subjugated European continent in a pragmatic and humane manner. Second, as General of the Army, he was convinced he could fashion an imposing military that was powerful but respectful of its role in the new world. Matt had a grudging respect for him.

"Herr Dr. Vogel and I were in the dining room having *abendessen*...dinner, discussing the disposition of the young enforcers who arrived late on Wednesday night when the alarm sounded. The *Führer* quickly rose and ran down the hallway to his office, picked up the telephone, and ordered the ordinance commander to arm the four V-3 rockets and transport them to the launching platform. I followed him to get his instructions concerning the five operatives."

"They had demanded to see the *Führer* the previous night, but I decided to keep them in confinement until after I conferred with him in the morning. The leader, Fräulein Hoffman, was quite agitated and insistent so I confined them in a locked ward. I called the *Führer* in the morning, but he did not want to see them until he finished his final instructions for the initiation of **Operation Destiny**. During the conversation he became extremely troubled."

"Why did he get angry?" asked James.

"I think it was because I told him that Fräulein Hoffman had some files from Konstanz that she wanted to discuss with him. That's when he told me to continue to detain them and he would decide what to do with them later."

"I have those files in my satchel," Matt interrupted. "They're explosive... and clearly explain why Karla Hoffman killed Vogel. One file contained a personal account of his thoughts and actions beginning in 1943 when he was convinced that Germany was going to lose the war."

"It seems that he was the one who designed and built the Liège bunker and also destroyed it. It was a simple matter of jealousy. He thought he should be head of the successor government, and when Hitler selected Karl Hoffman as *Führer-in-Waiting*, he bombed the compound and devised a plan to use the children of the dead leaders as pawns in his scheme to establish a Fourth Reich. He treated them well and systematically propagated a fanatical hatred of America and the Allies by telling the children that we killed their parents."

"He proceeded to train them to be spies, scroungers, couriers, lookouts and assassins, etc. He unleashed them a year or so ago to gain revenge on specific groups like the *SOE*, *OSS*, prominent war leaders like General Sinclair, Prime Minister Churchill, President Eisenhower, and us. He also expressed his belief that these killings would distract us from his real purpose."

"How did he know about us?" asked Abby.

"From Pat Kendall," came the bitter reply. "He details how Pat was tortured and gave up a great deal of war and MI6 information before he died. You may or may not want to read this part of the diary. It's disgusting."

After a short pause to let everyone regain their composure, Matt directed the Neo-Nazi General to continue his account of the raid and Karla's retribution on Vogel.

"Herr Dr. Vogel instructed me to keep them in the locked room, but somehow they got out and appeared outside his office about ten minutes after the alarm sounded. They were angry and threatening."

"Fräulein Hoffman shouted at the *Führer* and asked if he killed their parents and tricked them into a false-hearted life for no reason. He got up and ordered the two guards to shoot them. Karla's disbelief turned to rage, and they fired first, killing both soldiers. She then raised her weapon and shot him three times as he tried to run. I stood looking at them and they lowered their firearms and asked for directions to the escape tunnel. I pointed the way out and they left quietly."

"Why didn't you go with them?" asked James.

"It was my duty to remain with my men," he answered.

The General was then led away to the interrogation room, and Matt again picked up the narrative.

"We arrived in the administrative area maybe an hour after the underground battle began and found Vogel dead and General Wagner on the telephone talking to the missile launch group. Vogel's orders had apparently been misinterpreted and they were actively in the process of initiating the launch sequence. The General was trying to stop them, but they had already fired the first rocket with a Sarin gas warhead at Washington, D.C. He prevented the launch of a second nerve gas rocket on New York and two nuclear missile attacks on Russia."

This was shocking news to everyone in the room. There had been no word of this from 10 Downing Street or the White House, much less in the press. Surely there were mass casualties and panic in the United States.

Matt allayed their fears.

"While Vogel's scientists and engineers were skilled and their calculations generally correct, they were unable to fully test the propulsion system without alerting the world to the conspiracy. They miscalculated the fuel necessary to cover the forty-five hundred miles to Washington. The rocket fell harmlessly in the Atlantic Ocean about a hundred miles south of Nova Scotia. There were some reports of an odd sighting, but they were explained away as another UFO hoax. The Prime Minister and President didn't want to alarm the world and agreed to keep the failed conspiracy hidden."

"What about Karla?" asked Marie.

"The General told us what happened and pointed the way toward the tunnel that led to the river. While we took off after them, it didn't seem likely that we could catch up to them. Captain Anderson radioed the troops stationed near the dock and alerted them to the fleeing group of assassins. He reported that they had already rounded up dozens of scientists and combatants but had not seen the group-of-five yet."

"It took us ten minutes to get to the tunnel entrance, and maybe another five minutes to reach the dock. As we got there, we caught a glimpse of them getting into a small craft out of sight of our soldiers. They apparently got delayed due to the commotion on the dock. As they took off for open water, I yelled to a sergeant with a bazooka and he fired at the boat hitting it dead center, right at the water line. It completely disintegrated and we saw bodies flung in the air and into the river."

"What about survivors?" quizzed Marie.

"There were none. There was a strong current that swept away the bodies. No one could have survived."

"There are still some loose ends to be cleaned up by the military and federal police," mused James Rosino, "but it looks like we averted a worldwide calamity. You guys did a fantastic job. Just think, Matt...an obscure attempted murder in a far-away country uncovered and prevented a worldwide conspiracy. What are the chances?"

Their task complete, James, Abby and Ruth took a military charter back to the USA where they returned to new assignments in the FBI, NSA and Minneapolis General Hospital. General Stuart Menzies and Duncan Giles peacefully slipped back into retirement. Hugh Kensie and Marie Spenser headed back to their academic responsibilities in London and Durham.

A tired and pensive Matthew Seiberling Kane sighed a breath of relief that his ninety-day *Alice-in-Wonderland* ride was finally over. He would take a few days in London to reflect and envision his future before getting back to his comfort zone in Minnesota and resuming his journalism career.

Chapter 32
May 31, 1955

It was a calm and relaxing day on Lake Minnetonka as Matt and Marie Kane and their circle of old and new friends gathered on Lake Minnetonka for a day of celebration. Matt had just received a Special Award from the Pulitzer Prize Committee for International Investigative Journalism for his exposé on the pharmaceutical industry. Present on *The Rose* were lifelong friends John and Sandy Oleson and Tony and Pat Erickson. His new friends from the past year included Rich and Ann Johnson and James and Ruth Rosino. There was no mention of a failed assassination attempt or Neo-Nazi conspiracy.

It had been a whirlwind year for Matt and his new friends. Last August, after appropriate farewells to his colleagues, Matt quietly left MI6 headquarters and checked into the Savoy Hotel on the Thames River in London to rest and consider his dilemma. Providence provided his answer.

At midnight, the telephone rang, and James Rosino was on the other end. James called to ask one simple question.

"What are your intentions regarding Ruth?"

James had become increasingly enamored with Ruth over the past three months and realized on the flight home that he was absolutely smitten. She was strong and understanding, she was beautiful, and she didn't seem intimidated by the perils of his FBI life.

Matt was relieved. He cared very much for Ruth, and owed her a great deal for coaching him through his physical trauma, but he ached for Marie. Now both men had a chosen path.

The next morning, Matt dashed from London to Durham and asked Marie to marry him. They were married the next Saturday in the historic Durham Cathedral.

James took the next flight he could get from Washington, D.C. and showed up on the doorstep of Ruth's Minnetonka Boulevard apartment and asked Ruth to marry him. She had strong feelings for Matt, but she knew that James was her destiny. She just hadn't known how it would happen. After James related his conversation with Matt, her angst was relieved, and she accepted his proposal.

One final time, providence intervened. The position of Special Agent In-Charge of the Minneapolis Division of the FBI was open. James requested and received the promotion on January 1, 1955. Ruth and James married the next day, and were expecting a child in November.

Meanwhile, a tall, attractive blonde in her mid-twenties stepped down the ramp at Lambert Field in St. Louis and walked into the terminal with a slight limp. Destination unknown.

About the Author

Dr. Donald J. Lloyd has had an extensive career as a medical executive, health care consultant, professional speaker, college professor, and author. His publications include numerous professional articles, as well as the following books.

Healthcare 2010: A Journey to the Past

Trials to Triumphs

Smile and Jump High: The True Story of Overcoming a Traumatic Brain Injury

The 1950s was a decade marked by contradictions. While it was generally a time of world-wide reconciliation and budding prosperity, there was also an undercurrent of domestic and international unrest...the consummate environment for treachery, deception, and conspiracy. The complexity of this postwar era provided the author with the perfect background for exploring one possible scenario in this enigmatic period ...***OPERATION DESTINY***.

Made in the USA
Coppell, TX
25 May 2021

56180796R00184